ALL TOGETHER NOW!

ALL TOGETHER NOW!

PREVIOUSLY PUBLISHED AS
SORTA LIKE A ROCK STAR

A NOVEL BY
MATTHEW QUICK

Ⓛ Ⓑ
Little, Brown and Company
New York   Boston

Copyright © 2010 by Matthew Quick
Reading Group Guide copyright © 2011 by Matthew Quick

Cover photo © by Imagescource/Photolibrary. Cover design by Tracy Shaw and Jenny Kimura. Cover copyright © 2020 by Hachette Book Group, Inc.

Little, Brown and Company
Hachette Book Group
1290 Avenue of the Americas, New York, NY 10104
Visit us at LBYR.com

Originally published in hardcover and ebook as *Sorta Like a Rock Star* by Little, Brown and Company in May 2010
First Media Tie-in Edition: August 2020

Little, Brown and Company is a division of Hachette Book Group, Inc. The Little, Brown name and logo are trademarks of Hachette Book Group, Inc.

The publisher is not responsible for websites (or their content) that are not owned by the publisher.

ISBNs: 978-0-316-49991-0 (pbk.). 978-0-316-08858-9 (ebook)

Printed in the United States of America

LSC-C

10 9 8 7 6 5 4 3 2 1

FOR MR. SCOTT FLEMING,

HERO OF TEENAGERS,

HERO OF MINE

★ ★ ★

ALL
TOGETHER
NOW!

PART ONE

Feel the Pain

CHAPTER

1

Lying down, shivering on the last seat of school bus 161, pinned by his teensy doggie gaze, which is completely 100% cute – I'm such a girl, I know – I say, "You won't believe the bull I had to endure today."

My legs are propped up against the window, toes pointing toward the roof so that the poodle skirt I made in Life Skills class settles around my midsection. Yeah, it's the twenty-first century and I wear poodle skirts. I like dogs. I'm a freak. So what? And before anybody reading along gets too jazzed up thinking about my skirt flipped up around my waist, my lovely getaway sticks exposed, allow me to say there's no teenage flesh to be seen here.

I have on two pairs of sweatpants, three pairs of wool socks, two pairs of gloves, a big old hat that covers my freakishly little ears, and three jackets – because I don't own a proper winter coat and it's extremely cold sleeping on Hello Yellow through the dismal January nights.

I can see my breath.

Ice sheets form on the windows.

My teeth chatter.

Sometimes I wake up because my lungs hurt so bad from taking in so much freezing air. It's like gargling chips of dry ice.

My water bottle freezes if I take it out of my inner coat pocket.

Forget about peeing, unless you want to shiver your butt off – literally.

And it's pretty lonely too.

Because I am holding him up above my head, Bobby Big Boy (Triple B) looks down at me, panting with his perfect pink tongue hanging out of his mouth. His breath stinks like the butts he's always trying to sniff whenever he's around any dog women – BBB's an awful flirt even though he is totally monogamous and loyal to Ms. Jenny – but I want to kiss him anyway, because he is a sexy mutt and the most dependable man I know. He'll never leave me – ever – which is why I don't mind the smelly doggie kisses. Plus he's wearing his dapper plaid coat, which I also made in Life Skills class, and his doggie jacket makes him look beautiful. His hair is mussed around the ears like Brad Pitt, or maybe like he needs a bath, but his eyes are loyal and kind.

As I finish my confession, I keep him waiting, suspended above me, his little legs running like he thinks he's on a treadmill or something. There's no rush. We are alone, we have all night, and Bobby Big Boy digs air running above my face.

I've been sleeping with Triple B for somewhere around a year now. I found him in a shoebox half starved – no tags. No lie. He looked like a sock that had been flushed down the toilet – having traveled through all those gross pipes – only to be spit out of some sewer grate into a wet orange Nike box set up sideways like some elementary school kid's diorama. PATHETIC ALMOST DEAD MUTT, the exhibition would have been labeled, had some little tyke taken it into the science fair. Needless to say, I rescued his butt from the curb and nursed him back to health, mostly with scraps of meat I initially stole from Donna's dinner table until she caught me and started buying BBB dog food.

Did I put up Lost-Dog-Found posters?

I'll put it to you this way—if I ever meet the people who let Triple B get so skinny, watch out.

Bobby Big Boy is still air-running like a champ, and will keep at it until I lower him.

Regarding time, the parking-lot streetlights go out around eleven, and then there is no reading or writing—because I can't risk some curious passerby seeing me using a flashlight. That would blow our cover. With no lights—all alone—things can get quite weird, which is why I like to keep Bobby Big Boy around. But it's only nine-something now, so I'll have plenty of time to do my homework, after I'm done confessing to Triple B, who doubles as my at-home priest, of course, because Father Chee is only God's servant and not God, so therefore, not omnipresent. I have priorities, and keeping my soul white with a nightly confession is high up on the list. I'm a pretty good Catholic; I'm still the big V. Momma Mary and me are, like, five-by-five; I'm a holy teenager of God, sucka! And Mom won't be back until after the bar closes, and maybe not even then. She's gone a fishin' for men, as Jesus says.

"Today, I kicked Lex Pinkston in the shin," I tell 3B, his legs still going like mad, "which I know is a sin, especially since God made man in his own image, so He probably does have sympathetic (divine) shins prone to the unmerciful ache of a swift kick to the holy shin bone, and those Roman thugs probably kicked good old JC in the shins a few times before they nailed Our Lord and Savior to a tree, making Him equally sympathetic to the plaintiff's case, but before you go telling God all about my sin of punting teenage-boy shin, Father Big Boy, let me stress that there were extenuating circumstances. Lex made Ricky echo something filthy again—and I warned that plebian, Lex, like fifty times—so I let him have it. I kicked him square in the shin, and he started hopping on one leg—his friends laughing like hyenas, or maybe apes. Scratch that. Primates are cute, and way smarter than Childress Public High School football players, who suck and never win any games, because they are too busy being morons."

I could be wrong but—with his legs still running—Father BBB sorta smiles at my story, like he might even appreciate a good shin-kicking inflicted on an exceptionally evil classmate—which makes Father Thrice B seem almost human for a second. Or maybe I just want him to be human.

So anyway, what happened was...while I was throwing away my trash, Lex told Ricky to tell Ryan Gold that her "boobies are lovely," which Ricky did, of course—not because he is one of God's special children but because he is a guy who can get away with such things because he is special—and Ryan Gold turned bright red before she started to cry, because she's still a prudish virgin pre-woman, like me, and Ricky just started robot laughing—"Hi! Hi! Hi! Hi!"—like he does whenever he is upset and confused, and boy, did it make me mad. Especially since Ricky knows better, and is trying to earn the right to take me to prom. Donna would be devastated if I told her what her only son said today in the cafeteria.

I lower Bobby Big Boy down to my chest. He stops running

and licks my under-chin in an effort to console me. The weight of him on my chest makes me feel less alone – sorta loved – which I realize might be whack, but we get love wherever we can, right? At least that's what Mom says anyway.

"So am I forgiven, Father B3? Off the divine hook? Bark once for yes."

"Rew!" BBB says, just like I taught him. He's a good little doggie. Truly.

AA, 2009

★ ★ ★

When I finish writing the above essay, I rip it up and sigh. It kicked apple bottom, and yet I had to rip it up.

Bobby Big Boy runs south, ducks his little head, and burrows up under my jackets and shirts, snuggling up against my barely bumpy pre-woman chest and keeping me quite warm without scratching up my belly so much, because he is a frickin' gentleman.

Maybe you think I had to rip up the essay because it was sorta a confession, and therefore private, but the truth is that I trust Mr. Doolin, my English teacher, the guy who asked our class to write a slice-of-life story. He's pretty hip and lets us express the truths of our lives in our writing, gaining our trust so that our words can be more authentic, which is cool of him, because I'm sure our writing honestly—the truth—pisses off some teachers and parents, even though all freaky teenagers keep it real when we can.

Maybe you think I ripped up my essay because I didn't want

to narc out my friend Ricky or those moronic football players, but I don't really care about narcing them out, because when you say or do repellent stuff in the lunchroom, that's public knowledge as far as I'm concerned. True? True.

I wouldn't want to turn in an essay that made Ryan Gold look bad, because she is a nice person, but I would have turned this essay in if Ryan was the only thing stopping me, because sometimes — when it comes to writing — you have to sacrifice the feelings of other people to make a statement. Serve the greater good and all, which Mr. Doolin says almost every day.

But the truth is that I don't want anyone to know that I am living out of Hello Yellow — that my mom's last boyfriend, A-hole Oliver, threw us the hell out of his apartment, and that my mom has to save up some dough before we can get four walls of our own. I mean, it's a pretty pathetic story, and I'm not really all that proud to be my mom's daughter right now. Homelessness reflects badly on both of us. True? True.

I'm sure there are people who would let us crash at their houses, because the town of Childress is full of good-hearted dudes and dudettes. Word. But charity is for cripples and old people and Mom is sure to come through one of these days. I still have Bobby Big Boy, and Mom still has her job driving Hello Yellow, all of our clothes and stuff fit in the two storage bins between the wheels, below the bus windows, so it's all good in the hood.

Except that sitting here with my legs up and BBB on my chest, I can't think of anything else to write about — especially since my original essay was so killer.

The quiet of an empty Hello Yellow can drive you a little nuts.

Bobby Big Boy and I just cuddle until the streetlight blinks out and everything goes black.

I can rest my eyes, but I can't really sleep until Mom gets back from fishing, because I worry about her.

She's still pretty.

Bad things happen to pretty women who have daughters like me and can't afford to do jack crap for 'em, which makes said pretty women desperate for a Prince Charming—only Prince Charmings marry hot young chicks my age, or maybe a little older. Mom's almost forty, so she's pretty screwed when it comes to men. Sometimes I like to think about her marrying an old rich dude, who would act all grandfatherly and leave Mom tons of money when he croaked. That would be cool, but it ain't gonna happen. Truth.

Another thing: Mom's taste in men is akin to a crackhead's taste in crack cocaine. Any old hit will do. And it sucks for all nearby loved ones (me) when mi madre is hitting the man-pipe again, because she sorta loses her frickin' mind—to put it bluntly.

All alone on Hello Yellow, I think about Mom for a long time.

She sucks at being a mom. Emphatically.

She's so ridiculously irresponsible and socially dumber than Ricky—who is diagnosed with autism—but I still love her. I'm a sucker for love and having a mom in my life. Call me old-fashioned, maudlin, or mawkish.

When I hear Hello Yellow's front door being keyed into, I freeze and hold my breath.

Should be Mom.

Must be Mom.

What if it's not Mom?

I'm in a creepy parking lot outside of town; it's full of eerily similar school buses parked in perfect lines. Too much symmetry can be daunting. There are train tracks on one side of the parking lot and creepy woods on the other. Bad stuff happens by train tracks and in woods, because some men are inherently evil, and left unchecked, these dudes will do bad hooey — at least according to such cool cats as Herman Melville, who illustrated this exact point through that evil Claggart character from *Billy Budd,* which we just read in my Accelerated American Lit class. The Handsome Sailor. Budd Boy spilling his soup on Claggart in the mess hall — when Billy does that, it's a metaphor for accidental homosexual ejaculation according to Mr. Doolin, who has coitus on the brain 24/7, and sees a sexual metaphor in just about any old sentence. "Handsome is as handsome did it too." Herman Melville. Funny stuff. Truly. But being in a bus alone at night near train tracks and woods ain't so ha-ha, believe me.

Plus there have been a few rape-murders on the outskirts of town lately and the cops haven't caught the bad guy yet, which has lots of people freaked out and for good reason.

Madman nearby — beware!

Finally, I cannot take it and completely blow any chance I have of surviving an encounter with the local psychopath, mostly because I am only seventeen, and a chick, even if I am a junior now. "Mom?" I say.

"Amber? Did I wake you up?"

Whew. It's Mom. "No. Some crazy lumberjack train conductor was just about to abduct me and make me his slave, but you scared him off. Thanks."

"That's not even remotely funny."

"How was fishin' fo' men, any bites?"

"Nope. Nothing."

"A good man is hard to find."

"Damn skippy," my mother says, like a used-up chippie who will never find her Prince Charming, but you can tell — by the tone of her voice — that Mom is faking something, trying to sound hopeful enough to make her daughter feel as though she will not be sleeping on a school bus forever, so I give her a little credit. She's had a harrowing life.

"Always tomorrow," I say through the darkness, as my mom pats my forehead like I am Bobby Big Boy. I like dogs, so I do not take offense.

"Does your puppy need to go out before I hit the hay?"

"Bob probably could squirt a few drops."

"Please don't call him Bob."

"That's his name."

"Your father was — best to forget him, and — "

"Well, Bob here has to take a squirt, and I have school tomorrow, so can we skip the broken-record talk and get doggie duty over with, please? I can't sleep without my pup."

"Come on, little dog," Mom says, clapping her hands. And Bob bursts forth from my pre-woman chest, widening the neck holes of — like — four shirts, and scratching the hell out of my neck. He loves to piss. It's his favorite.

"Use his leash!" I yell, because I don't want 3B to get lost in the dark.

"Okay," Mom says, but I know she doesn't use the leash, because I'm on it—it's under my butt.

My mom lies to me all the time. She sorta has a problem. She is a fabricator of falsehoods. Or maybe she is just drunk again, which is no excuse.

Sometimes when I am losing faith in Mom—which is, like, all the time lately—I like to think about one of the top-seven all-time Amber-and-her-mom moments. These are little videos I have stored in my brain—all documenting the mom I knew before she sorta gave up on life, before Oliver broke Mom's spirit and got her drinking so heavily. Here's the number-seven all-time Amber-and-her-mom moment:

Back in the 80s—when Mom was in high school—she was a big-time softball player who helped her team win a state championship, which was the highlight of her entire life. She used to talk about softball all the time, and even used to play on a local bar team in a beer league. I used to go and watch Mom play softball against fat men with huge beer bellies and foul mouths. There were only a few other women who played in the league, and Mom was a million times better than all of them. Mom was better than most of the men too, for the record. She couldn't hit the ball that far, but she knew how to hit through the holes in the infield, and she was one hell of a second-base woman—never making any errors.

Anyway, when I was a little girl, Mom got it in her head that she would train me and make me into a killer softball player just like her, so she took me to the sports store and bought me a glove and a bat and a ball and a hat and cleats and even a pair of batting gloves, even though I hadn't asked for any of these things. This was well after my dad took off on us, and we never had all that much money, so this purchase was sorta a big deal, which I understood even as a little girl, so I just went along with the idea, even though I really didn't want to play softball.

The next day, Mom took me and all of my new gear to the park. She showed me how to swing a bat and throw and catch a ball, but—even though she was a really good coach—I just couldn't get the hang of any of it, and trying made me feel like a complete idiot. For weeks I swung the bat and never hit any of the balls Mom threw me; all of the balls she hit went over my head, through my legs, and occasionally nailed me in the face or stomach, and all of my throws went to the right or left of Mom or hit her feet. Mom never yelled at me or anything like that, but after a few weeks of steady failure, after swinging the bat and missing for the bazillionth time, standing at home plate, I burst into tears.

Mom ran off the mound and toward me. She picked me up and kissed me on the cheek. "Amber, this doesn't happen overnight—you have to work at it if you want to be a good softball player. It takes lots of practice. It took me years!"

"But I don't *want* to be a good softball player. I hate softball. I really do."

Mom looked me in the eye, and I could tell that she was surprised by this news—I could tell she had never even once thought that maybe I wouldn't want to play softball.

"I never want to play softball ever again!" I yelled. "Never again. I hate this! All of it!"

"Okay," Mom said.

"What?" I said, shocked, because I thought that Mom would make me keep trying, because that's what adults usually do.

"Amber, it's just a game. I thought you might like it, but if you don't want to play, well then, you don't have to play softball."

"You won't be mad at me?"

"Why would I be mad at you?" Mom said, and then laughed.

"Because you spent all that money on equipment, and now I don't want to play softball."

"If you don't want to play, you don't want to play. It's okay."

"Really?"

"Really."

We left the field, got some Italian hoagies at the local deli, and ate by the lake sitting on a park bench. We fed parts of our rolls to ducks, and it was really nice to just sit with my mom after telling her how I felt. It was good to know that I could tell my mom what I truly felt inside and still be able to feed ducks with her afterward. I really love ducks. I like watching them waddle around on land, and their quacking noises crack me up. True.

I remember the sun reflected in the lake so brightly, it hurt to look at the orange water.

"Thanks for not forcing me to keep playing softball," I said.

Mom put her arm around me.

She never ever again tried to make me play sports, although we ate many more hoagies on that bench and fed flocks of ducks for years to come—and the feeding-ducks memories are something I truly treasure.

Quack, quack.

Ducks.

Pretty killer.

Back in the present moment, when Mom and BBB don't return to Hello Yellow right away, I'm just about to get up and take care of business myself, making sure my best friend doesn't get eaten by a rogue coyote or some other dastardly carnivorous mammal, but then Bobby Big Boy is tearing through Hello Yellow, jumping up into my shirts again, warming my belly and chest, and all is well under the comforter Mom had thrown over me before she left the bus, even though I had left it out on the adjacent seat for her, because we have only one comforter.

Bobby Big Boy's pretty warm from running around and a little lighter without a bladder full of pee. I hear my mom lock up Hello Yellow and then walk toward me.

"This is only temporary, Amber," Mom says.

"I like it. It's like camping, only on a school bus, and without fattening marshmallows, a cancer-causing campfire, or the pesky Kum-Ba-Yah singing."

"Did you get enough food today?"

This question pisses me off, especially since she probably blew what little dough she makes on cigarettes and vodka tonight, providing no dinner whatsoever for me or B Thrice. Mom only works four hours a day at nine dollars an hour, and she'd happily buy you a drink at some crappy bar before she'd buy a meal for herself or me. So depressing.

"Watching my figure," I say, stealing Franks' joke, "but Bobby Big Boy had a steak I swiped from Donna's dinner table."

"Ms. Roberts," Mom corrects me, because the drunk has

some sardonic notion of proper etiquette when it comes to surnames.

"Right," I say, like a total bitch, because I can be a cat.

My mother kisses me on the forehead real nice, says, "Sweet dreams, my love," and so I let go of the day's frustrations, push my palms together into prayer position, and I silently hold up all the people and dogs in this world who I absolutely positively know need me to pray for them: Mom, 3B, Ricky, Donna, Franks, Chad, Jared, Ty, Door Woman Lucy, Old Man Linder (my manager), Old Man Thompson, Joan of Old and all of the old people down in the Methodist home, Father Chee, The Korean Divas for Christ, Mr. Doolin, Private Jackson, Ms. Jenny, Prince Tony, the Childress Public High School faculty, and the whole damn town of Childress, even the football team, even Lex Pinkston, EVEN my absentee biological father, Bob, who may or may not even be alive for all I know — I hold them all up to JC in my prayers, asking God to help everyone be who they need to be, and then I simply listen to Mom breathe across the aisle until Triple B and I find sleepy land together, and I dream of the real bed on which Bobby Big Boy and I will rest one day. My future bed's going to be an ocean of mattress, maybe even a queen-size, sucka! Word.

CHAPTER 2

Waking up at a normal time in Hello Yellow isn't all that bad, because of the many windows—warm sunlight cubes reach everywhere. This happens on the weekends. True. But on school days, we have to rise before the sun comes up so that none of the other early-rising bus drivers will catch us sleeping on Hello Yellow, which would surely cost Mom her job. So we get up super early—way before dawn. I've been doing this for a while; I usually wake up automatically sometime between four thirty and five. But no matter how much she drinks, Mom is always up before Triple B and me.

Today, Mom's inhaling a Newport just outside of Hello Yellow, her dyed blond hair full of fading moonlight. (I keep my hair naturally black and I do dig the way it sometimes shines iridescent like crow feathers. True. I'm an inch or two shorter than Mom when she stands up tall, which is like never. While my skin is freakishly white, her skin is sort of yellow from smoking so much.) Mom's orange cherry glows brighter with each pull.

Like always, she's shivering mentholated smoke out of her nose and mouth.

BBB runs right past her, off the leash in the morning new-ness where there are no coyotes, local rapist-killers, or other unnamed monsters. He lifts his tiny leg and merrily pisses on the front driver's side tire of school bus 260, marking his all-time favorite wheel.

"Hey, Mom," I say.

"Good morning, sweetheart," she says from within her dark smoky shadow.

Mom looks really thin.

Skeletal.

True?

True.

When did you last eat? I think but do not ask, because I don't really want to know the answer, nor do I want to hear another one of Mom's stupid lies.

She won't even eat the food I bring her from Donna's house.

Bobby Big Boy pushes out a few grape-size pellets of poo, squatting somehow regally with a seriously determined look on his face, as if he were a mini sphinx thinking up some kick-ass riddle. I learned all about sphinxes freshman year, when we read *Oedipus Rex*. If you don't know this already, Oedipus had sex with his mom, which is very very whack—even more so than Billy Budd spilling soup on Claggart. We have to read crazy books in high school, let me tell you.

I walk to the storage bin under the windows of the passenger side of Hello Yellow, open up her underbelly, and pull out my trash bag of clothes. I sniff armpits and crotches until I find my purple scoop-neck sweater and a basic pair of jeans. Bra and underwear were changed yesterday, so no worries there.

Changing outside sucks because of the cold and the snowy slush underfoot, making your socks wet no matter how hard you try to balance on your boots when changing pants.

Dressed for school, still wearing three jackets instead of one winter coat, I walk back into Hello Yellow, BBB trailing in his dapper plaid coat; I grab my backpack, exit Hello Yellow, BBB trailing, and say, "Will you eat something today, Mom?"

"Oh, sure," she says, lighting up a fresh cancer stick. She forces a smile, but she is looking at something just above my hair and will not make eye contact. I'm afraid she might start crying, so I kiss her on the cheek, walk away, lift BBB over the fence and then hop my way out of the school bus compound.

Mom's not-eating started at an exact moment, which I can pinpoint. It's a good moment gone bad. Here is the all-time Amber-and-her-mom moment number six:

Two Thanksgivings ago, when A-hole Oliver was just beginning to show his true colors and Mom was just beginning to slip, she decided that she was going to make this killer traditional Thanksgiving meal with a real turkey and stuffing and cranberry sauce and gravy and wine and candles and everything else that most people have on Thanksgiving. This might not sound like a big deal to you, but Mom and I had never had a real Thanksgiving dinner before, and buying all the ingredients wiped out what little savings Mom had. True.

We got up very early on Thanksgiving morning to get the bird into Oliver's oven. And then we began preparing all of the side dishes while listening to this CD of Frank Sinatra doing Christmas music, which Mom had bought at the grocery store when she was splurging, because she is a big Sinatra fan.

This very morning—cooking with Mom—is one of my all-time favorite memories, because I had never seen her so happy, the two of us listening to Old Blue Eyes, as Mom calls Frank Sinatra.

Oliver got out of bed around ten and immediately went down the hall of the apartment building to drink with his friend and watch football, which was fine with Mom and me, because we were having such a great mom-and-daughter moment and I hated Oliver from the get-go.

I set the table really nicely, even making origami-swan place cards, and got the candles going so that Oliver's dingy small apartment actually felt sorta festive and alive.

When the turkey was ready mid-afternoon, Mom had me go down the hall to get Oliver while she cut the meat, but when I knocked on the door of his friend's apartment, no one answered.

We waited an hour for Oliver to come home before we started eating without him.

I knew that Mom was really sad that Oliver blew off her big meal—what she had spent all of her hard-earned savings on and spent so much time preparing—so I tried to make a big deal about everything and ate until I felt I was going to puke.

Mom hardly touched any of her food and just sorta stared at her plate while I shot so many compliments at her.

Oliver still wasn't home by the time we had put the leftovers into Tupperware and washed the dishes.

So Mom and I sat down on the couch and watched TV.

Jurassic Park was playing on one of the few channels we got, and I was all snuggled up in a blanket with my head in Mom's lap, taking in all the awesome dinosaurs, when she started to cry. So I sat up and held my mom for a long time while she cried and cried.

When she finished crying, she wiped her eyes and said, "Amber, you're the best thing about my life."

Oliver walked in all drunk right then, and Mom hustled herself into the kitchen to fix him a plate of food. I watched her dote on him, pretending not to care about his blowing off her meal, while he stuffed his drunken face. From the couch, as I watched them, I knew that I would never allow a man to treat me how Oliver treated my mother. And I began to believe that Mom knew this too—that I really wasn't going to be like her—and maybe knowing that I would not have an Oliver in my future somehow made her life a little bit better.

I liked being the best thing in my mother's life, even if I did wish that her life was a whole lot better than it actually was. Her telling me that on the couch as we watched *Jurassic Park*, it was sorta like a moment for me.

Back in the present, as I walk the cold mile to Ricky's house, B Thrice circles my heels like a maniac, and sometimes he runs through my legs when I take a long stride. Because I'm a chick, I like to pretend I'm Dorothy, BBB is Toto, and we're walking on the frickin' Yellow Brick Road, just about to meet some interesting friends who will help us melt the Wicked Witch. It's a pretty dumb fantasy, especially since Judy Garland was so super-mega beautiful and most boys would rather kiss the Tin Man—or even a flying butt-monkey—than swap spit with yours truly.

But I like skipping and singing.

It's maybe even my favorite.

There is no one out on the streets at the crack of ass, so I let loose with a couple of verses and suddenly I'm off to see the wizard in my mind. I'm a freak. True. But it ain't like I'm hurting anybody, and Bobby Big Boy gets a big bang out of the fantasy too, I know because the very second I start singing and skipping he goes mad, jumping like some tiny furry ballerina. And BBB can JUMP—like—three feet into the air, which is pretty good considering that he is only maybe twelve little inches tall.

And then I'm at Ricky's, so I key into the back door, using my very own key that Donna made for me a while back.

By the refrigerator, BBB has a little setup—two bowls that are Phillies red, because Ricky likes the Philadelphia Phillies and so does Donna. Donna spoils B3 with the wet stuff in cans. No dry crap for him. I feed my pup and he eats merrily, his little tail going like a frickin' windshield wiper.

Next I unload the dishwasher, which doesn't take all that long.

Today is omelet day, so I crack a half-dozen or so eggs into a big old silver bowl, add milk, and then whisk the hell out of it all. I find tomatoes and mushrooms and a red pepper in the vegetable drawer, so I chop that hooey up like a pro, using one of Donna's super expensive knives and a thick-ass chopping board.

All those sliced veggies go into my silver bowl.

I add pepper, salt, a dash of hot sauce, and a shot of tequila from the liquor cabinet, which is my newest secret omelet ingredient. When it comes to cooking, I can get quite loopy. The alcohol will get cooked out, and it's only a single shot split between three servings, so no worries about getting drunk before school or anything like that.

I spray the frying pan with Pam, and then let it get good and hot, while I halve oranges and put Donna's automatic juicer to use.

Bobby Big Boy has finished his breakfast and is lying on his back in the middle of the kitchen floor so that his tiny legs are in the air and I can see he has a stiffy, which is gross. But I don't want him to feel self-conscious, especially since lying on his back with a full belly is his second favorite, next to pissing, so I pretend I do not notice.

It takes three to four oranges to make a tiny glass of juice, and I end up using twelve, just so Ricky, Donna, and I will get all the vitamin C we need to fight frickin' colds and whatnot.

The pan is not quite hot enough yet, so I retrieve the newspaper from the driveway, remove the plastic wrapper, and put the paper on Donna's seat.

I set the table and put on coffee.

The pan is popping now so I pour some omelet jizz onto the metal and let it spread out into a perfect O.

When it gets hard enough, I fold over the yellow O into a D and flip it a few times, until the outside gets golden brown.

"Amber, someday you really have to let me cook for you. I'm getting to feel like Thomas Jefferson every time I come down into my kitchen and see you slaving away. You're robbing me of all my Mom-ness and making me feel like writing some sort of proclamation or something."

I just smile dumbly at Donna and shake my head—spatula in hand—like a moron.

Donna is my hero—plain and simple.

Sometimes, when she is being extra cool, I can do little more than marvel at her.

I admire Donna more than anyone.

I want to be Donna.

She grew up on the other side of the tracks, as they say. Her father was a truck driver, her mother died of cancer when she was seven, but she kicked butt in school and got a scholarship to Bryn Mawr College, which is a school for women who do not need a man to take care of them. She kicked butt at Bryn Mawr, earning a scholarship to Harvard Law School, where she became a lawyer. She wanted to have a child but not a husband, so she purchased some sperm and had Ricky, who turned out to be autistic, which did not freak her out at all, even though the sperm was supposedly screened for potential birth defects or something like that. She loves the hooey out of Ricky, and will kick your butt if you mess with her boy.

Donna is model tall with naturally blond shoulder-length hair. She wears these very cool business suits that are sexy in a serious womanly way, and she sports these killer heels every day. Men must seriously dig her, I'm sure. She drives a black Mercedes SUV that can fit all five members of the Franks Freak Force Federation—which is one of the awesome team names me and my closest friends, my boys, call ourselves—we all fit in the SUV if we put Chad on someone's lap, and Donna is always carting us around, because she digs freaky teenagers like me and the rest of The Five.

Ever since I first made friends with Ricky back in elementary school, she has let me call her Donna, and she is always doing cool things for me, like buying Bobby Big Boy food and letting him crash in her home when I am at school, even after he ripped up her leather couch, because he gets separation anxiety when I'm not around.

Plus, I used to steal her makeup, when I first went through puberty and started feeling the need to look pretty, and Donna wears—like—only the most expensive department store hooey too. I'm not proud of stealing her stuff, but one day when I was—like—fourteen, I went into her bathroom looking to score some makeup, and when I opened the medicine cabinet, there was a little sign that read "Amber's Shelf," and on it were all the top makeup brands that she wears. Brand-new gear everywhere. I felt so guilty, I started sobbing in the bathroom, and when Donna heard me, she actually came in and hugged me. I held on to her for at least ten minutes, I felt so shameful. When I stopped crying, she looked me in the eyes and said, "If you ever need something, just ask. Okay?"

That was it.

No reprimand.

No threats to tell my mother.

No guilt trip.

I've never stolen anything since—not even a piece of paper from school—and never will ever again, no matter how bad things get. Word.

As I finish cooking the last omelet, Donna scans through the business section of the paper and mumbles stuff about all her stocks shitting the bed.

I marvel at her—a woman with stocks and business suits and her own house. And then, I'm secretly wishing that she were my mother, which I realize is a terrible thing to wish, but I can't help it.

"Amber Appleton uses hot sauce in her omelet. Yes. She likes to cook omelets on Tuesday mornings. Yes. Amber Appleton is very pretty and I would like to kiss her under the apple tree because she is Amber Apple-TON! Yes."

"Good morning, Ricky," I say to my friend, who is wearing his Tuesday Chase Utley home jersey—number 26.

"Amber Appleton is going to take Ricky Roberts out of Ricky Roberts' house tonight but he doesn't know where and Mommy Roberts will not tell him. Mommy Roberts will not tell him where. Yes!"

"We're going to do a mission tonight. Remember?" I say to the now-seated Ricky while placing an omelet in front of him. "And when the Franks Freak Force Federation does a mission, how does Ricky Roberts receive information?"

"Ricky Roberts receives information on a need-to-know basis. Need to know. Yes," Ricky says, and then begins eating his omelet. "Need-to-know basis."

We can't tell Ricky secret hooey, because he says whatever he thinks, and therefore can't keep a secret to save his life.

I remove a plate from the oven and place it in front of Donna. "Can you still make it tonight?" I ask her.

From behind the business section, she says, "As your attorney, I advise you to videotape the proceedings."

"But we don't have a—"

"As your attorney, I have taken the liberty of securing a video camera and will be personally documenting everything that takes place tonight." She drops the paper and looks into my eyes. "Just make sure your boys know their lines. I'm counting on you to make this mission successful, because you're the leader of The Five, right?"

Donna winks at me and I almost crap my pants as she samples my omelet.

"Does this have tequila in it?" Donna asks.

I nod once and swallow.

"Nice. Coffee?"

I all but run to the coffeemaker and pour Donna a large cup. She drinks it black.

"Thanks," she says. "Are you not eating?"

"Can I use your bathroom first?"

Donna nods once and disappears behind the business section again.

Upstairs, in the bathroom, I strip down quickly, brush my teeth with the toothbrush stored permanently on Amber's Shelf, floss, use mouthwash, and then I'm in the shower washing my hair, using Donna's expensive conditioner, trying to keep my long black hair shiny. I do this all super quickly, so I don't use too much of Donna's hot water, because hot water costs money. I towel off, use the deodorant and perfume and makeup that Donna buys for me, redress, and then return to the kitchen, where BBB has fallen asleep on the little braided mat in front of the sink.

My hair is soaking wet, but neither Ricky nor Donna say a word about my needing to use their shower. Ricky is used to my using his place as a second home, and Donna is too classy to bring up the sore subject of my needing to freeload off her.

I wolf down my omelet and then do all the dishes and clean

up the kitchen while Donna reads the rest of the paper and Ricky does math equations in his workbook. He is a frickin' math genius. I take BBB out for one last pee, and then I kiss him goodbye just before I lock him up in his room, which is an unused first-floor bedroom with a doggie bed, tons of chew toys, a water dish, and even a radio, which we keep on the classical station to calm B Thrice's nerves. (B3 loves Chopin. I know because my pup starts jumping in the air like a maniac every time some Chopin-playing dude tickles that piano.) Just like every other morning, BBB starts crying and scratching at the door as soon as it's shut, which breaks my heart and makes me feel bad about Donna's door getting all clawed up, even though she says she doesn't give a crap about that room and has tons of money for buying new doors or whatever.

We hop into her Mercedes — heated leather seats, which are pretty killer. True? True. We rock out to Dinosaur Jr., which is an obscure indie band of olden days. Donna digs unheard-of bands like Dinosaur Jr. She even has cool taste in music. We listen to "Feel The Pain" three times, because Ricky likes that one, and then we are at Childress Public High School, so Donna shuts off the tunes.

"Amber, what do you have after school today?"

"The Korean Divas for Christ at three thirty."

"You can get Ricky home first?"

"No worries."

"Ricky, are you going to be good today?"

"Yeah-sssss," Ricky says in his goofiest robot voice.

"Are you going to repeat dirty words?" Donna asks.

"Nooooooooooooooo!"

"What happens if you do?"

"Amber Appleton will not go to prom with Ricky Roberts. Yes."

"That's right. So behave your little behind. Be the gentleman I know you are." To me, Donna says, "Tell Franks Freak Force Federation that we meet at my house at seven sharp. I'm not picking all of their little butts up individually, because I'm in court all day—murder trial. But if they pull off the mission without screwing up too badly, we're going to Friendly's afterward."

"Yes, ma'am," I say, like a moron.

"Friendly's. Reese's Pieces Sundae. Yes," Ricky says.

"All right. I have to get to the courthouse. Kisses and then out."

Ricky kisses his mother as I hop out of the backseat and onto the sidewalk. Ricky gets out of the Mercedes, slams the door too hard, and then says, "Going to play Halo 3 with Mr. Jonathan Franks! Yes! Halo 3."

CHAPTER
3

Maybe you want to know how The Five came to exist? True?
History of The Five.

It all began when Jared and I failed fifth grade.

Well, neither of us technically failed, but we were both held back, dropped into Chad's, Ricky's, and Ty's class. Jared—because he used to have this awful stutter back in the day and could hardly complete a frickin' sentence without repeating just about every syllable a bazillion times. Word. And me—I was held back because I missed too many days of school, even though I technically passed all of my tests when I eventually took them. If you miss so many days, you automatically get held back, or at least that's what I was told. The reason I missed so many days of school was because we were living with Good Boyfriend Gerald at the time, who was Mom's best pick by far, if you ask me.

GBG was a truck driver and used to make these long hauls across the country, and Mom used to go nuts for road trips, so whenever she didn't want to be left alone without GBG, she'd have one of the bus driving subs cover her route for a week or so and she'd let me skip school to ride across the country with GBG in his big old red tractor-trailer truck, which he called Melissa. Since GBG was making these trips all the time, I missed tons of school.

When we'd head west, we would drive right through the night, hardly ever stopping, because Good Boyfriend Gerald got paid more if he got the load there early. We'd all sit in his truck, Mom in the middle, holding both of our hands, and it was fun to drive on the highways of America like that, sorta like a family. GBG was pretty damn old and didn't ever say much, but he had a kind, wrinkly face—he loved to smile, and even though he was really big and was rough-looking with a gray bushy beard, he was the type of guy you trust right away, sorta like Santa Claus or something like that.

After he'd drop his load off, we'd drive back east a little more leisurely, and GBG used to take us to see cool stuff too. The best thing he ever showed us was the Grand Canyon. Word. We went there in December when there was snow all around the edge, and looking down into that big beautiful gap in the earth was sorta like a spiritual experience for me. I remember that there were so many shades of brown and tan inside that majestic hole that it didn't even look real. And the clouds—those were like looking at something too beautiful, like it actually hurt your eyes to see something so gorgeous. I wanted to hike down into that canyon, and will one day—word—but Mom was against it, saying that it wasn't safe in the winter, even though tons of other people were doing it with huge backpacks and spikes strapped onto their boots. Hard-core.

GBG paid for a hotel in Arizona, and after eating dinner at

this little greasy diner of sorts, Mom and I went for a walk while GBG took a shower in the hotel room, because he never could shower if I was in the room, saying it wasn't proper, which was sorta noble of him, like he was a knight from olden times. I remember walking, holding hands with my mom in this dumpy little town, and once we got away from the main drag, once we walked far enough down this empty road, my mom told me to look up.

Holding her hand, I tilted my head back and then watched my gray breath climb up toward a billion stars. Tiny blue diamonds the color of gas flames were everywhere. It was *so* beautiful. My mom and I just stood there in the road looking up for—like—forever. And looking up at winter stars in Arizona—this is Amber-and-her-mom moment number five. It was very cold, but I didn't care. I had never seen so many stars—and out in the open, with no one else around, I remember praying to JC, thanking him for the stars and my mom and that moment and for sending us GBG so that we could see things like the Grand Canyon, which is one of God's masterpieces if you ask me. It was a nice moment. Word.

That winter we took a lot of trips like that with GBG, who never said much but seemed to like having us around. I really thought he was going to be the one for Mom—the one who would make her an honest woman. But then one day at the end of the school year, GBG went on one of his trucking runs and simply didn't come home. Mom held out hope for weeks, saying he would be back, but then the landlord visited us, saying that the rent hadn't been paid for two months, and soon after that Mom and I moved in with yet another one of her boyfriends—Crazy Craig, whom I don't even want to talk about, that's how crazy he was—and GBG was nothing but a memory.

I often wonder what happened to GBG, the silent abandoning one who got away.

The second week of fifth grade, take two, I was removed from class by a strange woman who wore a frilly blouse. In the hallway, the woman said, "I'm Mrs. Pohlson. I'm not a teacher, but a social skills coach, and I'd like to invite you to join a very special club."

"Am I in trouble?" I asked her, because it seemed like Mrs. Pohlson might be lying to me.

"No. Why would you think that? Did you do something wrong?"

"You don't have to do something wrong to be in trouble," I told her.

She nodded appreciatively and led me to a small room at the end of the hall that had no windows and sorta reminded me of a big closet. Inside the room was a round table that took up almost all of the space, and seated around the table were four boys, the very boys that would eventually become *my* boys—Franks Freak Force Federation.

None of them said anything to me when I sat down at the table and said, "Hello."

"Boys, this is your classmate, Amber Appleton. Don't you want to say hello to her?" Mrs. Pohlson said.

"Ricky Roberts says hello to Amber Appleton. Hello. Yes."

"H-h-h-h-el-el-o."

"Hi, Amber," said the boy in the wheelchair.

"Hey," said the black kid.

"This is Ty, Jared, Chad, and Ricky. All classmates of yours, although they are in the other two fifth grade classes. We'd like you to join our club," Mrs. Pohlson said.

The only black kid in town. The kid who couldn't speak properly. The tiny wheelchair kid with a big head. The retarded kid (I didn't know what autism was back then). And suddenly me. I wasn't so smart back in the day, but even I knew that I'd landed squarely in Club Freak. I wasn't all that upset about being admitted into Club Freak, because I was a freak too, and I sorta knew it — word — but I was worried that there would be punishments, like extra homework.

"What sorta club is this?" I asked.

"We play board games twice a week in this room," Mrs. Pohlson answered.

"Why?" I asked, and then looked around at the other boys who were all looking at their laps. "Won't we get in trouble for missing class?"

"Don't you like board games? We can play Monopoly, Scrabble, Life."

"Why would you take us out of class just so we can play games?" I asked.

"Well," Mrs. Pohlson said, "we also practice speaking properly and interacting appropriately with our friends."

"Interacting?"

"Playing."

"So this is a club where we learn to play games with each other?"

"Kind of," Mrs. Pohlson said. "Yes."

All through elementary and junior high school Mrs. Pohlson took the five of us out of class twice a week. Sometimes we played board games, sometimes we read books aloud, and sometimes we just practiced having conversations with each other.

I began to notice that The Five hardly talked outside of Mrs. Pohlson's room—but when we were there, we sorta talked a lot, or at least more than we did in the lunchroom or gym or in the schoolyard, maybe because there weren't so many other people to compete with for talking time. I began to really like going to Mrs. Pohlson's room, and it wasn't long before our parents were scheduling after-school and weekend events for The Five. Soon I was over at my boys' houses, like, all the time, and it was like we had been friends since birth. We got tight quick. Word. Suddenly I sorta had four brothers and all these extra parents looking after me. Suddenly, I had Donna too.

Eventually, Jared stopped stuttering, but nothing else major happened through Mrs. Pohlson's intervention—except that we all became best friends.

CHAPTER
4

Almost magically, just when we had to leave Mrs. Pohlson, our group social sessions, and the elementary/junior high building behind, Franks was hired to teach marketing at CPHS, so he was sorta like a freshman too (only a teacher freshman) when we started high school, which is exactly when me and The Five first started hanging with Franks. Jared and I were in his marketing class, and because Franks was so cool, allowing us to play video games during class and whatnot, we were soon bringing the rest of The Five to his classroom before school and during lunch. The rest is history, as they say.

Franks' windowless classroom is in the basement of our high school, and you can access his room from outside by descending down into the earth via a set of old concrete stairs, and then knocking on a metal door seven times. Three quick knocks. Two slow, and then two fast. This lets Franks or whoever is inside know that a Marketing Club member is on the other side of the door. There are only five Childress Public High School M.C. members, and all five just happen to belong to Franks Freak Force Federation as well.

After Ricky knocks, we back up two stairs. Two seconds

later, Jared kicks open the door, which doesn't have a knob, but a silver bar that opens it, and then he sprints back to his seat behind one of the six televisions set up high on roller stands—every one of them connected to an Xbox and each Xbox connected to the rest via a crazy web of chords. Ty and Jared are both seated behind the television closest to the outside door—eyes glued to the ass-kicking alien action on the screen. On the other side of the room Franks is sitting next to Chad's super robotic wheelchair, which we call Das Boot, even though we don't even know what the hell *Das Boot* means exactly. All four of them are holding controllers and are trying to kill each other's spacemen in a virtual world that the televisions bring to their brains.

Ricky sits down at a third television set and turns on a third Xbox. "Ricky Roberts wants Ty Hendrix and Jared Fox to die so that Ricky Roberts can enter into the Halo 3 game and join Mr. Jonathan Franks' team, because Mr. Jonathan Franks is Ricky Roberts' very favorite teacher. Yes."

"Your wish is my command," Franks says. And then something happens in the virtual world that makes Jared and Ty moan and hold their heads.

Chad and Franks are high-fiving now, and Ricky is clicking buttons on his controller, entering into the virtual world.

I know my window is tiny, because once the game starts my boys are gone, so I say, "Franks, we doing a Marketing Club announcement today?"

Marketing Club is basically an extension of Franks' marketing classes. Only once a year we compete against other schools in these debates about marketing strategies and also we do these marketing presentations in front of judges for points. My boys and even Franks wear suits to the competitions and I usually wear one of Donna's killer business skirt suits. Pretty wild stuff. If you get enough points, you can win and go on to the national competition. We've never made it past regionals.

Franks is always trying to get more people to join M.C., because his job is always on the line when it comes to district budget cuts. His marketing classes are electives, and while they are usually full—because he teaches classes like Marketing Video Games, Make and Market Your Own Movie, and my personal favorite, The Business End of the Rap Game—he's not exactly a PTA favorite, nor do many of the Childress parents take him all that seriously.

Franks is maybe only five-six, he weighs close to three hundred pounds, and he hasn't cut his hair in years—sporting the gray ponytail look. To make matters worse, he wears these little photosensitive glasses that make him look sorta like a cross between Buddha and Lennon. (John—like, of The Beatles—not to be confused with that Russian dude, Vlad.)

"You write it, and I'll read it," Franks says, his eyes locked onto the screen ready to do space battle with teenage boys.

"Cool," I say, sitting down at Franks' teacher desk near the whiteboard.

"You can have half of my Sausage Egg McMuffin. It's in drawer number two," Franks says to me. "I'm watching my figure. And the top drawer is filled with peanut M&Ms, as always."

"Donna fed me," I tell Franks.

"Cool," he says.

Aside from the occasional curse words muttered and the post-killing taunting, it's easy to write when the boys are playing Halo 3, because the game distracts them and keeps them all pretty quiet.

Ricky never kills anyone in the game, and no one kills him, because he is diagnosed with autism and just likes running around in the virtual world, stimming out. And I have to say I love that my boys are cool with this—I love their letting Ricky play Halo 3 in his own pacifistic way. My boys are good people. Word.

So I write up the ad for Marketing Club, trying to make Franks sound hip, but also trying to write something that he won't read over the morning announcements, because I've never stumped him yet. There is an art to this, because I know he isn't going to read curse words or anything like that, so writing profanity into the ad would just be cheap and point-less and the opposite of urbane.

I'm halfway through the writing of the ad when I look up at the big-framed picture on Franks' desk. His little mean-looking redheaded wife is on the beach surrounded by Franks' six little redheaded children. Franks' head is sticking out of the sand by their feet—big head, little glasses. They buried him to the neck and then had someone snap the photo. I think about what would happen to Franks' kids—who are all less than ten years old—if he got canned.

"Yo, Franks!" I say, but he doesn't answer me, because he is playing the dumb video game, but I know he hears me, so I say, "You going to the school board meeting tonight?"

Silence.

"Franks?"

The sound of buttons being pushed rapidly by boy thumbs.

"FRANKS!"

"It's of this world," Franks says, which is what he says about everything. He means that he only worries about what will happen after this world, when God takes him to heaven, because he's a Catholic like me, and he has a super faith in JC.

Now I have faith in JC too, but I also know what it's like to live on a school bus.

"Maybe you should go, Franks. Think of your children, bro," I say, because tonight's when they are deciding whether to cut the marketing department's funding and if they do that, Franks will lose his job at the end of the year. But no worries. Me and The Five are not going to let that happen. We have a killer plan. We're doing a mission.

My boys, all except Ricky, shoot me nervous glances, because they don't want Franks to know what we are doing for him—they prefer to be anonymous do-gooders. So I flash them a thumbs-up to reassure them I know what the hell I'm doing.

"My family's never missed a meal," Franks says, like a man who has never missed a meal, because he doesn't know what it's like to be homeless. But it's all good in the hood, because I'm not going to let any bad hooey happen to Franks or his redheaded kids.

"Can I give you a hug today, Franks?" I say, because I've always wanted to hug Franks ever since we met in his The Art of Marketing Junk Food class.

"Against school policy," he says.

"Someday, I'm going to give you a big old hug. Teddy bear–style."

"Maybe when you graduate," he says just as Ty and Jared start moaning again. "Undefeated Halo 3 champs! Our streak is still alive, brother!"

From his wheelchair, Chad says, "Who's your poppa?"

Chad and Franks slap hands and then touch elbows before slapping hands again. Man stuff.

Just as I finish the last line of the MC ad, the five-minute warning bell sounds, so I stand by the door and, as they exit, I hand each one of my boys a piece of paper folded into a swan— origami style. Inside all of the swans are coded instructions regarding where to meet and at what time, plus their individual speeches for tonight, written by yours truly. Jared made up our code two years back and we all have it memorized. (It's just each letter plus 1, so that *A*s are written as *B*s and *B*s are written as *C*s and so forth. Not overly secure, but it stumps most of the morons in our school. True.) And as they walk through Franks' door, I give each of my boys a pat on the butt too, like I am a football coach or something. The pat on the butt makes my boys blush and smile. I have to pinch Chad on the cheek because he's in a motorized wheelchair and all, but I get him blushing too.

"Ricky Roberts wants a paper swan–coded message like everyone else in the—"

"How does Ricky Roberts receive information?" I ask him.

"On a need-to-know basis. Yes."

"You only have five minutes to get to homeroom," I say, and then Ricky is off.

Back inside of his lair, I hand Franks the Marketing Club ad and say, "Read that over the loudspeaker—if you dare."

"Cool," Franks says with a smile.

"Hug?"

"Homeroom," Franks says, raising his chubby hand.

I slap his red palm, and then I'm on my way to homeroom.

★ ★ ★

"Rub-a-dub-dub, it's Marketing Club! What's the rub, bub? Nada. MC for real, with plenty of zeal—and that's the appeal! Do you have what it takes—to slake—the growing desire for marketing and advertising fo' hire? We meet in the basement every day, hey, so what do you say? Drop on down, give Franks a pound. Become a Marketing Club man or woman today. Peace out, homies! And keep hope alive!"

Sitting in homeroom, I smile to myself. Franks read my announcement verbatim, just like he promised. He's an honorable man, a man of his word, which is rare in this world, or at least that's what I've observed after seventeen trips around the flaming ball in the sky. (That's the sun, sucka!) Everyone around me is talking and totally not paying any attention to the announcements; not even my homeroom teacher, Mrs. Lindsay, listens or gives a crap, but I know that there are at least four teenage boys sitting in homerooms hysterically laughing at my advertisement and Franks' awesome delivery—and I know that it might be the only laugh they get today. Franks Freak Force Federation will get a little fuel from this, and maybe that will be enough for them to make it through the school day. "Keep hope alive." I'm pretty sure Jesse Jackson said that when he was running for president back in the 80s. Yeah, we learned that hip catchphrase in my U.S. History II class a few months ago.

The day passes uneventfully—boring Spanish III, lame-ass gym, boring pre-calc, boring chemistry—and since Mondays and Tuesdays are Ricky's socialization days, we don't eat our lunch in Franks' room, but in the cafeteria, because the special education department thinks that Ricky should interact with the student body more. Great idea, special education people who have no idea how evil the student body can be to special people like Ricky Roberts.

When I'm in the lunch line, watching over Ricky, protecting my boy, Lex Pinkston elbows me in the back and coughs out a disgusting single syllable word for a woman, which I'm not even going to repeat. He pretends to cover his mouth and cough, because he is a moron, but it is clear that he is calling me this worst of all words, so I say, "Like you'd even know what one was."

"I've seen your mom's," Lex says, five moronic football players standing behind him. "Everyone in this town has."

I slap his face hard enough to turn his head—*SLAP!*—and it makes me smile, even though I'm a Catholic and JC is not down with violence.

And then Lex's hand is on his face. He cannot believe that I frickin' slapped him.

The football morons are shocked as hooey—their pieholes wide open, like their eyes.

Ricky is screaming, "Hi! Hi! Hi! Hi!"

The lunchroom monitors show up, get between us, and the next thing I know I'm in Prince Tony's office, waiting for him to finish some stupid phone conversation. When he finishes, he looks at me from across his battleship-size desk and says, "What now?"

"Your quarterback called me a disgusting single-syllable word for a woman — which I'm not even going to repeat — and then implied that he had sex with my mother, so I slapped his kisser," I say, and then add, "Prince Tony."

"It's Principal Fiorilli to you, young lady."

"Come on, Prince, we're behind closed doors. Just us here," I say to the tiny man, because he is weak and can be swayed if you flirt with him the right way — not in a sexy way, but in a father-daughter sorta way.

He turns red, and I know I have him.

"I heard you kicked him in the shin yesterday. His father called to complain and —"

"Lex Pinkston is an evil boy who —"

"I know exactly who Lex Pinkston is and his father —"

"I prayed for you last night, Prince Tony."

"You did?" He doesn't know how to react to this one. Church and state and all. This is a public school. "Why did you *pray* for me?"

"I pray for you every night. True."

"Thank you," he says, blushing again.

"When are you going to start protecting the good people of Childress Public High School?"

"What would you have me do?"

"Expel Lex Pinkston."

"For what?"

"For being evil."

"It's not that easy."

"So you are admitting Lex Pinkston is evil?"

"*I said* it's not that easy."

"Yeah, it is."

"First, Mr. Pinkston is a school board member and we have to be delicate when — *why am I explaining myself to a seventeen-year-old girl?*"

"I'm going to say one thing to you, Prince Tony, and then I'm going to walk out that door."

I stare into his eyes, and I see him swallow once. He digs me, and he knows that Lex Pinkston needs to be kicked in the shin and slapped every so often, if only to maintain the balance of power within the student body so that evil doesn't get out of control; the boss man sees this because deep down, Prince Tony is a good man — even if he is a wimp who plays both sides of the political fence — and like Billy Budd, Prince Tony needs a Captain Vere to protect him from the evil people in the world. I fancy myself a more adroit and less dreamy, less starry Captain Vere. Captainess Appleton, at your service. Word, all you lime-suckers.

"You're a good man, Prince Tony," I say, "and I believe that you will eventually clean up this school and protect the common students from the selfish interests of school board members like Mr. Pinkston. My money's on you, Prince Tony. *My money is on you.*"

I get up and start walking out of his office.

"You simply cannot assault students in my building, Ms. Appleton. I will not endure your vigilante approach to—"

"Search your heart, Prince Tony. You know what's the right thing to do. I believe in you. And I'm praying for you. Every night."

I walk out of his office, and his ancient wrinkly secretary Mrs. Baxter—who wears the reddest lipstick I have ever seen on any woman, and looks like a patriot with blue hair and white skin—asks me, "How'd it go in there?"

Mrs. Baxter is pretty nice, and I think it's safe to say she's an Amber Appleton fan.

"I'm praying for your boss," I tell her. "He has the ability to turn this school around."

"If he only had the chutzpah," she whispers, with her hand shielding her ancient lips so that only I can see.

"Viva la revolution, Mrs. Baxter," I say as she writes me a pass, and then I jog up two flights of stairs so I can check out Doolin's Accelerated American Lit class, where I learn all about civil disobedience and that cool cat Henry David Thoreau, whom I admire a whole bunch, because he represented hard-core and even went to jail for his beliefs, which is saying something. True? True.

CHAPTER 5

Practical Life Skills class, where I work on my prom dress.

Semi-boring history, and then I'm at Ricky's locker.

"Amber Appleton slapped Lex Pinkston in THE FACE. Bad girl! Bad girl! Bad girl!"

"If you don't stop saying bad girl, I'm going to tickle you."

"No! Ricky Roberts does NOT like to be tickled. No tickle-tickle."

This is as close as Ricky gets to making a joke, because tickling is his favorite. I get him good under his armpits, and he doubles over and yells "Hi! Hi! Hi!" until some bearded teacher I don't know comes out of his classroom and asks if everything is okay.

"Beautiful," I say to the beard.

"Amber Appleton is my best friend. She makes omelets with tequila and takes me on missions and I am taking her to prom in a limousine! Yes," Ricky says.

The beard nods once, real serious—as if Ricky told the beard that he needed to donate a kidney to the president because it was the beard's civic duty or something—and then the beard walks back into his classroom.

Truth be told, there are a lot of teachers who are scared of Ricky, because he flips out sometimes and punches himself in the head, which can get a little intense.

As we walk to Donna's house together, Ricky counts aloud, and I enjoy the afternoon winter sun on my face.

Bobby Big Boy always pisses himself whenever we are reunited, so I pull a few paper towels from the roll, and then let him out of his room. In the tiled hallway, he circles me seven times, like he has been snorting cocaine all day, and then he pees on the floor, so I wipe up the yellow puddle and give Thrice B a kiss. He tries to slip me the tongue, but he doesn't make it into my mouth or anything.

I give Ricky a sleeve of Fig Newtons and a blue Gatorade.

He's already doing his math homework, because he frickin' loves math.

"I have to go see The KDFCs," I tell him, but he doesn't look up from his math. "I'll be back to cook dinner. Okay?"

"Ricky Roberts is doing math. Do not talk to Ricky Roberts when Ricky Roberts is doing math!"

"Cool," I say, and then lock the door behind BBB and me. Ricky will do math problems forever if you let him, so no worries leaving him alone.

I take Donna's ten-speed bike from the garage and put B3 in the little basket Donna bought for him that is attached to the handlebars. He fits perfect so that just his head sticks out. It's pretty frickin' adorable.

We are flying through the cold January air, out of town, across the tracks, and into the ghetto. There are a lot of down-

and-out people in this town, and they usually stare at me when I ride my bike through.

The first time this happened, it scared me a lot, because it sorta looked like these people wanted to kill me, but I have since learned a trick.

Whenever someone looks at me like they want to stomp my face in, I now look the person in the eyes, smile really huge, wave, and say, "Hope you're havin' a great day!" It's pretty wild, because doing this really works. If you don't believe me, try it yourself. Even the meanest-looking people will get this really stunned look on their faces, but then the smile blooms, and they usually wave back and say something nice like "God bless you!" or "Same to you!" It's a pretty cool trick, and maybe even a pretty killer way of life, if you are a crazy spiritual ho like me. True? True.

Today I yell, "Hope you're havin' a great day!" eight times, and I get two "Thanks!" one "Jesus loves you!" two "You go girl!"s two "Same to you!"s and one "You a sexy bike girl! Ride on, girl, ride on," which made me laugh, because the man who yelled this had to be at least ninety-seven.

And then I'm at the Korean Catholic Church, which is an old shoe store turned house of God, and sits nestled between a McDonald's and a liquor store. In his penguin suit, Father Chee is waiting outside for me, because the men in front of the liquor store sometimes say bad things to me, and the "Hope you're havin' a great day!" trick doesn't always work on them so well.

Technically, I got hooked up with Father Chee through my high school guidance counselor, who says I have to do a load of community service if I want to get into Bryn Mawr College, which is where I want to study English, because you can go to law school if you major in English and do really well at Bryn Mawr College. That's what Donna did anyway. But to tell you the truth, I don't really give a crap anymore about fulfilling the community service requirements, which are of this world, as Franks like to say. I still want to go to Bryn Mawr and all, but doing what I do with Father Chee has become part of my religious practice, which I realize might sound truly whack to some, but I believe in what FC and I do, like—for real. Word. And I had been praying for a chance to make a difference in the lives of people who needed it most, because that's really all I want to do with my life—help people who need it, just like JC told us to do.

About a year back, Father Chee contacted the high school looking for someone to teach English to the women in his church who wanted to learn. At first, I tried to simply straight-up teach them vocab and grammar and whatnot, but it was so boring and depressing for the women that I had to think up a killer alternative or quit. Lucky for FC's church members, I'm pretty good at thinking up killer hooey. Also, Father Chee and I work well together—we're an awesome team—and ever since I implemented my new teaching technique, my enrollment has more than doubled.

Father Chee holds open the front door and I ride Donna's bike right into the church.

My Man of God locks the door behind us, which is sorta weird since it's a church and all.

"Hello, Bobby Big Boy," Father Chee says, patting 3B on the

head. Triple B licks Father's hand, because they are boys, and then FC is pulling BBB out of the basket so that they can get a man hug in, which is cool, because B Thrice loves to hug Men of God.

My dog is Catholic. And if you say dogs don't have a soul and therefore don't go to heaven, I will slap your face silly. Word.

Maybe—before I get into the story of The Korean Divas for Christ and Father Chee—you might want to know how I became a Catholic and a crazy-serious religious person?

Well, the only thing my father, Bob, left behind for me when he took off was this series of children's books called Jesus Was a Rock Star. They were these big picture books for kids—twelve in the series—and each was about one of the killer adventures Jesus had on earth, how Jesus rocked the world and then got crucified for being so cool. These books were pretty awesome because Jesus was always doing miracles like turning water to wine and walking on water and even bringing people back from the dead, which is definitely a pretty killer thing to do. Also, in the pictures, Jesus was very handsome (sorta like Jack White of the White Stripes) with His long rock-star hair. JC always had an entourage around Him, He never freaked out when people let Him down or things went wrong—JC was always so very cool—and He loved everyone and went around saving people like Mom and me, people everyone else had already given up on.

My favorite Jesus adventure was when He stopped the crowd from stoning a hooker. You probably know that one already, but all these mean men were actually going to throw rocks at the woman's head until her skull caved in and she was dead, but Jesus did this Jedi-mind-trick thing and just wrote words in the sand until the mean men noticed and asked what the hell JC was doing. Then—so cool, like a rock star—Jesus says that the person without any sin can throw the first rock at the woman. And then the men start to feel guilty and freak out and leave—which is the best part. Jesus didn't even have to raise His voice, let alone throw any fists. Who would have thought that writing words in the sand would work? And then JC doesn't even yell at the woman for having too much sex. He just saves her and tells her to live a good life, which is pretty cool of Jesus. No guilt trip or anything.

I still have my Jesus Was a Rock Star books, and the pages are all worn out from my reading them so many times. True.

My mom never really dug Jesus too much, maybe because my dad was big on JC and he broke Mom's heart—shattered it—leaving her all alone with newborn me and an endless train of loser boyfriends.

So Mom never took me to church or anything like that.

But when I was in eighth grade, Ty was always complaining about his mom making him attend these religious classes about Jesus so that he could join the Catholic Church and avoid getting sent to hell. I asked if I could go with him, and this excited Mrs. Hendrix very much. So I started attending Jesus class with Ty at St. Dymphna's, which is this big old church with killer stained-glass windows, ancient wooden pews full of comfy red cushions, and a massive organ that can blast your eardrums until you go deaf—St. Dymphna's pretty much has the works.

Only the priest there—Father Johns—told the Jesus stories all wrong. Father Johns was always going on and on about how Jesus was going to be disappointed in us if we sinned or didn't do enough charity, and the way he talked about JC made the Son of God seem more like a mean, pissy old lady than a rock star. But the one thing that really hit home with me was Father Johns telling us that we would go to hell if we didn't join the Catholic Church, do enough charity work, and live a good life. That bit sorta scared me and made me want to join for real.

Needless to say, I was baptized, did the confession thing, had my First Communion with all of these little kids whose parents were good Catholics and therefore didn't let their sons and daughters get to middle school before they have their First Communion, and then Ty and I joined the church as his parents watched all proud. Mrs. Hendrix was my sponsor—and she even bought me a white dress and white shoes for the big day. I took Mary for my confirmation name—not too original, I admit—and then I went to a big party at the Hendrix house, where Ty's relatives actually gave me presents simply because I was an official Catholic now.

Mom didn't come to see me baptized, nor when I became a member of the church—probably because of my religious dad leaving her.

For a year or so, I went to church with the Hendrix family every week, but then I just stopped going for some reason. I think it was because the priest kept on messing up the Jesus stories—talking about Jesus as if he were this boring arrogant person who didn't rock, which we all know is not the case. I didn't feel anything when I went to church, and I could read about Jesus at home and pray anywhere, so I just stopped going to Mass. I think I really let Ty's mom down, but religion and JC aren't for impressing people's moms. True.

I was going to try another church to see if they talked about Jesus any differently, but then I met Father Chee—and instantly, I knew that I had found my priest for life. Word. FC rocks, just like JC.

Inside Father Chee's church, there is a small room where you can hang your coat, which is where I park Donna's bike, and then there is the sanctuary. A big crucifix hangs front and center over a little altar and a simple podium. The walls are cinder blocks painted puke yellow, and there are no windows and no pews, but only long white lightbulbs in the ceiling—the kind that look like lightsabers—and rows of flesh-colored fold-up chairs, which are currently occupied by a dozen or so Korean women, all of whom jump up and start smiling just as soon as I walk into the church.

I don't want to brag, but I'm sorta like a rock star to these people.

The first thing that happens whenever I enter The Korean Catholic Church:

Every single one of The KDFCs gives me a big old hug and then they speak their homework sentence in English. I give them a prompt at the end of each class, which I copy down a dozen or so times because I don't have access to a photocopy machine. Father Chee usually explains the prompt in Korean, which is sorta like cheating, but it's also good because we want The KDFCs to do the assignment so that their English will improve and they can start branching out into America and whatnot.

Last week they all failed to do the assignment correctly.

I had asked them to state what they would most like to do in the world and to describe how doing it would make them feel, using one killer adjective. But all of these kind-hearted women—every single one—said what they would like to do for their husband or their children or their parents.

"I would like to buy a big house for my son or daughter."

"I would like to buy my husband an expensive car."

"I would like to send my nice parents to Hawaii."

So I failed them all and told The KDFCs that they had to use better adjectives and say what they wanted for *themselves*, because having dreams for yourself is totally American, and if they were going to live in America, they needed to think like American women.

So I say, "Na Yung, did you do your homework?"

"Yes, Amber," Na Yung says.

"And?"

Na Yung, who is old enough to be my mom, gets all nervous whenever she is speaking English around me, which is why I called on her first, so she can get it over with and relax.

"I would like see live handsome movie star in Hollywood—like *delicious* men I see in photo American magazine."

"Nice job," I tell Na Yung. "Very American! Good pronunciation and delicious is truly a killer adjective! A-plus. How about you, Sun?"

"I dream to fly in beautiful fat *rotund* air balloon so hair will blow warmest behind my ear."

"That's *damn* good, Sun. Rotund is *very* good. I'd like to fly in a beautiful fat rotund air balloon too. That would be truly killer."

As I listen to the dreams of all the Korean women present, Father Chee smiles at me so that I can see every one of his teeth. I can tell he really really digs me, in a non-sexual good-guy priest sorta way. Maybe he wishes I were his daughter, because he's not allowed to make a daughter for himself. He would be a cool dad.

The KDFCs love it when I praise their English, and you can tell that they really dig expressing themselves in my class too, which is pretty cool. I'm having a good time listening to their dreams, but then suddenly everyone has spoken and The Korean Divas for Christ are lining up in two rows by the altar—songbooks in hand—so eagerly, because they pretty much come for the soul singing. FC and I know that they like singing better than learning English, which is why we invented this awesome alternative class in the first place.

"Shall we?" Father Chee says, offering his arm like a frickin' gentleman.

Just like always, he walks me arm-in-arm to the front of the church, as if he were about to give me away on my wedding day.

When I am in position, Father Chee bows to me once, and then takes his place at the old beat-up piano to my left, opening his songbook to the number we always start with.

"Okay, ladies," I say. "What do we need to work on this week?"

Back when I first started teaching, I let each one of The Korean Divas for Christ choose an English language name the way my

Spanish teacher let us pick Spanish names back in Spanish I. (I went with Juanita.) After I started English the fun way, I had each one of The KDFCs take the name of a famous R & B singer.

Hye Min—who goes by Tina—raises her hand, so I nod in her direction. She says, "A selling the word."

"That's right, Tina. You need to sell the frickin' words. And how do we do that, ladies?"

Front-and-center Kyung Ah—aka Diana—raises her hand, and when I nod at her, she says, "Hips and the hands."

"It's all about the hips and hands. And?"

A back row exceptionally tall woman named Sueng Hee—we call her Beyoncé—yells out "Shoulder dips!" without my calling on her, which sorta pisses me off, because I find her outburst threatening to my authority, but I appreciate the unbridled enthusiasm, so I let it slide.

"Shoulder dips. *And?*"

The oldest KDFC, a wrinkly grandmother we know as Ella, waves at me, so I point at her.

"The souls clap," she says.

"The super-duper soul clap. That's right," I say, and then start clapping slowly, soulfully.

All of The KDFCs follow suit, because they are all frickin' pros.

So I add a shoulder dip and a step to the right—clap!

The KDFCs don't miss a beat and move with me.

Shoulder dip, and a step to the left—clap!

We repeat this for a few times, and then I yell, "Work those hips, ladies! Work what God gave you—meaning yo' apple-bottom booties!"

So we all let our booties snap with our heads.

Left—slide—clap!

Right—slide—clap!

When we are nice and warmed up, I yell, "Hit those keys, Chee!"

Father starts playing piano, and then The KDFCs are rocking "You Can't Hurry Love" by The Supremes. The way they sing sounds very staccato, because they are Korean and don't know English all that well, but they sell the song with the moves I gave them, and I have to say that I am proud of these chippies today, because they are sorta rocking my socks off.

Before we all got so damn good at soul singing, Father had the church buy us twenty copies of *The Supremes Complete Songbook* and then—using Korean-English dictionaries—the Korean Divas for Christ and I translated all the songs, writing the Korean under the English, so that my students would know what the hell they were singing. Then we worked on pronunciation, and then finally, selling the songs onstage.

I didn't know that Father Chee could play piano when I thought up the singing-to-learn-English idea, but on the day that we were first going to start singing, the piano magically showed up in the church. When I asked him where the piano came from, Father Chee said that God had put it there. When I asked him who was going to play the piano, Chee said God would play through Father Chee's fingers. Maybe some corny hooey to you, but I like the way Chee keeps God magical, sorta like Santa Claus when you are a kid. More priests should take this approach, because there is a frickin' reason why Santa is more popular than Jesus nowadays.

I take The KDFCs through "I Hear a Symphony," "Stop! In the Name of Love," "Baby Love," "You Keep Me Hangin' On," and a few other classics, before we make the power circle, which is when all the women put arms around each other's shoulders so that we are all linked up in a super-powerful woman circle, and then I yell some empowering hooey I made up a while back.

"What are we?" I yell.

"Strong!" The KDFCs yell back.

"Who are we?"

"The Korean Divas for Christ!"

"Who loves us?"

"JC!"

"Who wants us to be happy?"

"God!"

"Who rocks?"

"The Korean Divas for Christ!"

"Who are the best Korean soul singers in the world?"

"The Korean Divas for Christ!"

"Hell yeah?"

"Hell yeah!"

"HELL YEAH?"

"HELL YEAH!"

And then I break off and run around the inside of the power circle giving each Korean Diva a super high five, which is a two-handed slap above the head. The KDFCs go crazy for this sorta pumped-up ending. They like to hug me before I go, and since I really dig hugs, I go wild with the hugging too. Every KDFC gets a big old hug from me, which takes like ten frickin' minutes.

When it's time to go, it's usually dark, so—in his penguin suit—Father Chee jogs next to me and BBB as I ride my bike through the ghetto. He likes to make sure I get home okay. I smile at damn near everyone in his neighborhood and do the "Hope you are having a great day!" trick, which makes Father Chee laugh and glow in a fatherly proud sorta way.

While I'm riding, I usually confess my sins.

"Forgive me, Father, for I have sinned," I say to Father Chee.

"Confess your sins and Jesus will forgive you," FC says.

"I kicked Lex Pinkston in the shin yesterday and slapped his face today. But he called me a disgusting single-syllable word for a woman—which I'm not even going to repeat—said he had sex with my mother, and made Ricky say something sexual to a classmate."

Still running, Father Chee nods wisely—like—a million frickin' times. "Jesus offered us an example. Turn the other cheek, He told us."

"That's why I'm confessing. Do you think I haven't read the Bible?"

"You are forgiven."

"No penance?" I ask.

"You've done it already. Teaching English to my church members."

"But I *enjoy* doing that."

"God wants us to be happy!" FC says, which makes me smile.

When we get pretty deep into my neighborhood, he says, "I'm going to return to the church now."

I stop riding my bike and we look at each other, smiling face-to-face, both knowing that we kicked butt for God today—making The KDFCs happy and hopeful.

I pretend that Father Chee is my dad, and maybe he pretends I am his daughter.

"Can I get a hug, Chee," I say.

"Of course," he replies, and then he hugs me like any good father would.

"How 'bout some love for B3?"

Father Chee pats BBB's head, so lovingly, and I say, "You're a good man, Chee," just before I pedal away.

I look back, and—as always—Chee is there watching, making sure I get to Donna's okay, and that makes me smile and feel like there is so much good in the world.

CHAPTER 6

When I arrive home, Ricky is still doing math problems at the kitchen table, so I feed Bobby Big Boy some wet canned stuff and start cooking Donna's dinner. I decide to go with rice, red peppers, and chicken. So I defrost the chicken in the microwave, chop up two red peppers, boil some rice, and dig out the wok.

After I cut up the chicken and the red peppers into thin strips, I put it all in a big old silver bowl and douse it in a load of soy sauce and sesame seeds.

Next, I get a shot of Jack Daniels from the liquor cabinet and dump that onto the chicken and red pepper.

"What the hell," I say, and then pour some Jack onto the now-hot wok, which makes a sizzling noise and produces a good warm wheat smell.

I stir-fry it all up, and it smells pretty delectable.

Ricky is STILL doing math problems, and BBB is chillin' on the kitchen mat, looking up at me, watching my every move, because the dashing mutt's totally in love with me.

Donna comes home at exactly six thirty; she is one regimented woman.

"Like I've told you a million times before, you don't have to cook for us, Amber. But it sure smells good," she says as she tosses her keys into an old crystal ashtray that she keeps on a stand by the kitchen door, and sets down her bags and hangs up her overcoat.

She runs her hands through Ricky's hair and kisses him on the forehead, and I get a little jealous, I must admit, because my mom is so uncool compared to Ricky's.

"How's my boy?"

"Doing math problems. Do not talk to—"

"What time is it?"

Ricky looks at the clock on the wall and then shuts his workbook. "Time for Ricky Roberts to eat his dinner with Mommy Roberts and Amber Appleton."

"That's my boy," Donna says to Ricky. To me she says, "How was your day, Amber?"

I nod and then shrug, like a tool.

"Okay," Donna says. "Can we eat?"

I serve everyone, and we begin to eat.

"Is there Jack Daniels in this?" Donna says after tasting my newest dish.

"Yep," I say.

"Tastes divine," Donna says. "Got you a present, Ricky."

"Mommy Roberts got Ricky Roberts a present!"

"See that bag by my briefcase? Over there by the door?"

"Ricky Roberts sees a bag!"

"Why don't you go see what's in that bag."

Ricky stands and walks over to the bag. He picks it up and shakes it like a Christmas present. He even holds it to his ear. A hand finally goes in and comes out full of camouflage. "Ricky Roberts gets a shirt."

"What does it say on the shirt?" Donna says, fork in hand.

Ricky holds the shirt above his head and reads the words written in hunter orange. "Franks Freak Force Federation!"

It is the coolest shirt I have ever seen.

"How many are in that bag, Ricky?" Donna says.

Ricky counts. "Seven!"

"One for every member involved in the mission."

I swallow hard; I love Donna so much. She was in court all day—a murder case—but she still got us team shirts for the mission. She rocks!

"There are *FIVE* members of Franks Freak Force Federation. Mommy Roberts brought *SEVEN* shirts. Seven."

"Well, your attorney needs to dress the part. And I thought Franks might want one, so I had my assistant make up seven. What the hell, right, Amber?"

I nod dumbly. I want to have an assistant someday who will make freaky teens cool T-shirts so that they can do good things in style. I want to be Donna. So frickin' much.

Donna winks at me, and then eats some more of my stir-fry.

Ricky strips off his Utley jersey and puts on some camo. "Franks Freak Force Federation!"

"You like?" Donna says.

"Ricky Roberts likes very much!"

"Amber?"

I nod fifty times, like a moron.

"There's one in there for you," Donna says.

I sprint to the bag and find that there is a fitted girly tee in there for me, so I go into the other room and put it on, checking myself out in the hallway mirror. The cut makes my boobs look perky, and the coloring makes me look dangerous — sorta like Sarah Michelle Gellar playing Buffy the Vampire Slayer or maybe Uma Thurman in *Kill Bill: Vol. 2*. I feel so ready to fight for good tonight.

I walk back into the kitchen and Donna says, "You look like a knockout. How am I going to wear a fitted tee if I need to stand next to young sexy you?"

"Amber Appleton is sexy!" Ricky says.

"True?" I ask, and then blush like a moron.

"True," Donna says, and nods in this killer gangsta way that makes me believe her.

BBB barks once in agreement. "Rew!"

"Cool," I say, smiling.

I eat my dinner, and then Ricky and I clean up the dishes while Donna answers a bazillion e-mails on her Blackberry. Her thumbs move at the speed of light, and I dig how she mouths the words she is typing, like a little kid would.

Jared shows up with his brother Chad strapped to his back like a toddler in a baby backpack. Chad never really grew, and his head is almost as big as his body. We told him to leave Das Boot at home for dramatic effect. Ty is right behind the Fox brothers, and all are totally psyched to put on their new shirts.

The boys talk about Halo 3 while I take BBB out to pee and Donna gets changed.

After I have B Thrice locked up in his room and listening to classical music, I hear Donna calling my name so I walk upstairs and into her bedroom.

She has a frickin' king-size bed even though she is thin and single. It is very kick-ass. When I enter, she's checking her makeup in the mirror and wearing her fitted camo tee with a black skirt and knee-high leather boots with blocky two-inch heels.

"Sit," she says to me, so I sit on the edge of her bed. "Those boys downstairs, would they be doing what we are about to do tonight if you weren't around to lead them?"

I shrug. My heart is beating like mad.

Donna looks me in the eye. She is a goddess.

"They wouldn't be doing anything tonight if they didn't know you. They'd be playing video games or jerking off or doing whatever teenage boys do when left to their own devices."

I don't know what to say, so I say nothing.

"I see something in you that I like very much, Amber. You're not like most people. You are going to do something very special with your life. You're going to do something very special tonight, because it's what you were born to do."

I almost crap myself, and I can feel myself shaking a little.

"Here's a little secret between old friends," Donna says, and then bends down to whisper into my ear. "Most people—even adults, even grown men—are like teenage boys, only they pretend they are not." Donna stands up and winks at me. "People like you and me need to tell them what to do, so that the world won't get too messed up. They want you to give them instructions. They need you to do this. And you know what needs to be done, because you have a good heart—and you have courage. I've seen your good heart at work time and time again over the years. You're all good. One hundred percent. So trust your instincts, and speak your mind tonight. Be brave. Those boys look up to you. You're the shepherd. Herd the sheep. Understand?"

I nod thirty times in ten seconds and blink back a few tears, because no one really talks like this to me ever, and I think I understand what Donna is saying, because I get this feeling in my chest sometimes, and I'm not really like other people.

"Let's do this," Donna says, and I follow her out of the bedroom.

When we get to the living room, the boys stop talking and take in Donna's hotness. It mutes them instantly. Donna lets them take in her presence. I study Donna, and this is one of her tricks. She waits for people to take in her hotness before she speaks—always. She is the greatest person I know, and if she weren't an atheist, I'd say she was perfect, or maybe even God incarnate.

★ ★ ★

On the way to the school board meeting, I can tell my boys are tense. I'm in the back with Ty, Jared, and Chad—and their collective nervous quietness is freaking me out a little. Also, Donna is not rocking any music, nor is she saying anything, which is strange, because she always seems to be talking or listening to music when we drive, which is how I know she is now testing my leadership abilities. Ricky is quietly counting the streetlights we pass—oblivious.

I start to wonder if my boys need a pep talk, so I say, "How does everyone feel?"

"Cool," Ty says.

Jared and Chad nod. Chad is sitting on his brother's lap.

"Did you memorize the speeches?" I ask.

"Yeah," Chad says.

"Can we nail them tonight?" I ask.

"No worries," Jared says.

"This is Franks' livelihood we're talking about. If Franks gets canned, no Halo 3 next year," I say.

"Yeah," Ty says, "we get that."

"And Franks' six kids," I add. "Think of them tonight. We don't want them living on the streets, right? Use them as motivation. Picture them in your mind."

"We got it," Jared says.

"Have we ever let you down before?" Chad asks.

They aren't nervous at all, maybe because they are teenage boys and therefore do not know how much is at stake. None of them has ever been homeless either. None of them has ever missed a meal. Their lawyer and banker fathers are around to provide houses and clothes and food and all the other good stuff. These boys don't understand what I understand.

Following my own advice, I think about Franks' redheaded kids as we park, and my chest starts to burn—my eyes start to water.

"Leave your coats in the car, boys," Donna says. "I want everyone to see your shirts."

We take off our coats, get Chad into the babypack on Jared's back, and then Donna says, "We bust in. I make a brief introduction, and then you boys follow Amber's lead. Understood?"

My boys nod. They understand.

"Ready to start filming?" Donna says.

"Wait," I say. "We should pray first. Before we go in."

"If you must," Donna says, and then walks toward the door, Ricky following his mother, because Ricky is also an atheist, just like his mom.

We are all shivering in our T-shirts, because it is cold out, but we are also geared up for the mission.

Chad, Ty, and Jared don't really dig on JC as much as I do, but they all believe in God, so they bow their heads and close their eyes as I grab Ty's and Jared's hands, and say, "Dear God, we are gathered here tonight for a good cause. Franks' job is on the line. We believe that CPHS needs Franks, that he does much more good than harm in that building, which is cool and important. If our cause be just, give us the strength to use the talents with which you have already blessed us. Help us rock the worlds of those board members. Peace out, God. And peace be with you."

We all drop hands and open eyes.

"Ready?" I ask.

"Hell, yeah!" Chad says from behind his brother's head.

We walk toward Donna, who has the video camera out and recording now, which makes me realize that she videoed my prayer. I'm not sure I like her videoing my prayer, but I don't say anything about that.

Donna says, "Introduce yourself, boys."

"Chad Fox, aka the Desert Fox, ready and willin' and chillin'."

"Ty Hendrix. Tower of Power even if I am only five-ten."

"Jared Fox. Just Jared."

"My name is Ricky Roberts. The macking mathematician,"

Ricky says, which makes me smile because I made up that name for Ricky.

"Amber Appleton. Just a girl with God on her side."

Donna holds the video camera at arms length and films herself saying, "Donna Roberts, attorney at law. We're at the Childress Public High School board meeting. The time is 7:46 PM Tuesday, January 27, 2009. The rest will be self-explanatory."

Keeping the camera on herself, Donna walks into the converted-into-offices house next to the elementary school, and into the boardroom where the school board meets.

There are community members and one or two local reporters seated in folding chairs; Prince Tony is in the front row with a few other administrators, and the school board is seated behind this long table front and center. Pretty standard adult stuff abounds.

We're all in camo, hunter orange letters proclaiming who we are quite loudly. But wearing a three-piece suit that actually has a pocket watch chain draped like an evil gold smile across the man's belly, as if he is stepping out of some old corny movie about waiting for trains to show up, Mr. Pinkston stands, removes his pocket watch from his vest, and—while reading the time—he says, "Who are you and what the hell do you think you are doing?"

Donna just stands there in front of Mr. Pinkston, front and center, wearing camo, filming herself, confidently letting all present take in her hotness.

"Sit," Donna says, as if she were talking to Bobby Big Boy.

Amazingly, Mr. Pinkston looks up, surprised, and then sits.

The room is dead quiet.

"Ms. Roberts," Prince Tony says in a calm, soothing voice. "What's going on here? We don't allow these meetings to be videotaped. Surely you can understand why."

Donna completely ignores Prince Tony and addresses the room. "Boys and ladies. I'm with Roberts, Bradley, and Wong. If you haven't heard of our law firm, I guarantee your lawyers have, and those boys will want to know what has been said tonight, so take notes. It's come to our attention that you are considering cutting funding for Mr. Jonathan Franks' marketing classes. I'll be representing Mr. Franks and all five of the students who will be speaking tonight. All pro bono, for as long as it takes. You need to know two things before we begin. One. Roberts, Bradley, and Wong. That's not alphabetical order. Two. Name one. The one in charge. Roberts. That's me. Amber?"

Donna starts filming me.

I'm in total frickin' awe.

"Amber?" Donna says.

Ty elbows me in the back.

"You're up," Donna says.

I look at all of the school board members. With such freaks as us in front of them—represented by one of the most feared lawyers in the tri-state area—they are in total panic mode. I can see it plainly all over their faces. All of them are impressed with Donna, except Mr. Pinkston who looks sorta like Dick Cheney and is glaring at me like he might want to roast my carcass alive and eat me for dinner. Like father, like son. Suddenly, I find my swagger.

"As my colleague clearly stated." *I called Donna my colleague.*

Was that a mistake? Too much? "We are here on behalf of Mr. Jonathan Franks. You may—"

"Okay. Enough foolishness. This school board is within its legal rights here tonight," Mr. Pinkston says, completely interrupting me. "It's perfectly legal to consider—"

"Don't you ever interrupt my client again, Mr. Pinkston." Donna locks eyes with Mr. Pinkston. She is unflinching. "And I think my client knows a little bit more about the law than you or anyone else in this room, because I've informed Ms. Appleton of her rights. As a taxpayer and a concerned citizen, I'm trying to help you avoid making yet another classic and extremely costly blunder."

Donna turns the video camera on Mr. Pinkston.

"Don't you dare film me!" he yells.

Donna smiles, keeps the camera on Mr. Pinkston until he turns red, and then she turns it back on me.

I clear my throat and then say, "You may think Mr. Jonathan Franks is expendable, but he serves at least two great purposes, one of which is to protect you from lawsuits. Lawsuits? I can hear you asking. Lawsuits. I'm the poorest girl in the high school. I haven't been to the doctor or dentist for a decade because my mother cannot afford health insurance. For all I know, I may have cancer or may be in need of a lung transplant. But I'd never know it, because we cannot afford to go to the doctor. Maybe if she worked for a good employer, I'd have health insurance. But she works for your school district—for fifteen years now—driving buses, which doesn't pay so hot. No benefits either. So I don't have money for the sorta fitting-in clothes your sons and daughters wear, nor do I have money to fix my messed-up teeth, and this has led to some serious self-esteem problems. But can I see one of the quality therapists some of my classmates get to see? No. Because I don't have health insurance. Word. This high school is a daily hell for me, let me tell you, but there is one place where I am always welcome—where I don't feel like going on a freaking rampage—and that is Mr. Franks' room. I am the Marketing Club team leader, and I oversee the Childress MC chapter. I personally won second place in the marketing fast food competition last year at the regionals. Mr. Franks runs this club for little to no pay when you break down the hours and the costs of the trophies, ribbons, and pizza parties he throws to boost MC morale. And it is the only thing in this school that gives me any sense of self-esteem. So don't take away the one good thing in my school day—or I might just snap, and start needing all that therapy you don't provide the children of your employees. Ty?"

I take a step back. I survey the school board and catch a few sympathetic eyes. One large woman even nods at me and gives me a wink, like she is my mom or something and is proud. Cool, I think. We're moving people tonight.

Ty steps forward and says, "I have a dream. I dream that some day in the near future Childress Public High School will diversify the faculty and recognize Martin Luther King Day. I'm the only black kid in the school, and the only place I feel comfortable is in Mr. Franks' room. If Mr. Franks lost his job, there would be no refuge left for me in this school, and I think I might have to start writing letters to the local papers about how hard it is to be black at Childress High School, a place that does absolutely nothing to celebrate my heritage. A place that inadvertently says to me every day that white is right. No black authors in the English curriculum. Coaches always asking me to join the basketball team. Mrs. Watts always trying to get me to sing Negro spirituals in her all-white choir. I'm sick of it, yo. The only thing I've ever done through CPHS in celebration of my heritage was to raise money for the United Negro College Fund, because a mind is a terrible thing to waste. I ran a charity Ping-Pong tournament last year and do you know who was the faculty member that helped me market and chaperone that tournament? Mr. Franks. He also made the biggest faculty donation too. Don't fire Franks, or you'll be sorry when MLK day rolls around and you don't observe the holiday again! Because I'm speaking up this year if Franks gets cut."

Ty steps back, looks over at me, and I nod at him, which makes him smile, so I give him a wink, Donna style, and say, "Jared and Chad."

"I'm just a regular white kid—I love Franks and all, but you probably noticed that I'm carrying around my younger brother in a backpack," Jared says. I worry that he is going to forget the *Scarface* line, but then he remembers and says, "So say hello to my little friend!"

"Hello," Chad says over Jared's shoulder. "Maybe I would have driven my electronic wheelchair in here if the building was wheelchair accessible. But it's not. Nor are the gym locker rooms, really. And Das Boot—my two-wheeled ride—don't fit through the library aisles, so I can't browse the books or anything like that. If I want to pick out a book to read, I have to be carried through the library, which is humiliating. No one—besides the kids in this room—really talks to me at school. I'm late for every class because I have to take the elevator and all the kids push the buttons on every floor when they walk by—ha-ha—so I have to wait forever. You people suck at accommodating the special-needs people of the world. But you know who makes me feel like I am wanted, every day? Mr. Franks. Yeah, we play video games, but you know what? In the video games I have normal legs and arms. I can run around and jump and walk in a virtual world that Franks sets up for me using his own equipment that he buys with his own money because you people do nothing to fund his program. Try not walking for seventeen years, and then tell me that video games are stupid. If Franks goes, there will be no more Xbox in school and therefore no place in the high school where I can socialize or interact normally with other teens doing something age appropriate."

"We don't have Xbox at home," Jared adds, and then the brothers step back.

I give them each a nod and a wink when they look at me. My boys are rocking tonight. I'm so proud. "Ricky?"

Donna hands Ricky a prepared statement, and tells him to read it, which he does. "My name is Ricky Roberts. I am the only Childress Public High School student diagnosed with autism, and I do not like the special education teachers very much. Also, school board member Mr. Pinkston's son Alexander Pinkston torments me on a daily basis, which makes me sad and angry sometimes. But I love Mr. Franks, because he always lets me into his room and makes me feel like I am wanted and that I have many friends, and that my friends are also wanted in the school. I do not like eating in the lunchroom, because Alexander Pinkston torments me. I like eating my lunch with Mr. Franks. Mr. Franks is my favorite teacher. Please do not fire him. Please. Thank you. Yes."

Donna steps forward and says, "And I am a tax-paying community member. Mr. Pinkston's son likes to trick my son into making sexual overtures to female classmates. My son will repeat almost anything he is told, especially when encouraged by the captain of the football team, so this is quite an easy task to accomplish. On Monday, Mr. Pinkston's son told my son to tell sophomore Ryan Gold that her *quote* boobies were lovely *unquote*. So Ricky did, which resulted in Ryan Gold's bursting into tears in the middle of the lunchroom."

Mr. Pinkston stands and says, "How dare you burst into our meeting and accuse my son with unfounded—"

"Sit down, Mr. Pinkston!" Donna says.

Mr. Pinkston scans the crowd for support, finds none, and then sits.

"We visited with Ryan Gold and her parents yesterday," Donna says. "Ryan Gold is a member of the National Honor Society. She goes to church every week. She is the nicest, most well-spoken girl you have ever met. And she is willing to testify in a court of law. Now I have talked with Principal Fiorilli several times and have even sent him letters regarding the harassment Mr. Pinkston's son has inflicted on my son and other students. These letters are documented, of course. I have responses. So if you fire Franks, or if this man's son—with malicious intent—comes within thirty feet of my son or Ryan

Gold or any of these good kids here tonight, I will launch a lawsuit on this school that will drain your budget so fast, you'll have to fire every damn teacher in the district to get it passed. Am I clear?" Donna's eyes scan the crowd. She lets them take in her hotness. "And if any of these children have any sort of uncomfortable experience during the next few school days, this digital document gets copied and sent to every newspaper and television station in the area. Have a good meeting, boys and ladies. Keep Franks. Avoid legal trouble. It's a win-win."

When Donna strides out of the room, we follow, and when we are outside, Donna distributes the celebratory high fives, and my boys are all smiles.

"What do you think, Amber?" Chad says.

"Did we deliver the speeches okay?" Ty says.

"Do you think it will work?" Jared says.

For some crazy reason, instead of answering, I smile and give each one of my boys a big old hug, which makes Ricky say, "Hi! Hi! Hi!"

And Donna says, "Let's go to Friendly's!"

So we all pile into her Mercedes.

When we arrive at Friendly's we get a big booth and Donna orders one of every sundae on the menu and six spoons, and we eat ice cream as a team, sword fighting with long ice cream spoons, laughing our butts off, getting chocolate sauce and whipped cream and caramel all over our teenage chins as we shuffle around the sundaes and sample all of the delicious concoctions—replaying the night, talking about how cool we all were, and how Franks is sure to keep his job now, and how Franks Freak Force Federation rocks hard-core, especially in our new camo shirts, which we all agree to wear to school tomorrow like the sports teams do before big games. But when people ask us what the shirts are about, we won't tell them, because it's our secret. True? True.

So I try not to get any sundae on my new shirt and catch myself looking at Donna a lot. She's not really saying anything, and she doesn't eat very much ice cream, but she's smiling in this very satisfied way, and every so often she runs her nails through Ricky's hair, which makes me jealous again. God, I really wish she were my mom. I'd be so much cooler and smarter and—but then I remember to be thankful for what JC sent my way today, and I smile and run my nails through all of my boys' heads of hair, which makes them say, "Stop! Ice cream hands! You sticky ho-bag!" So I laugh at them and keep on trying to run my hands through their hair, pretending to go for one, and then at the last second, going for another boy's hair, which results in a lot of grabbing wrists and screaming.

The waitress comes over when we almost knock over Chad's high chair. She's a teen from another high school, who says, "You must chill, or Kevin is going to—like—freak."

"School night, kids," Donna says, and then pays the bill while we all try to mess up each other's hair on the lawn outside of Friendly's. As we wrestle, I think about how much I love these boys. They are good people. I really really love these boys. All of them equally. My boys. My friends. Franks Freak Force Federation.

After Donna drops off Ty, Jared, and Chad, I say, "How did you know that Lex made Ricky say that stuff to Ryan Gold?"

"Lex Pinkston is a bad boy!" Ricky says. "Bad boy! Bad boy! BAD BOY!"

"Hello?" Donna says. "Son diagnosed with autism. No secrets in the Roberts household."

"Did you really talk to Ryan Gold and her parents?"

"Yep."

"But you had a murder trial today and—"

"I sent Jessica to represent our interests regarding the Golds."

Jessica is Donna's young and pretty and extremely smart assistant, whom I hate, because Donna is always going on and on about what a great future Jessica has.

"Cool," I say, totally wanting a Jessica of my own someday, who will help me do even more killer good for deserving people.

"You're not really self-conscious about your teeth, are you?" Donna asks.

"No. I just made that up on the fly. I'm cool with my teeth."

"Good, because they really do look white and straight."

"Thanks."

"Will I be driving you home, Amber?"

"Got to pick up Bobby Big Boy, because I can't sleep without my pup," I say.

"How about I drive you and Bobby Big Boy home after that?"

"No, thanks."

"It's pretty cold outside," Donna says.

"Yeah, but I have to stop by Franks' house."

"Mr. Jonathan Franks!" Ricky says.

"Oh?" Donna says, because she knows I'm totally lying. I'm pretty sure Donna knows I'm living out of Hello Yellow. She's super smart. When I don't say anything, Donna says, "Amber, I know how you feel about taking help from me, but I *can* help you and your mom if you need it. I know people who can—"

"We don't need your help," I say, and am surprised that I sounded like a cat saying what I did. I feel badly about this—especially after all Donna has done for me—but I can't help adding, "Not everyone needs your help, you know."

I am such a bitch.

But Mom is going to come through one of these days. I've got my money on mi madre, and mi madre on my mind, sucka!

"Pride is not pretty," Donna says.

"I'm not a pretty girl," I say, because I can't help myself, and I dig Ani DiFranco.

"You're gorgeous," Donna says, "you shine, only you don't know it yet."

This is a weird thing for Donna to say, so I clam up and listen to Ricky counting aloud and wonder about what he could possibly be counting.

CHAPTER
7

When we get to Donna's house, I let B3 out of his room, mop up his welcome-home puddle, put his plaid coat on him, and then find Donna in her room changing.

"Donna," I say.

"Yeah?"

"I'm sorry I was a bitch in the car."

"You weren't a bitch in the car."

"You rocked the school board meeting pretty hard," I say.

"No, *you* rocked the school board meeting pretty hard," she says.

"I couldn't have done it without you."

"Yeah, you could have. You just don't know it yet."

"I'm going to leave now," I say, because I don't want Donna to patronize me, even if she is trying to be kind. I could never do what she does. I sleep on a school bus. I'm a freak. I couldn't even take first place at the Marketing Club regionals.

"Okay," Donna says. "See you tomorrow morning?"

"True," I say, and then leave without saying goodbye to Ricky, because—all of a sudden—I'm feeling sorta down for some reason.

It's cold outside. North Pole cold. And I don't have a proper winter coat.

As I'm walking toward the school bus compound, I remember what I said about visiting Franks' house, and since I don't want JC to think I am a damn liar, I make a detour. Franks lives in the neighborhood, in a grasshopper green rancher with a big old addition on the back—bedrooms for all of his redheaded kids.

It's kind of late for a school night, but B Thrice and I walk up his driveway and knock on his basement window. Franks is playing Halo 3 in his basement, probably against Ty of the Franks Freak Force Federation and people all over the world, which boys and men do through something called Xbox Live. He looks up at me, then points to his watch and shakes his head. But before I can knock again, I hear Franks' mean red-headed wife say, "I'm calling the cops if you don't get off our property! I know who you are, Amber Appleton. Go home and leave my husband alone! He's not working now!"

"I'm totally in love with your man," I say to Franks' wife, just to get her riled up. "He's going to leave you and marry me as soon as I'm of age!"

"I'll kill you with my own bare hands!" she yells, stepping out of the kitchen and into the cold night. She's wearing a depressing bathrobe and slippers, which makes her look really sad and homely.

"Just kidding, Red. Your husband is an honorable man, and he loves you to death and would never leave you or the kids. Not for a million bucks. That's why I want to hug him so much. I don't expect you to understand, but please know that I'm praying for you and your family every night."

"What are you talking about?" Mrs. Franks says.

"You're a lucky woman," I tell her, and then BBB and me walk away.

B3 is a little lackluster at night. He's a morning dog. So I usually talk to JC on my long walk home to Hello Yellow.

"JC," I pray. "You see us at the school board meeting? Whatcha know about that, sucka?" I laugh because it's sorta fun to call JC sucka when I'm praying. "Were you proud of me, Heavenly Father? Did your daughter do you proud?"

I look up into the sky and there are no stars. Just streetlights and blackness.

I don't really feel like JC is listening tonight, so I stop praying and start to cry.

I cry a lot when I am alone, probably because I am a chick and all, but maybe because I'm not strong like Donna, and I think about stuff too much — like, for example, sometimes I get this idea that my dad has really been watching over me the past seventeen years sorta like a guardian angel or something, only he's really alive and waiting for me to earn the right to have a dad, and once he sees me doing enough good, he's going to run up behind me and surprise me with a big old fatherly hug, picking me up off the ground and spinning me around like in the damn movies. Sometimes, after I have done something pretty kick-ass, I turn around really quickly, because I sorta believe that he might be there ready to hug me. But he never is.

I don't want to turn around tonight, because I'm seventeen, so I realize that the fantasy is silly and even delusional maybe, but as I'm walking home tonight, I think about how I protected Ricky from Lex Pinkston today, and how happy The KDFCs looked when we were performing "You Can't Hurry Love," and I know that Father Chee is definitely proud of me, and I got my boys to save Franks' job, which is something that any good father would be proud of, and as I'm walking down the street, I start to feel like my father is really behind me—I even think I hear his footsteps.

I don't want to turn around and be disappointed once again, but I also still believe in hope and the possibility of beautiful things happening in this world. I still believe that JC and God have a kick-ass plan for every one of us, so I say, "Dad?"

With so much hope in my heart, I spin around in the middle of the sidewalk and there is no one there—like always.

And so I cry—so hard that BBB gets scared and starts barking, so I pick him up and carry his butt back to Hello Yellow.

Mom's asleep under the comforter, so I let her be.

I don't do my homework.

I sit in the quiet darkness for a long time.

For some reason I start thinking about the time I asked my mom for a tent, which is all-time Amber-and-her-mom moment number four:

When I was maybe seven or so, I saw this sitcom on television where the mom and daughter spend the night in the backyard. The little girl gets a tent for her birthday and then she wants to sleep outside instead of her room, so the mom sets up the tent for her, and they have these great times pretending that they are explorers pioneering across America back when it was inhabited by Native Americans, back in the day. It looked like fun, so I begged my mom for a tent.

Mom didn't get me a tent, but she made me one out of blankets and broom handles one summer night and we attempted to camp behind the apartment complex we were living in at the time, back when Mom was with a different boyfriend, Trevor, who was only around for a few months or so.

By flashlight, Mom and I read books I had checked out of the library, and then she told me silly ghost stories before we went to sleep.

I woke up in the middle of the night feeling some sorta slime on my face.

"Mom?" I whispered. "Mom?"

"What's wrong?" she said.

"I think there's something on my face."

"Go back to sleep," Mom said.

"I really *really* think there is something on my face. Can you check?"

Mom turned on the flashlight and started to scream.

I sat up and started to scream.

There were slugs all over the inside of the blanket tent, all over our sheets, and a few were even on us.

Both of us ran out of the tent, and we couldn't stop screaming.

Eventually, the cops showed up with their guns drawn, because someone reported a disturbance.

We were so freaked that we couldn't even talk.

Mom just pointed to the tent.

The cops actually aimed their guns at the tent and started to talk very mean to the slugs. "You're surrounded. Come out with your hands up. We can resolve this peacefully."

It was pretty funny to hear the cops talking to slugs like that, so I started to laugh.

The cops didn't like that, and started questioning us, and soon they understood that they had drawn their guns on a tent full of slugs, so they had to laugh too.

After Mom had explained the situation, she offered to buy the cops a cup of coffee to make up for the misunderstanding, and when they agreed, we got to ride in the cop car. I asked the officers if they would put on the lights and sirens, and they said, "Sure."

We rode super fast to the all-night doughnut shop, where Mom flirted with the cops and I got to eat doughnuts in the middle of the night, which was pretty killer.

When the cops dropped us off back at the apartment building, we went inside and, since Trevor had to work in the morning, Mom slept in my bed with me, which was really nice, especially since the bed felt so comfortable after trying to sleep outside on the grass for a night.

What I wouldn't do to be in a bed tonight.

In the present moment, after taking BBB out for one last pee worrying the whole time that the local rapist murderer will get me, back on Hello Yellow — even though I really don't feel like it — I force myself to pray for everyone on my list, asking God to help us all be who we need to be. And I pray really hard, even though I can't feel God tonight, and I wonder if He is mad at me or something, which makes me feel as though maybe my day wasn't so kick-ass after all.

I'm cold without the comforter, but BBB keeps me

warm—his little body inhaling and exhaling against my chest—and I eventually fall asleep.

When I wake, I cannot remember my dreams—but Mom is outside smoking a Newport, and everything begins once again.

PART TWO

Freak Scene

CHAPTER
8

After another frickin' freezing night in Hello Yellow, my butt has finally thawed and is now all nice and toasty. I'm singing in the back of Donna's Mercedes. Again, heated leather seats. So nice.

We're listening to Dinosaur Jr.'s "Freak Scene," which is my favorite D. Jr. song, pretty much because it is also Donna's favorite, and I like watching her sing it like a teenager.

Donna is driving too fast, bobbing her head to the beat, singing all of the lyrics at the top of her lungs, her hands pounding out the beat on the steering wheel as Ricky counts inaudibly.

I think it's funny that Donna listens to songs about freaks, because she is so cool and hip and stylish and smart and together and she is definitely what every woman wants to be as far as I'm concerned—certainly not a freak like me.

Maybe she just listens to music like this so she can relate to her son Ricky and The Five.

Maybe.

But she is rocking pretty damn hard this morning—so

much that she even blows through a stop sign, but I don't say anything, because I don't want to kill the mood, which is totally rocking, and how often does one truly get to rock out hard-core? Let alone a high-powered attorney who has a murder case to worry about. Sometimes you just have to let crap slide when it comes to adults acting like kids, because that can be a beautiful thing. True? True.

When we arrive alive at the high school, Donna kills the music, kisses Ricky, and tosses me the XXL camo shirt for Franks.

"Your boy Franks should be proud today," Donna says, and then winks at me before she turns up the tunes again and pulls away.

"Going to play Halo 3 with Mr. Jonathan Franks!" Ricky says, and then we're knocking on the outside basement door.

Ty kicks open the door this morning, and then Franks and Chad kill off Ty's and Jared's spacemen so that Ricky can join the action—just like every other morning.

Before I lose my boys to video games, I say, "Franks, check this out," and then hold up the camo shirt.

"For me?" Franks says.

"Mommy Roberts made a shirt for Mr. Jonathan Franks and all five members of Franks Freak Force Federation!"

"Cool," Franks says, taking the shirt from me, admiring the orange lettering and rubbing the material between his thumb and forefinger as if the shirt were made of precious fabric—like it's the original American flag sewn by frickin' Betsy Ross or something. "*Very* cool," Franks says.

"You do see that we are all wearing the same shirt?" I say.

"Also cool," Franks says.

"We playing a game, or what?" Ty says, and then all of the boys are logging into the virtual world.

Did my boys forget all about last night, or did they already discuss the school board meeting with Franks?

Before I can bring up the subject, just before their minds are sucked into the various Xboxes positioned around the room, Lex Pinkston knocks on the hallway door and sticks his head in. "Um, Mr. Franks, may I come in and say something?"

"Mr. Pinkston, all students are welcome in my room. Enter."

Lex enters slowly. He is tall and full of muscles and dumb-looking, but today he has this very sincere look on his face. "Listen," he says to the room. "Sometimes I say dumb things because I like feel I have to in front of people or something because there's a lot of pressure on me, being that I'm the QB and all, and well, I know that what I've been telling Ricky to say is well, um—not cool."

"Are you trying to apologize?" I say.

"I'm sorry that I said those things to you, Amber."

"I'm praying for you every night," I say.

"Why?"

"Because you need it."

"Well, I'm also sorry for telling Ricky to say those things to Ryan. I'm sorry, and it won't happen again. Okay?"

"Did your daddy make you come down here this morning?" I ask—like a total cat.

"Listen, I said I was sorry. It won't happen again. Okay?"

"No. It's not okay, because you can't just erase—"

"Do you like playing Xbox, Lex?" Franks says.

"What?" Lex says.

"Are you a gamer?" Franks says. "Do you like video games?"

"Yeah. Who doesn't?"

"Are you any good at Halo 3?" Franks asks.

"Beat anyone in this room," Lex says.

My boys all exchange glances and restrain smiles.

"Why don't you play a game with us," Franks says.

"Right now?"

"Homeroom doesn't start for fifteen minutes."

"Are you serious?" Lex says.

"You're on Ricky's team," Franks says. "Amber, why don't you pull up a chair?"

I pull up a chair next to Franks and for the next ten minutes I watch my boys' virtual spacemen kick the crap out of Lex's virtual spaceman in every way imaginable. If I had to guesstimate, I'd say Lex gets killed an average of five times per minute, and never even records one kill.

My boys are unmerciful.

My boys are triumphant.

My boys are beautiful.

"You guys are really good," Lex says when the game is over.

"Bring your friends next time," Franks tells him. "We play every day before school and at lunch. All are welcome."

When the warning bell rings, my boys skedaddle like someone yelled fire or something—the lab rats—but I hang back.

"Why did you tell Lex he could hang in *our* room?" I ask Franks.

"This is everyone's room. All are welcome," Franks says.

"*Lex Pinkston?* Do you know that just yesterday he called

me a disgusting single-syllable word for a woman, which I'm not even going to repeat?"

"Maybe if he were in this room more, he wouldn't have called you that name. Maybe you'd become friends?"

"Are you for real, Franks?"

"No, I'm an illusion," he says, and then laughs at his own joke—like a moron.

"Have you heard how the school board voted last night?"

"No."

He doesn't bring up our saving his job, so I assume my boys didn't tell him.

"Aren't you worried about the vote?" I ask.

"It's of this world."

"Your wife was pretty pissed when I came to your house last night."

"You shouldn't come to my house, Amber."

"She doesn't really think I'm in love with you, does she? Why can't I hug you, Franks? Just once."

"Why do you do that? Why do you insist on making me feel uncomfortable whenever we are alone?"

"A hug is a good thing, Franks."

"Not always."

"Like—when is *a hug* not a good thing?"

"When it makes someone uncomfortable."

"I'm down with hugging," I say. "I hug everyone indiscriminately."

"Not everyone wants to be hugged."

"Well, that's just dumb."

"Why, because you say so?" Franks says. "Would you hug Lex Pinkston?"

I'm sorta getting pissed at Franks, especially after everything I did for him last night—not to mention how he invited Lex and his buddies into The Franks Lair—but the second bell rings, which means I'm late, so I just leave without answering and go to homeroom, where there is a pink slip waiting for me, so I about-face and walk my little behind down to Prince Tony's office.

All of my boys are on the bad-boy bench, except Chad who is in Das Boot.

"Amber," the red-lipped Mrs. Baxter says to me just before I address my boys, "can you come over here?"

So I walk over to Prince Tony's secretary's desk.

"I heard about last night," she whispers. "You certainly have chutzpah."

"Thanks," I say, and then join my boys, who are more than a little bit fidgety sitting on the bench of discipline.

"We better not get in trouble," Ty says.

"Ricky Roberts needs to go to calculus in how many minutes?"

"This don't seem so good," Chad says from Das Boot.

"Beats going to gym," says Jared.

"Guys, it's Prince Tony," I say. "Just let me do the talking. No sweat."

"What if he calls us in one at a time?" Ty asks.

"No chance," I retort.

"How do you know?" asks Jared.

"How many minutes until math?"

"I know Prince Tony. He'll want to save time. He's efficient to a fault."

The door opens. Prince Tony says, "The lot of you. Inside."

I give my boys a knowing glance, as if to say *Told ya!*

Inside we all take seats in the various corners of the office, Chad motorizes Das Boot front and center, and Prince Tony sits behind his huge desk.

"The school board voted to keep the business department."

We all clap and cheer!

"You'll be pleased to hear that Mr. Franks will be getting an increased budget."

I smile and nod my head confidently. Score!

"Now, all of those other things you were complaining about last night," Prince Tony says, "were you serious? Do you really feel strongly about those other issues, or was it just a collective front to save Mr. Franks?"

"Pretty much just a front," says Ty.

"We just really like Franks," Jared says.

"How many minutes until math?"

"Halo 3 during lunch and before school. Is that too much to ask?" Chad adds.

"So this matter is resolved?" Prince Tony says. "No more busting into school board meetings? You're satisfied?"

"Pretty much," Ty says when no one else speaks up.

"Good," Prince Tony says, and then adds, "you kids were impressive last night. Truly. Now off to class."

All of my boys jump up and happily follow Das Boot and Chad out of Prince Tony's office, but I stay seated and shake my head sadly.

Even after all the slaying they have done in their virtual Xbox world, my boys just don't have the killer instinct.

"Ms. Appleton?"

"Is that how it works with adults?" I say.

"I'm not sure I follow."

"It takes a bunch of threats to get what you want, but no one really cares about anything that doesn't concern them? No one cares about doing what's right for the sake of doing what's right?"

"What are you talking about? Mr. Franks' program is secure for at least another year—through your graduation. You've accomplished your goal. You should be happy."

"Maybe."

"What's wrong?"

"I don't know."

"You can talk to me, Amber," he says, like any old adult would.

"Don't you think that we should recognize MLK day and diversify the faculty? Don't you think we should make the entire school handicap accessible and friendly? Don't you think that kids shouldn't have to endure harassment from people like Lex Pinkston?"

"Of course. Yes to all of those."

"Then why don't you make all that stuff happen?"

Prince Tony leans forward, looks me in the eye all fatherly, and says, "Don't you think I would if I could?"

"But you're the principal of the school. You can do anything you want."

Prince Tony smiles sorta sadly, and says, "You're a good kid, Amber. And you are going to be a great woman someday."

"Why does everyone say that to me? Like I'm a bottle of wine or something."

"Someday you'll understand."

"That's such a BS answer."

"And someday you'll give that same answer to someone younger than yourself."

"No, I won't."

"Better get to class, Ms. Appleton," Prince Tony says, and then he starts opening his mail, like I'm not even there anymore, and I wonder if anything we did last night meant anything at all.

CHAPTER
9

Lex Pinkston actually brings his football buddies down to The Franks Lair during lunch, my boys merrily play Halo 3 with the enemy, and—to make matters even worse—under Franks' supervision, everyone seems to get along, which pisses me off, so I go back into the lunchroom and read *The Crucible* by Arthur Miller.

Now, John Proctor was a man I can admire. Going to the gallows instead of giving up his friends to the witch hunt. Proctor was a man of principles, unlike Prince Tony and my boys, who jumped at the first chance they got to play video games with the cool kids—the same kids who called me a disgusting single-syllable word for a woman and made Ryan Gold cry less than forty-eight hours ago.

It's all so depressing.

Confusing.

Messed up.

★ ★ ★

After school I collect Ricky at his locker and go to Franks' room. Franks usually has to pick up his kids after school—because his wife isn't a teacher and works regular adult hours—so Franks doesn't stick around too long after the last bell, but I catch him in the hallway just before he is about to leave for the day.

"Did you even hear about what we did for you last night?" I ask him.

"Yeah," Franks says, his hands full of folders. "Principal Fiorilli filled me in."

"And?"

"And?"

I try to shrug off his lack of gratitude, but I can't control the shocked expression on my face, which says, *Aren't you even going to say thanks?*

"I appreciate your speaking on my behalf, Amber. And you too, Ricky."

"Mr. Jonathan Franks is Ricky Roberts' favorite teacher."

Franks gives Ricky a quick but heartfelt high five.

"So why aren't you like—more touched by our gesture?" I ask.

"Well—I'd like to think I'm keeping my job because I'm a good sales and advertising teacher, and not because you threatened the school board without bothering to ask how I felt about your doing so. Maybe the school board voted the way they did simply because they think I am a good teacher."

I can't even believe that he isn't thanking me properly and

freaking out with happiness. I thought Franks would hug me for sure. I really thought this was going to be our moment.

Something inside me snaps.

"What?" I say. "*We* saved your job, Franks. *We did it.* Us. Franks Freak Force Federation. Are you even serious with that good teacher crap? You play video games all day and offer kids easy electives so they can pad their GPAs. We saved your butt. Don't you understand that? They would have fired you if it weren't for us."

As soon as the words come out of my mouth, I am sorry.

"Why did you *really* go to the school board meeting, Amber? For me, or for you? I don't need saving. *Do you?*" Franks says very coolly. Then he adds, "If you need help, I'm willing to help you here at school. Anytime between 6:30 AM and 3:15 PM. Just ask. My door will always be open to you. But stop coming to my house. It crosses the line, Amber. *It crosses the line.*"

And then Franks walks away from us.

"Amber Appleton is crying. Why is Amber Appleton crying? Where is Amber Appleton going? Why is Amber Appleton crying? Why is Amber Appleton crying?"

I cry raging tears all the way to Donna's house with Ricky trailing me.

"Why is Amber Appleton crying? Why is Amber Appleton crying? Why is Amber Appleton crying?"

He only stops repeating the question when he opens his math workbook and sits down at the kitchen table.

I let BBB out of his room; he pisses for a full minute—making a yellow river—and then jumps up into my arms.

I give him a long squeeze before I mop up the river with paper towels.

Before I leave, I give Ricky a bowl of pretzels and a can of mandarin orange seltzer, and then I'm on Donna's bike, BBB in the basket.

"Stop crying," I say to myself. "You have old people to cheer up. They believe in your ability to keep the tears at bay. They are depressed enough already about being old. Buck up, Amber! Buck up! You can't battle when you're crying. You need to defend your title. Stop crying!"

At the last second I remember to stop at Alan's Newsstand and buy a large cup of hot cocoa and a Snickers bar, and when Alan asks if I have been crying, I say, "What?" and laugh crazily, so he won't ask me again. Then I finally pull it together as I pedal the last few blocks to the Methodist Retirement Home.

I got this Wednesday gig here after I saw an ad stapled to one of the big old trees in front of the retirement home. I was walking by after work and the hot pink paper of the ad caught my eye, so I took a closer look. The ad read something like this: "Today is the perfect time to make a new friend. Seniors have wonderful stories to tell and are always ready to share their grand array of life experiences. If you want to be a senior pal, if you want to be regaled by stories of olden times, please inquire within. Make a new friend today." I'm totally down with making friends, I'm a very good pal, and I absolutely love being regaled, so I inquired within and signed up for the program. I became a regular at the Methodist Home once Rita's closed for the season and I stopped scooping water ice after school.

When I first went to the old folks home, I was told by the staff that I was simply to talk with the old people in the common room — do puzzles, listen to stories about grandchildren, the Depression, the cost of milk seventy years ago, all of which started to make me feel really depressed. These people didn't need someone to listen to their crappy stories; they needed a spark, something to remind them that they were still alive. And it was pretty obvious that the staff paid them little to no attention, especially since people die here, like every day. Every week I come back someone's missing. But for the longest time, I wasn't sure what I could do to liven up the joint.

Then I met Joan of Old, who — on the outside — is the meanest person you ever met, but on the inside, she's actually pretty philosophical, which you have to discover by breaking through the meanness by being mean yourself, so she will respect you. I discovered this by accident one day when I told her I wanted to go to Bryn Mawr College and she said I'd never get in because I wasn't smart enough.

Her rudeness surprised me because old women are supposed to be really grandmotherly and nice, so I lost my cool and cursed her out really badly, calling her some pretty nasty things, which made her smile, which was weird, but led to my having a kick-ass idea: turn the common room into a word-battle arena where hope dukes it out with despair once a week, which sounded crazy loopy at first, but I've always trusted my visions, so I pitched my idea to some of the older men — who were always putting their arms around me and squeezing my shoulders—and they ate the plan up and made it happen.

Because she loves being evil, Joan of Old agreed to play her part right away, and it has really improved morale at the home very much—or at least that's what the residents tell me anyway.

The front of the Methodist Retirement Home has these huge slavery-times plantation columns and a porch with wooden rocking chairs that look out over a big old rolling lawn, but I use the back entrance, where you have to sign in and pass through security, which—on Wednesday afternoons—is pretty much Door Woman Lucy.

So I park Donna's bike behind a bush—hiding my ride, so it won't get stolen—grab BBB, and then walk into the visitor's entrance with my pup in one hand and the hot chocolate in the other.

"Ain't no dogs allowed in this building," Door Woman Lucy says from behind her desk, shaking her head slowly, staring into my eyes. "You know the rules, Ms. Appleton. I don't make 'em, and I need to get paid, so that funky little rat's gonna have to stay outside."

"DWL." That's what I call Door Woman Lucy to her face, and I think she likes the nickname, because she always smiles when I say it. "It's cold out."

"Sure is."

"Too cold for a dog to be outside."

"Wouldn't know."

"Bet it gets cold every time that door opens."

"Sure does," Door Woman Lucy says, lifting one eyebrow.

"I just bought this hot chocolate here, but I'm not really feeling much like drinking a delicious wintertime beverage right now. But it would be a shame to throw it away. I'd really hate to chuck a fresh cup of hot chocolate."

"Ms. Appleton, as you know, I'm not allowed to accept bribes from visitors, but if you left that drink on my desk, knowing that it won't change the fact that that dog of yours must stay outside the building, I'd maybe see it don't go to waste."

Very slowly, I place the cup on her desk, lay the Snickers across the lid as an added bonus, sweetening the deal—because I really do dig Door Woman Lucy—sign the clipboard with all the lines and names of people who have visited today, record the time of my visit, and then I step away slowly, making my way into the building, BBB under my arm.

"Thanks for leaving that dog outside, Ms. Appleton. I'm sure you understand that rules are rules," Door Woman Lucy says.

"Oh, I understand," I say.

BBB barks once to convey that he understands as well.

And then B Thrice and I both walk through a second door and into the home.

We make our way through some depressing hallways with dusty fake plants in the corners, but we don't see any staff members.

There is a great cheer when I walk into the common room.

I don't want to brag or anything, but I'm sorta like a rock star to these people.

I slip BBB to Knitting Carol, who hides my pup in a lap full of yarn. B Thrice loves to sleep in yarn, so no worries. Knitting Carol loves dogs, so it's a match made in heaven. With B3 in her lap, she's smiling like a little girl on Christmas morning. True? True.

"All right, kid," Old Man Linder says to me, massaging my shoulders from behind. "The old broad has been mumbling nasty things about you all week. She's coming at you hard today. Don't let her rattle you with any low blows, because the wrinkly bag's brimming full of 'em, as you are well aware."

Old Man Linder is my manager. He's something like a hundred and fifteen years old and has to drag around an oxygen bottle that pumps pure air through these clear tubes that are stuck up his nose. His breath stinks and he has spots all over his face, but he is a kick-ass manager, and he hasn't thrown in the white towel on me yet. He's tough as nails, so I trust him to manage my corner.

Big Booty Bernice has shut the common room doors, so the staff won't hear the cheering and come break up the battle in the middle of my exchange with Joan of Old.

All of the old people are slowly pushing chairs and wheeling the wheelchair-bound into position, so that everyone can see and hear, which means that everyone has to be really super-mega close to the battle, because old people don't see and hear too well. Word.

White hair abounds, along with homemade sweaters, no-name dress sneakers, cough drops, ear-hair, yellow fingernails, shaky limbs, wrinkles, diapers, and an intense hospital smell that dries out your nasal passages in—like—ten seconds.

Joan of Old is in her wheelchair, front and center, staring me down with her wrinkly pink eyelids, trying to psyche me out. She might weigh eighty pounds if her clothes were soaking wet. She's wearing all black like always, still mourning her husband who died—like—thirty years ago. True.

Joan of Old wiggles an old pink finger at me and then shakes her head so that her black bonnet falls a little to the left, so she straightens it with her bony shaky hands.

Joan of Old has no manager, mostly because everyone in the home hates her. She is such a downer most of the time, and she likes to quote depressing Nietzsche 24/7, which, of course, wins her no friends.

I take my place by the sunniest window in the room, and Old Man Linder says, "Remember, the crowd doesn't always get your newfangled MTV kid references, so keep your jokes age appropriate. You're battling for our happiness. This is the only thing we look forward to all week. Besides this weekly battle, our lives bore us to death. This is the one thing that's different and exciting, so don't let us down. You making that old crusty broad smile—this is something to believe in. It breaks the awful chain of days. So for us, please just keep going at her until she smiles. No mercy!"

I nod once and roll my head along my shoulders, crack my knuckles, and jab the air a little—like Cassius Clay. (Also known as Muhammad Ali, sucka!)

All of the old people are seated and waiting for the battle to begin, so Old Man Thompson—who actually wears a bowtie every Wednesday, just to play the role—stands and turns to face the audience. He's hunchbacked but sprightly.

"Welcome once again to the Wednesday Afternoon Battle between Hope and Pessimism. To my left we have the indomitably hopeful one, the girl of unyielding optimism, the teen of merriment, the fan favorite, the girl you wished were your granddaughter or maybe even your great-granddaughter, the only minor who visits the home on a non-holiday, the undisputed Wednesday Afternoon Champion, Amber the Princess of Hope Apple-Tooooooooooooooooon!"

I raise my hands in the air and hop a little.

The people clap and all the old dudes with front teeth left whistle.

"And now the challenger," Old Man Thompson says, and everyone starts to boo. "This woman needs no introduction. The woman in black. The constant mourner. The self-proclaimed nihilist. The one who says the building is too cold and forces management to keep the thermostat so high that we have to dress as though we are all back in the spring of '36 when we had that record-setting heat spell. The woman who once faked a heart attack because she thought we were having too much fun at last year's Christmas party. You know her well. You have no doubt suffered her insults at least once in the last twenty-four hours. The brittle broad you love to hate. Joan! Of! Old!"

Boos abound. Someone throws a crochet hook at Joan, but misses her head by at least four feet.

Joan's little raw bony hands swat at the many booers, whom she cannot identify—because she is blind.

"All right, ladies," Old Man Thompson says, "front and center."

Joan of Old wheels herself over, and I step to her.

"Now we want a clean battle," Old Man Thompson says, his breath smelling like he powdered his tongue with the dust found at the bottom of a Tums bottle. "Politics and religion are off limits. This is a Methodist home, so let's keep the cursing to a minimum. You know the rules. Joan of Old smiles and the young lady wins again. Amber Appleton cries, and the old broad wins her first battle. The challenger calls the flip."

"Tails," Joan of Old says.

Old Man Thompson flips and catches a quarter, smacking it down on the back of his spotted and veiny hand. "Heads!"

"How do I know you're not lying?" Joan of Old asks. "I'm blind, you know."

"Feel the top of the coin for all I care," Old Man Thompson says, offering the back of his hand to Joan of Old.

She feels his hand and the coin, and then says, "Damn it!"

"You kicking or receiving?" Old Man Thompson asks.

"Kicking," Old Man Linder answers for me, and then slaps me on the butt before saying, "Go get 'er, kid," and then he sits down.

"Let the battle begin!" Old Man Thompson says, and all of the old people clap and hoot.

"The problem with women of your generation," JOO opens with, "is that you waste all your time doing community service, harboring dreams of a college education, when you should be trying to find a husband who will put a roof over your head and food in your refrigerator. Smarten up, chippie. Coming here is a waste of time. We'll all be dead in a few weeks anyway. The time to find a husband is now, while you're still skinny, because you'll be a heifer in less than ten years. Do you really want to end up a spinster?"

"Ooooo!" the crowd says, and Joan of Old nods confidently.

"Okay. Okay," I say. "Joan of Old is so ancient."

"How ancient is she?" my manager yells, just like I taught him.

"She's so ancient her elementary school teacher had to chisel her report cards in stone, and Joan had to ride a dinosaur to school every day."

"Hey!" the crowd says, and cheers, repeating my silly joke to each other, nodding their approval.

This joke may not be funny to you, but you have to consider my audience—old people love safe corny jokes.

No smile from Joan. Nothing.

"When I was a young woman there were no dinosaurs about, but there were lonely plain homely girls who never got asked to dance by handsome promising boys. All of these ugly girls ended up living lonely virginal lives in depressingly small government-subsidized apartments, because no man would have them. When I was your age, we usually found these dinosaur-faced girls at the old people's home, doing community service."

"Oooo!" the crowd moans.

I swallow hard. That one sorta cut me.

Do I really have a dinosaur face? And how would she know, since she's blind? Did someone tell her I have a dinosaur face?

It's true that boys don't ever ask me to dance. I'm not all that jazzed up for boys or anything—why would I be after seeing what A-hole Oliver and company did to my mom—but I don't want to be alone for the rest of my life either, after all of my boys (The Five) marry stupid women, younger versions of Joan of Old.

And I really don't want to end up like my mom.

I swallow once and look over at my manager. Old Man Linder has the white towel draped over his shoulder, but he is nodding confidently, showing me his old pink palms, saying, "Relax," so I roll my head along my shoulders, look out into the crowd, and can see that they look very concerned.

"Joan is so old," I retort, "she farts dust."

"Hey!" the crowd roars, and I lift my hands in the air.

But Joan of Old is undaunted. She's not smiling.

"Friedrich Nietzsche once wrote," JOO says, " 'The thought of suicide is a great consolation: by means of it one gets successfully through many a bad night.' I offer that little tidbit to you as a form of future consolation, when we are all dead and buried and you are all alone in some federally funded box of an apartment—manless and childless—thinking about your barren womb."

"Below the belt!" my manager yells.

"Watch yourself, Joan," Old Man Thompson says.

"Joan, didn't you used to date Nietzsche, back in the 1800s? After your husband died," I say, and a few old men cheer, but most of the old people moan, so I know my joke didn't go over so well. Spoofing on dead husbands is sorta off limits around here. Unwritten rule.

"Watch yourself, Amber," Old Man Thompson says. "Let's keep this wholesome. Good clean fun."

"What do you know, child?" Joan of Old says. " 'Life always gets harder toward the summit—the cold increases, responsibility increases.' Also Nietzsche. You haven't even begun to feel pain, young woman, but you will. You will feel pain. Life is hell, and your life has only just begun."

Joan sorta stares at me through her pink wrinkly eyelids, and suddenly, this old Nietzsche-quoting woman chills my bones. Maybe she's right. Maybe there is nothing but pain in my future. Endless pain and then you die. Can this be what's true?

The room is dead quiet, and I haven't got a joke left in my head. I feel that this might be the end, that I am about to be defeated by Joan of Old for the first time, and that hope is going to die shortly in the Methodist Retirement Home along with everything and everyone else.

But then I remember that I have God on my side, so I pray silently.

Come on, JC. Just one little joke. Let me keep hope alive for these old people who are all about to die. Let me give them a little hope—enough so that they can keep on believing until they croak.

And then I have it!

I walk over to Joan, say, "That's okay. Be as pessimistic as you want, JOO. I'll still love you anyway," and give her a big sloppy kiss on the cheek. Joan's mouth opens wide in this very dramatic way, and then I know I have her. Everyone howls with laughter. "You cute little old wrinkly incredibly depressing kook—I love ya!" I give her another big sloppy kiss on the other cheek, and then Joan is blushing, and—

"She smiles!" Thompson says. "Joan of Old smiled for the briefest of seconds. Do we have a witness?"

Half of the old people in the room yell "Aye!"

"That's my girl!" Old Man Linder says as he lifts my left hand into the air, proclaiming me victorious once again.

"Amber Appleton is the winner and your undisputed champion!"

The old people who can stand do, and all of them begin to congratulate me, which quickly yields to stories of grand-children who never visit—these tales are accompanied by endless wallet-fold pictures that show the grandchildren at various stages of their lives and are presented (usually) in chronological order, one picture per each year the child has attended school—talk about the cost of grocery items fifty years ago, the weather over the last eight odd decades or so, homemade arthritis remedies, the inadequacy of social secu-rity checks, who died this week, and, of course, recapping the trickier jigsaw puzzles recently assembled.

Before we leave the community room, Bobby Big Boy visits the lap of almost every old person in the building, and they all smile as they pat BBB's head and scratch his belly. My dog is great with old people—so gentle, so calm—it's like he actually knows that old people are brittle and fragile and about to die.

Just before I bust out of the old folks home, I walk over to the far corner where Joan of Old is sitting all alone facing a wall, which she thinks is a window.

"Joan?" I say.

"What do *you* want, Ms. Hopeful? Come to gloat? Come to rub it in?"

"Do you want to pet my dog before I go?"

"That filthy beast? Ha!"

"You almost made me cry back there. That bit about no boys liking me. That really cut to the quick, as you old people like to say. You couldn't see it—because you are blind—but my bottom lip was quivering. True."

"Truthfully?"

"Yeah. It was a close call. I felt the tears coming."

"You're just saying that to make me feel better."

"I'll probably cry about it later tonight, when I'm all alone."

"You don't have to say that," Joan of Old says, "but thank you."

"You really are pretty mean and depressing, JOO."

"Well, I try. And I really hate to admit it," Joan of Old says, "but you're pretty hopeful and funny, Amber Appleton. But that kiss was a cheap trick, and I'm going to protest the battle, just so you know."

I catch her smiling again, but I don't call her on it.

The smile vanishes like a flame in the wind, and Joan of Old says in this very sad voice, "Do you know that you are the only person who has ever made me smile since my Lawrence died back in '82?"

This is depressing news, even though I realize it is a weird sorta compliment.

I sigh. "I wish you were the only person who ever made me feel like crying, but I can't give you that honor, Joan of Old. Sorry."

"'Simply by being compelled to keep constantly on his guard, a man may grow so weak as to be unable any longer to defend himself.' That goes for women like us too. Remember that, Amber. Remember that."

"Nietzsche?"

Joan of Old nods once and then says, "I hope I don't die before I make you cry, Amber. I'm going to beat your young little hopeful butt one of these days."

"May we have many more battles," I say, and then go collect BBB from the lap of Agnes the Plant Talker. Agnes talks to any old plant and pretends it's her son, who lives in California and never visits.

As I put on my jackets, Old Man Linder gives me one more shoulder squeeze and says, "You were brilliant up there, kid. You keep us feeling young with your youthful ha-has and your skylarking."

"Can I get a hug, Old Man Linder?" I ask.

"Is the Pope Catholic?" he says, and then gives me this very long hug, his nasty breath making my neck sorta wet, which I tolerate, because he's got oxygen tubes up his nose and is probably going to die any day now, plus I really like hugs.

"See you next week, Old Man Linder."

"If I live that long!" he says, and then gives me a wrinkly wink.

"'Bye, all you crazy old people!" I yell across the common

room, and then BBB and I walk the depressing hallways with the dusty fake plants in the corners.

"How'd you get that little dog in my building?" Door Woman Lucy says to me when I walk past her, which makes me laugh.

"How'd you like the hot chocolate and Snickers?" I ask her.

"I don't even know what you're talking 'bout."

Door Woman Lucy and I share a smile. She's good people. Truly.

I retrieve Donna's bike from the bush, put BBB in the basket, and begin my ride back to Donna's house.

As I pedal, I start to get a bad feeling. I start to feel like I have everything all wrong, and that everyone—all of the many people who are not like me—everyone else is right, and all my hopefulness is just childish bullcrap.

I mean, yes, there are a few people who like to watch me do my thing—taking on the school board and Prince Tony, singing with The Korean Divas for Christ, defeating Joan of Old on a weekly basis—but it really doesn't mean anything, because there is only one of me and so many of the people who are not like me, and maybe I'm just an amusing distraction for those other people. Maybe I'm just a freak. A sideshow.

Speaking of sideshows, here's all-time Amber-and-her-mom moment number three:

When I was a little girl Mom always took me to see the circus every year, whether we could afford it or not—all through elementary school. There were years when we couldn't even afford to turn on the heat and had to go without eating meals from time to time, but Mom always came through with circus tickets for us, and when we were at the circus, she'd always buy me cotton candy, popcorn, peanuts, soda, and a souvenir—sometimes a stuffed elephant or monkey, sometimes a T-shirt or a hat or a poster of someone being shot out of a cannon or walking the tightrope or a million clowns getting out of a tiny car.

I didn't even really like the circus particularly, but I liked to look at my mother's face when we were there watching all the acts, because she always looked like a kid. She got so excited whenever the guy got in the cage with the lion, or the motorcycle guy rode around the inside of a metal ball super fast on his bike, or the trapeze artists swung and did flips. All that stuff amazed my mom—she'd be on the edge of her seat the whole time, and if you looked at the faces of all the kids around us and then looked at my mom's face, you'd see that same sense of wonderment.

I remember when I first *really* understood that my mom was a kid at heart—it was the last time Mom and me went to the circus when I was in sixth grade and was sorta outgrowing the circus and other little kid things too. I didn't really want to go to the circus that year, but since it was a tradition, I didn't say anything to Mom. And then we were there in the middle of it all, in the big tent, seeing the same tired acts, and I was bored out of my mind until I noticed how into the circus Mom was—how much going meant to her. You could tell just by looking at her face—Mom frickin' loved the circus.

I wanted to be able to light up my mother's face like the circus did.

It was an important moment for me.

So maybe that's when I started trying to be something more than I was, but truthfully—five years later—no one really takes me all that seriously. At best, I'm just an interesting blip in people's lives—an amusing footnote. Which is probably why my dad split and my mom can't stay sober and all of her boyfriends ditch us after only a few months or so. Sometimes I wonder why I try at all. What's the point?

In an effort to prep for my battles with Joan of Old, I did some research on Nietzsche at the library. He was an atheist like Donna and Ricky. And he once wrote: "What is it: is man only a blunder of God, or God only a blunder of man?"

That statement made me mad at first, because I am a Catholic. But it also made me think. How do we really know that we didn't just make up God? What proof do we really have of God's existence? And if God doesn't exist, is there really any reason to be hopeful at all?

I asked Father Chee these questions a few weeks ago, and he said this is what faith is all about—not knowing for sure. I would sure say that was a BS answer had it not come from FC, because my Man of God sorta has something cool going on. He seems enlightened, and not just because he's Asian. I believe in FC (and God) so I kept and keep holding on to hope for some reason, even though it does get harder and harder the higher you climb toward life's summit—like Joan of Old and Nietzsche both say. True? True.

All these thoughts have me down—so I really don't feel

like cooking dinner for Donna and Ricky. I can't even think up one recipe anyway.

Maybe I should skip dinner and go to Private Jackson's house?

His pad is on the edge of town close to the ghetto. It's where I go whenever I am feeling blue.

CHAPTER 10

I met Private Jackson last year when my history teacher assigned us real live local veterans. We were supposed to write these dudes on Veterans Day for homework points. We were instructed to echo this form letter that Mr. Bonds had typed up and handed out. Basically, he wanted us to copy the words in our own hand-writing, so it would seem like we thought up the carefully con-structed sentiment. It was all about how we were proud to be Americans and were thankful for whatever our fill-in-the-blank veteran had done in whatever fill-in-the-blank war in which they had fought, and that while we would never understand what they endured for our country, we appreciated the benefits of American citizenship—what they fought to protect.

So I was assigned Private Paul Jackson and was told he fought in Vietnam. I copied my letter and filled in the blanks, but it made me feel sorta funny. I mean, how did I even know he did something good in the war? Maybe he was a crappy soldier who did more harm than good, and here I was thank-ing him for doing it. How would I even know? I felt sorta mad about this when I was made to write the letter, but truth-fully, I forgot all about it after it was written, turned in, and sent—especially since most of the kids in my class got kick-ass thankful response letters, and I didn't get jack crap.

About a month later, after the holidays, Mr. Bonds had some of the Vietnam veterans we had written come talk to our classes. Private Jackson didn't come, but the four dudes who did told us some pretty wild stories that made most of us students cry, because the vets talked about their friends being killed in horrible ways and the anti-war hippie people spitting on our soldiers when they came home to the US of A and how much every Vietnam veteran hates Jane Fonda, who is an old-lady actress and is also known as Hanoi Jane because she posed with the enemy for pictures during the war, which is *so* whack. Word. When I saw these four dad-aged men fighting back tears—in front of a bunch of teenagers—still suffering from a war that happened so many years ago, I realized that our letters were pretty damn important to them, and I started to think a lot about Private Jackson and why he never wrote me back.

So I wrote him another letter, telling him about the men who had come to speak with our classes, asking him if he knew these dudes, only I did not call them dudes in the letter. And then I told him all sorts of stuff about my life: how my dad took off on me before I could even speak, and how I sometimes get lonely, but I am very loyal and would make a good pen pal if he were interested in writing someone who appreciated the sacrifices he made for our country back in 'Nam, but understood if he didn't want to talk about all of that—I just wanted him to know that Americans like me welcome him home now, and shame on anyone who made him feel otherwise, back in the day. The letter was very formal and heartfelt, but it was also pretty kick-ass too.

When I asked Mr. Bonds for Private Jackson's address, he wouldn't give it to me, but told me that he would read my letter and if it were appropriate to send, Mr. Bonds would mail it for me. I told him that was unacceptable, and we sorta got into a fight about censorship and freedom of speech, which is protected by the first amendment—one of the very things Private Jackson fought to protect. Finally, Bonds agreed to listen to me read the letter aloud and then—if the letter were appropriate—I could watch him address the envelope, after which we'd drop it in the mailbox together, so I'd know that he'd mailed it, but he wouldn't be forced to reveal Mr. Jackson's personal information, which was not listed in the phone book or anywhere on the Internet; I know, because I checked in the library. Word. The deal was that we students wrote the veterans introduction letters, and if they wanted to write us back, then we were free to write them whenever. Since my veteran hadn't written back, I wasn't supposed to get a second shot.

So I read Mr. Bonds my second letter, and because I am a pretty kick-ass corresponder and I skipped over all of the really personal parts about my dad and whatnot, Mr. Bonds said my letter was well-written and appropriate and worthy of a postage stamp, which he applied to a Childress Public High School envelope and then stuffed my words in that white rectangle.

When we got to the mailbox outside of the school, I asked if I could put the envelope into the box, because I love mailing things, which was a lie I made up, and he said, "Sure."

I glanced at the address just before I dropped the letter into the mailbox, and when Mr. Bonds went back into the school, I walked to Private Jackson's home.

Private Jackson lives in a very small barn-red rancher at the edge of town, near the ghetto, as I mentioned before. There is nothing particularly interesting about his house—he has some bushes out front and a young maple tree. He drives a regular car. You'd pass right by without even thinking twice if you were walking down the sidewalk and trying to guess which house belonged to a Vietnam veteran. I was sorta expecting there to be one of those black POW flags flying outside, but no dice.

So I had to look for the right number, the regular old address-finding way, and, when I found the 618, I went right up to the door and knocked.

No one answered, so I knocked again, and then again.

I was just about to leave, thinking, *Duh, the guy is probably at work*, when the door swung inward and this very normal-looking almost elderly man wearing a yellow button-down shirt, silver glasses, and tan slacks appeared. "Can I help you?" he asked.

"Did you get a letter from some crazy high school girl named Amber Appleton?" I asked him.

"Yes. Why?"

"What did you think of her letter-writing abilities?"

"Nothing."

"That's why you didn't write her back?"

"Are you Amber?"

"We learned about your war in school and I met some of your friends."

"My friends?"

"Guys who fought in Vietnam like you—they came to our class and told us all sorts of things." I didn't want to mention his friends being killed, or people spitting on him, so I brought up the part that most seemed to unite the dudes who came to speak to our class. "Like about that bitch, Jane Fonda."

He just looked at me like I was crazy.

"You know Hanoi Jane?"

"What do you want?"

"I wanted to apologize for writing you that crappy form letter. My teacher made me write it — but that was before your friends came and told us about what it was like to fight in the jungle. Had I known what it was really like, I would never have written you such a lousy form letter. I wrote you a better letter today — more interesting and personable. But my teacher made me mail it, so you won't get that letter for like — three days or so, I would guess."

Private Jackson just looked at me for a second, and then said, "Is this some sort of joke?"

"Hell, no! Seriously. I just thought that maybe you'd want to — like — get to know me?"

"Why?"

"Why not?"

"I'm not going to tell you war stories, if that's what you're after. I don't talk about the war anymore. I've let go."

"No. I'm totally not after Vietnam stories at all. I couldn't believe all of the things your friends told us when they visited our classroom, and it was really hard to listen to them, especially since they all cried at least once, and it's really hard to watch grown men cry. I've heard enough. True. Do you have any kids?"

"No."

"Can I come in?"

"I don't think that would be a very good idea."

"Do you want to—like—maybe take a walk with me?" I asked him.

"Why would I want to take a walk with you?"

"I don't know—I'm interested in learning more about the you of today."

"Why?"

"Because I don't like writing strangers, so since I was forced to write to you, I figure I should at least know something about you, so we can keep writing letters and maybe even hang out from time to time."

"I'm sorry," Private Jackson told me, and then shut the door in my face, which made me feel really sad—and like a peon.

So I pounded on his door with my fists and yelled, "That was mean!" even though he wouldn't open the door a second time. "You'll regret slamming the door in my face when you read my next letter, especially since it took me hours to write and is therefore very moving! And if you hadn't fought for our country in Vietnam, if you hadn't been in the jungle for a year or whatever, I'd call you a bad name right now! Goodbye!"

★ ★ ★

About a week or so later, when I had all but forgotten about Private Jackson, at the end of Mr. Bonds' class, when all of the kids were lined up at the door, my history teacher said, "Ms. Appleton. You got mail."

He handed me this envelope that was addressed to me C/O Mr. Bonds via Childress Public High School.

I opened the envelope and the sheet of paper inside had eleven handwritten words on it:

WALKING MS. JENNY
FIVE O'CLOCK P.M. TODAY
SHE RUNS THE DIAMOND
—JACKSON

I instantly recognized that Private Jackson had written me a haiku—which is a form of Japanese poetry that has three lines and seventeen syllables. I learned all about haikus in—like—third grade, back in the day. But I had no idea why Private Jackson had written me a haiku, nor what the hell his haiku meant. But I *did* know that I'd be going to his house later that day.

I realized that this was highly irregular activity—receiving haikus from a strange man—but I chalked it up to Jackson's being in Vietnam. A lot of men didn't come back right, but they're still our men, damn it! I felt it was my civic duty to check out what the hell Private Jackson's haiku was all about. As a citizen of the free world, I owed him this much.

So at five PM I stood outside of Private Jackson's house and waited to see what would happen.

Private Jackson emerged on schedule wearing a brown coat

and one of those Irish hats that old people wear forwards and black people wear backwards. PJ wore his the old-man way.

But the coolest detail about this moment was that PJ had this tiny little funny-looking gray dog on a leash. When I saw the dog, I ran over to it—all girly of me, I know—and I bent down to give the pup a big kiss and a pat on the head.

As you know, I go frickin' nuts for dogs.

"You pass the test," Private Jackson said to me from above. "She likes you. And she's a very hard judge of character."

"So this is Ms. Jenny?" I said, rubbing the crap out the little dog's head.

"Yes."

"What breed is she?"

"Italian greyhound."

"What did you mean by writing *she runs the diamond?*"

"You'll see if you take a walk with me."

We started walking down his street, following Ms. Jenny.

"So you dig haikus?" I asked him.

"Yes."

"Kind of interesting for a dude your age to be writing haikus."

"Why?"

"Aren't they for children?"

"Why would you think that?"

"Elementary kids write haikus when they study Japan. I had to read one while wearing a homemade bedsheet kimono at the Cultures of the World Festival, back in the day, when I was only a wee one."

"Do you remember the haiku you read?"

"No."

Private Jackson didn't say anything in response.

"Why did you write me back this time?" I asked him. "Why did you send me a haiku?"

"I don't know. I didn't want to. If we're going to be honest, I now wish I hadn't."

"Why?"

"I don't really like people."

"Why?"

"Dogs are better than people. I have a dog. That's all I need. Dogs are easy. People are complicated."

"Tell me about it. Dogs are way better than people."

"It was rude of me to slam the door in your face. My actions troubled me for days. It was rude. Unkind. I feel as though I have accrued bad karma."

"No worries. People are rude to me all the time. I'm totally used to it. My mom's boyfriend slams the door in my face all the time. At least you didn't call me a bitch, right? Oliver's a grade-A a-hole."

PJ didn't laugh at that joke but said, "You looked like the type of person who likes dogs."

"How can you tell?"

"You have a kind dog-loving look about you."

"Thanks."

"I wasn't complimenting you. I was just stating a fact."

"Un-thanks."

He laughed slightly at that one, covering his mouth, as if he had burped, and then said, "I thought maybe if I sent you a haiku, and you understood what it meant, that would prove that you'd like to see my dog run, and then — after you saw Ms. Jenny run the bases — we'd be even."

"That's a pretty elaborate plan, Jackson."

"Please don't make fun of me."

"I wasn't making fun of you. I was just stating a fact," I said, because I love a running joke.

"I'm not going to write you any more letters. This is a one-shot deal. I want to be upfront about that. I'm not looking to make a friend. I just wanted to erase the bad karma I created when I slammed the door in your face. I didn't ask you to come to my door, but the universe sent you and I acted poorly, so I have to reverse that before I go back into my house where I can be alone with Ms. Jenny."

"Cool. Letters suck," I said, even though I really dig letters. I was sorta figuring out that PJ was a little nuts by this point, but I still dug him. He didn't seem mean, and he was trying to make up for slamming the door in my face. People don't often make stuff up to me. "So why did you write me a haiku?"

"I write haikus all day long. That's what I do. All I do."

"What do you mean that's what you do?"

"I mean, I get up in the morning, walk and feed Ms. Jenny, write haikus until five PM — keeping my thoughts concentrated and pure — walk and feed Ms. Jenny, read the haikus of other more talented poetry masters at night — keeping my thoughts pure and concentrated — and then I go to bed at eight PM."

"Every day?"

"Yes."

"No bull?"

"It's what I do. Not very interesting, I'm afraid."

"Are you kidding me? That's the most interesting hooey I've heard in—like *weeks*."

PJ smiled at that one, but in a confused sorta way—like he maybe had to pass gas. "You're teasing me."

"No way. I really dig haikus. Five. Seven. Five. Seventeen syllables. That's the bomb."

"You're making fun of me."

"Why would I make fun of you?" I asked PJ.

"I'm not used to taking walks with people."

"Neither am I."

"We're here," PJ said to me, and when I looked up and around, I realized that we were on the town baseball field. *She runs the diamond.* "Watch this. It's beautiful. The opposite of a door slammed in your face."

When he let Ms. Jenny off the leash, the little thing started sprinting around the baseball diamond. She ran really fast and hard, but her legs were so little that it took her quite a long time to make it all the way around, which was so frickin' cute that I had to follow her on her second lap, which made her bark and start to run circles around me as we made our way around the bases. When I hit home plate, I looked over at Private Jackson and he was smiling at me in this very strange and almost eerie way, so I picked up his dog and held her to my face, giving her a kiss, before we walked back to PJ.

"So do you forgive me for slamming the door in your face? Are we even now?" he asked me.

"You bet. That was great!"

He kinda smiled in this really sad way, and then I couldn't think of anything else to say.

On the walk back to his house, Ms. Jenny peed on a tree and pooped by a bush, but neither of us said anything.

When we arrived at his house, I said, "If you ever feel like writing me another haiku, I'd love to read more of your work."

"Don't make fun of me," he said.

"I'm not. Can I send you some of my haikus? Maybe you could critique one or two for me," I said, even though I hadn't written a haiku since third grade. True.

"I just wanted to make up for slamming the door in your face, and now that I have erased the bad karma, I'd like you to leave me alone. Please. It's what I most want."

That bit muted me.

He turned and started walking toward his door, and I kept waiting for him to look back over his shoulder and say something nice, or give me some sorta sign that he really wanted to see me again and be my friend, but he didn't look back or anything, which made me feel sorta mad at first, but then that madness turned into a sadness that stuck with me for many days, until I got this crazy idea: I would send Private Jackson a hopeful haiku every day, and every one of the haikus would be about dogs, because that was the only thing I knew he liked.

I washed and waxed Donna's Mercedes for twenty bucks—she lets me do that sometimes—and then I used the money to buy a box of envelopes and two books of stamps.

I started sending Private Jackson one doggie haiku a day.

According to Private Jackson, here are my all-time top three doggie haikus (out of more than a crapload):

Pooping anywhere
You like outside, anytime
A dog's life rocks hard

A pup will never
Forget to kiss you goodnight
Even when you smell

Dogs have lots of fur
Does that count as wearing clothes
Or are they naked?

Okay, I suck at writing haikus, but I was faithful and wrote Private Jackson every day for more than a month.

He never wrote back even once.

Then one day I found this little wet furry thing in a Nike box, who I named Bobby Big Boy and nursed back to health, as you know.

> I found a doggie
> In a designer shoebox
> He was very sad

(I actually sent that haiku to Private Jackson but got no response.)

What you don't know is that BBB was all traumatized from his stint on the streets, living in a bright designer shoebox, and after I rescued him from the clutches of starvation, B Thrice was very sad for a time, even after we got him back up to his fighting weight.

I used to sing to BBB, give him extra spoonfuls of peanut butter, bathe him in Donna's tub, give him full body rubdowns, read him happy books, and I even made him a dapper coat. Donna bought him all sorts of toys and gourmet doggie food and Phillies dishes, but nothing seemed to cheer him up. I just couldn't figure out what would make BBB happy.

Then I saw these two goth kids making out hard-core in the A-building stairwell of our high school—they looked so happy and in love when they paused the spit-swapping and let me pass through, and for some reason right then and there I knew I needed to get Bobby Big Boy a girlfriend.

When I thought about the size and weight of BBB's perfect companion, Ms. Jenny came to mind, so I took B Thrice to the baseball diamond at five o'clock and introduced him to Private Jackson and Ms. Jenny.

We arrived when Ms. Jenny was already off the leash and doing laps, so she didn't notice us at first.

"Who's this?" Private Jackson asked, saying nothing about all the haikus I had sent him, which bummed me out a little.

"This is Bobby Big Boy."

Private Jackson bent down and patted BBB on the head. "Where did you get him?"

"I found him on the street in a shoe box," I said, wondering whether PJ had not received and read any of the haikus I had sent him about BBB.

"You rescued him," PJ said.

"Yes, sir."

"That's good karma."

That's when Ms. Jenny saw Bobby Big Boy and Cupid's arrow stuck. She came tearing ass off the baseball field and began sniffing BBB's butt. I had him on the leash, so he started crying.

"Let him off the leash," PJ said.

"What if they fight?"

"They won't. Ms. Jenny's a lover."

So I let BBB off the leash and the two little dogs began to wrestle and run around in circles and roll all about for at least a half hour as PJ and I just watched and smiled.

"This is the happiest I've seen B Thrice since I picked him up off the streets," I told Private Jackson.

"I think Ms. Jenny is in love," PJ said to me.

And then we both agreed that for the sake of our dogs' happiness, we would meet at the field at least once a week, for doggie playtime.

But when it was time to say goodbye, I couldn't help asking whether PJ liked the doggie haikus I had been sending him.

"Ms. Jenny will be looking forward to seeing Bobby Big Boy again," PJ said. He leashed Ms. Jenny and walked away.

I was pretty proud of BBB for not trying to hump Ms. Jenny on the first date, so I chalked the experience up as a victory, and left it at that.

We started visiting the baseball diamond pretty regularly, and after a few weeks or so we were walking Ms. Jenny and PJ back to their house, and then one day we went inside for tea, and I saw that Private Jackson had been hanging up my haikus on his living-room walls, and that he had completely covered one of four walls with *my* haikus!

"Why do you put my haikus up on the wall?" I asked him.

"Do you like green tea?" he replied.

"Yes," I said, even though I had never before even had green tea, and then we drank tea together silently, while BBB and Ms. Jenny took a nap, spooning on the rug under a glass coffee table.

A bit later on—after many house visits—Private Jackson started allowing me to read through his haiku notebooks, which impressed me very much, because he writes beautiful poetry.

Here's Private Jackson's best haiku, as far as I'm concerned:

> TOGETHER PLAYING
> GRAY AND WHITE-BROWN DOGS OF OURS
> WE WATCH QUIETLY

Simple and true. Like a frickin' snapshot. Jackson wrote that one for me and gave it to me on this really nice piece of paper for my birthday last year. I carry that haiku around in my backpack and I read it whenever I am feeling really down. I have it memorized, of course, but I like looking at Private Jackson's handwriting, because it is so meticulous—like a little kid's. It's as if he was trying so hard to remember how to spell each syllable, or maybe like he was giving each syllable so much importance, that every single letter had to wait an extra second to be born and is therefore spaced just a little too far apart. You've never seen anything like it, and his kick-ass handwriting makes the haiku even better.

To this day, if I ask Jackson any questions about his past or his family or anything like that he'll usually say some Zen bullcrap like "There is no past," or "I am here in the present," or "Like our dogs playing in the grass, I am." It used to piss me off a lot, before I got used to the Zen hooey. But now, I sorta like it. True.

And that's all I ever do with Private Jackson—run the dogs, drink tea, and read his haikus. I still write him haikus, only I hand deliver the poems to save money, because postage adds up and I'm living in Hello Yellow as of late.

Something cool: I've covered three and a half of his living room walls with doggie haikus. I'm going to cover all four before junior year ends. Word.

As we are riding Donna's bike back to her house from the old folks home I ask BBB if he needs some good lovin' and he barks once, so I make a detour and we ride toward the ghetto, toward Private Jackson's house.

It's past five, so no diamond running for BBB today, as we've missed Ms. Jenny's daily sprint around the bases, but B Thrice can still get some kissing and spooning in, so when we arrive, we stash the bike around back and then knock on PJ's front door.

When Private Jackson opens up, BBB sprints into the house in search of Ms. Jenny and disappears into the hallway that leads to the bedrooms. My dog can get quite randy from time to time. He needs a release every once in a while.

"I'll put on tea," PJ says to me as I enter his house and sit down on his old-ass couch.

I listen to PJ preparing tea in the other room—the sound of water running into a metal kettle, the clicking sound of the electric gas stovetop starter, the ignition of gas—I imagine the blue flames and the bubbles rising in the kettle, and I start to feel better.

Time sorta stops when I'm in PJ's house—it's sorta like stepping into a real church, not like Father Chee's converted-store-strip-mall church, but like some ancient holy stone church that smells of centuries worth of praying and hoping and believing, sorta like in the Catholic church where I was confirmed, St. Dymphna's, and PJ's house feeling holy is strange, because—after reading so much of Private Jackson's poetry—I've sorta gathered that he's in the Nietzsche-Donna-Ricky camp. I'm pretty sure PJ's an atheist.

Here is the saddest haiku I have ever read:

CUNNINGHAM PRAYS WHILE
BAGGING OUR CASUALTIES AND
I AM SO ALONE

Private Jackson wrote that one back in 'Nam. He doesn't know that I read it, because I flipped through the back section of one of his haiku notebooks when he was making tea.

He had said I could read any poem in the sections segmented by the blue and red and black plastic dividers, but he didn't want me to look at the pages between the green dividers. Of course, I turned to the green section just as soon as PJ was out of the room, and he seemed to stay in the kitchen for a very long time—way longer than it takes to make tea—so maybe he wanted me to read the Vietnam haikus, I don't know. But from what I have gathered from reading his haikus—because he doesn't tell me squat about his life—it seems like Private Jackson started writing haikus in the jungle, maybe as a means of staying sane, and he just never stopped writing haikus when he came home.

CHAPTER
11

"So what is bothering you today?" PJ says as he hands me a steaming hot cup of green tea.

"What? Can't I just visit you for no reason at all?"

"You only come when you're sad."

"Joan of Old hit me with a whole bunch of new depressing Nietzsche quotes, but I eventually made her smile," I say, and then sip my tea, which tastes like mown grass. Green tea is an acquired taste that I have not yet acquired, but I drink it like a woman for Private Jackson, mostly because it's all he keeps in his house other than water. He mostly eats rice and roots, so no snacking here either.

"How'd you get her to smile this week?" he asks, which makes me pause, because he usually never asks me any questions about anything. This is as lively as PJ gets when it comes to conversation. This is Private Jackson on speed.

"I kissed her. And I said a bunch of funny stuff too. Hey, do you think I have a dinosaur face? You can be honest with me. If you were seventeen would you want to get all hot and heavy with me, or no? And if no, is it because I have a dinosaur face? You can be totally honest with me."

"I think you are exactly as you should be. You are perfect for this moment."

"More Zen hooey."

"Do you have any poems for me?"

I reach into my pocket and hand him a sheet of paper housing eight doggie haikus written by yours truly.

Private Jackson reads my poetry very slowly as he slurps his tea with this very determined look on his face—almost like he is taking a dump or something.

"Which is your favorite," I say after—like five minutes. He's still reading, contemplating each set of seventeen syllables as if they were new constellations that suddenly appeared in the sky one night. He's a crazy serious cat sometimes.

"They are all perfect," he says without looking up.

"No Zen bullcrap. Which one is your favorite?"

"I cherish them all equally and will hang them on the wall just as soon as you leave, finding the perfect spot for your words."

"Which do you think is the funniest then?"

Private Jackson reads them all over again and then a little smile blooms on his face. He reads number four very dramatically, saying, "Dogs go into the—bedroom and get funky wild—humans drink green tea."

"Tried to capture the present moment," I say.

"You certainly have."

"You want to meet Donna?" I say, because I've been telling Private Jackson that I could hook him up with the sexiest woman he has ever seen in his life—and she's rich ta boot!

"No."

"You don't know what you're missing out on, and—"

"How do you like your tea?" he asks politely.

"Tastes like grass."

"Grass is natural. Grass is good."

And then we sip tea in silence until Ms. Jenny and BBB come out of the bedroom, walking like they are a little drunk or something, with this crazy look in their eyes.

"Only dogs can truly love," Private Jackson says.

"You could know love, my friend," I say. "Donna is a catch. She is—like—very hot."

"I will wash your teacup now," Private Jackson says.

I hand him the teacup and say, "Can I give you a hug before I leave?"

"I would be honored to shake the hand of such an accomplished poet," he says like always, so when he extends his hand, I hold it with both of mine for as long as Jackson will let me.

"You're a good man, Jackson," I say, looking him in the eyes, "and a great poet."

"I will wash the teacups now," he says, and then he drops my hand, turns his back, and walks into the kitchen.

And so BBB and I hop on Donna's bike again and ride it back to her house.

When we arrive, I don't really want to go inside for some reason, but B Thrice needs to eat, so I go in for the sake of my doggie's health.

Donna all but sprints into the kitchen when she hears the back door open and says, "Did something happen to you, Amber?"

"No. Why?" I say without making eye contact, even though I realize she was worried because I didn't make dinner, and then I make my way over to the cabinet where BBB's cans are kept.

I pop one open and feed B Thrice.

He starts pigging out, because he's always hungry after making love to Ms. Jenny.

"Did Joan of Old finally make you cry?" Donna asks, looking genuinely concerned.

"Almost, but I got her to smile with a big, sloppy sneak-attack kiss. She's protesting the battle, because she says kissing is illegal, but it's pretty much a bullcrap claim, and Old Man Thompson is never going to side with Joan of Old, because of that time when she called the cops and tried to get him thrown out of the home by placing a restraining order on him, because he was looking at her funny."

"Isn't she blind?" Donna asks.

"She is. Word."

"Then how did she know he was looking at her?"

"She didn't. He wasn't. Joan just made that hooey up."

"Why?"

"Because she's Joan of Old, evil incarnate."

"I have to meet this Joan of Old someday."

"Come to the battles. Any Wednesday afternoon. Better come before she dies though, because that could be—like—any day."

"Ricky told me that Lex Pinkston apologized to you, and then came to The Franks Lair for lunch."

"Can you believe that bullcrap?"

I realize that I am being sorta flip toward Donna, but I need to keep being flip or else I might start crying again. I don't want to be around Donna right now, maybe because she's too perfect, and I know I'll never live up. And that's a hard reality to swallow. True? True.

"Ricky was very excited about socializing with the football team. He said they were very nice to him for once."

"Yeah, because you threatened Mr. Pinkston with a lawsuit."

"Remember what I told you about teenage boys and men, how they need to be herded like sheep?"

"Yeah, so?"

"Are sheep evil?"

"No, they're sheep."

"So maybe you should give Lex Pinkston and his boys a try. I hear the rest of The Five enjoyed playing Halo 3 with the football team. It's good to make new friends."

"That's so messed up," I say, shaking my head, feeling the tears coming.

"You know who boys like Lex tease and call names? Girls they are secretly in love with. The kid probably has a crush on you. And if he's willing to play nice, why not let bygones be — Amber, where are you going?"

I'm frickin' out of there, BBB following behind, and then we're walking through the night, down the street.

My stomach is growling because I haven't eaten anything since breakfast, but I don't give a crap.

"You're going to have to take a rain check tonight, JC," I pray, "because I got nothing left over for you. I just can't pray tonight. Sorry."

I walk pretty quickly back to the school bus compound, BBB and I hop the fence, and I am surprised to find that Mom is home and awake.

"I made dinner," Mom says when I enter Hello Yellow, and then she proudly holds up a McDonald's bag.

"I could kiss you, Mom."

"Why?"

I hug Mom for a long time, until I start crying like a baby once again. Her body feels so skeletal, and I can actually feel her ribs through the back of her jacket, which makes me sob even harder.

"It's okay, Amber," Mom says, alcohol on her breath. "We won't be on this bus forever. I'm working on it."

I want to tell Mom that I really don't give a crap about living on a school bus, but that the world is beating me down and I feel like I'm battling everyone and no one is putting any fuel back into my tank and I'm not sure I'm going to make it to adulthood unscathed and still believing in hope because JC isn't doing me any favors as of late and everything is so frickin' messed up—but I can't stop crying, so I just let my mom hold me and pat my back for a half hour or so of pathetic sobbing.

When I finish crying, I open the McDonald's bag and find an ice-cold child-size Happy Meal: small Coke, a handful of fries, four chicken McNuggets, and some stupid toy promoting some stupid kid's movie.

"Did you eat?" I ask Mom.

"Oh, sure," she says, and then takes a sip from a Coke can, which I know is filled with vodka, because I can smell it.

"Mom, if you love me," I say, my stomach growling with

hunger, "will you please, please, please eat this meal while I watch?"

"I bought it for you, Amber. You're a growing girl and—"

"Please, Mom," I say, tears suddenly streaming down my face again. I hold a chicken McNugget up to her face and say, "Please eat this. Please. For me, Mom. Please. I want to see you eat."

Bobby Big Boy is watching me from an adjacent seat, wanting to eat the chicken nugget himself, but he's too good of a dog to go for it, so I don't worry.

Finally, my mother takes the piece of chicken from me, bites off a tiny bit, and then chews.

Mom swallows, and then says, "There. Are you happy? Now you should really eat—"

"Eat the rest. The whole meal, Mom. For me. Please."

"Amber, you have to eat something yourself and we only have—"

"I ate like—ten pounds of hamburgers at Donna's. Please let me watch you eat the rest. I've had a bad day, Mom. Please eat. Try. For me."

Slowly, my mom nibbles at the food, sorta like a suspicious mouse might nibble on rat poison, as I watch.

Mom really does try to eat, which makes me proud of her.

After ten minutes or so, she gets down two and a half chicken McNuggets—and then she starts to throw up.

By the time I get her off Hello Yellow, she has puked three times. After another bout of puking in the bus yard—which scares me a lot—finally Mom stops vomiting.

When she asks for her cigarettes, I get them for her and let her smoke. I even bring her the Coke can of vodka, because I'm terrified now, thinking my mom might die right here and now, and I know that vodka is what she most needs.

There are paper towels and some sorta blue spray cleaning stuff under the driver's seat, so I clean up Mom's throw-up, which is full of blood and tiny shredded pieces of chicken.

I gag all the way through.

I try to think of something nice to take my mind off the present reality, so I think about all-time Amber-and-her-mom moment number two:

I'm tiny.

I cannot talk.

My arms and legs are wrapped up in a sheet—like a mummy.

I'm in a baby stroller and it's late summer.

I'm shaded by one of those baby awnings above me—that rounded half dome that covers half of the baby stroller.

Bob is pushing the stroller and Mom has her elbow linked to my father's and I hear the cry of a seagull, so maybe we are near the beach.

Suddenly—we stop moving.

Bob leans down and kisses Mom.

Baby me watches Bob and Mom kiss—baby me smiles.

Now, I know that there is no way I could remember this moment because I was only a few months old when my dad took off, and he probably wasn't so in love with Mom before he took off, because why would he take off if they were actually in love?

So maybe I made the memory up?

It's still my number two—regardless.

Back in the present moment, while I was trying to remember, while I was cleaning up puke, BBB has been hiding on one of the back seats, because I have been sobbing the whole time, and that scares him.

By the time I am finished, I reek of throw-up, and since there is no sink or anything around, I'm going to smell like puke for the night unless I wash with the dirty black slushy snow in the bus parking lot, which would make me smell like gas and bus emissions. I don't even have a water bottle tonight. Nothing.

When I go back outside to throw the puke towels into the woods, BBB follows and starts his jumping routine—and I just can't take it right now, so I scream, "Stop jumping!"

He stops.

He looks up at me with his little ears pointing straight up—like I hit him or something.

And then he starts whining, as if he is crying too.

So I throw the puke towels over the fence, into the woods—erasing Mom's mess—and then I pick up BBB and give him a kiss on the lips.

"I'm scared, Bobby Big Boy. I'm scared. I can't keep doing this."

"Rew!" he says in agreement before we walk back to my mom.

"I have to go out," Mom says, exhaling mentholated smoke.

"Where?"

"I'm going to get medicine for my stomach."

"Where?"

"At the drugstore."

"The Childress Rite Aid?"

"Yes."

"Let me come with you," I say. "It's late."

"You have school tomorrow. I'll be fine."

"Mom. Are you going to get more vodka? You can tell me the truth. I won't try to stop you. I just want to know the truth."

Mom will not look me in the eyes. "Going to the drugstore. I just need some Pepto-Bismol. I'll be back in a few minutes. You just go to sleep," she says before she starts walking away from me, staggering a little.

I know that I should stop her, that I should maybe follow her to make sure she is okay, but I'm only seventeen—I'm still a girl, just a stupid confused chick—this is nothing new, and I have nothing left in my tank. I'm on empty, and so I go back into Hello Yellow and cry myself to sleep without even praying first. Sorry, JC.

CHAPTER

12

When I wake up, the streetlights are off. "Mom?" I say.

Silence.

"Mom?"

Somehow I know she is gone.

My heart is pounding.

I stand.

Slowly, as my eyes adjust to the darkness, I feel every seat in the bus with my hands and keep on saying, "Mom? Mom? Mom? Mom?"

BBB sniffs the entire bus floor.

Mom is not on Hello Yellow.

I know it is after eleven, because there are no streetlights on, but I have no idea how late it is. Mom goes out to the bars all the time, but for some reason, I have this very bad feeling that something horrible has happened. I can't really explain it—I just instantly know, or maybe I just feel it in my gut.

"Come on, B Thrice," I say, and then we leave Hello Yellow.

I know Mom went one of two places: Charlie's Pad, which is the bar on the edge of town, the first bar in the ghetto; or the liquor store next to Father Chee's church, where they sell big plastic bottles of vodka for very cheap—less than half the prices charged in Childress, plus the store in the ghetto is open later.

I'm not thinking too clearly right now—granted. I just know that something bad might have happened to my mom, so I'm sorta on autopilot—walking super fast.

I go right by Private Jackson's house, walk a few more blocks, and then I am in the ghetto, trying to open the metal front door to Charlie's Pad. The neon beer signs behind the high windows—which are covered with mesh wire to keep out burglars—those signs are off and the door is locked. "Hello?" I yell. "Hello?"

No one answers.

"Hello! Anyone in there? Mom? Mom!"

"Shut up, bitch!" someone yells, but when I turn around no one is there.

I don't see anyone on the streets.

Just trash swirling in the wind.

If the bar is closed, it must be well after midnight—I know this much. And since the bar is closed, the liquor store is definitely closed, but for some stupid reason, BBB and I start walking toward the liquor store very quickly, as if we might actually find my mom there.

I'm desperate.

I'm a little loopy tonight.

I'm alone.

I'm scared.

I'm stupid.

I pass a crazily bearded insane-looking homeless man who throws an empty beer can at me and yells, "Catch a cat by the tail 'till you spin around and drown! Catch a cat by the tail—"

BBB and I start running.

The icy wind cuts my face.

I hear car alarms going off in the distance.

When I get to the liquor store it is closed and the doors are chained shut. No one is around.

For some stupid reason I bang on the doors, yell, "Mom?" and then I bang on the doors of the Korean Catholic Church, and yell up to Father Chee who lives above the church, but no lights go on.

Then I remember where I am and what time it is.

I start to get really scared, especially when this crappy-looking car—with silver rims and tinted windows and booming bass and neon-pink lights that make the road under the car glow—this crazy car pulls up and idles right next to me.

I start to walk down the street, back toward the town of Childress.

The car follows, going only as fast as I can walk.

It follows me for an entire block—rap music blasting—before BBB and I start to run.

When I get halfway down the next block, the car speeds up and turns, and then screeches to a stop, cutting me off at the corner.

The door opens and this tough-looking white dude with a blond spiky haircut and too many gold chains gets out.

"Where's the fire? Where you going so fast, little girl?" he says, smiling at me.

He's wearing a white tracksuit that is very baggy.

Because I am so tired and confused and worried, I start to cry again—like a wimp.

"Don't cry. It's okay," he says, taking a step toward me, moving very slowly. "What's wrong?"

BBB is now barking at this man skeptically. Like Ms. Jenny, B Thrice is a good judge of character, but for some reason I want to believe that this guy is not evil—that maybe JC is sending me some help.

Blondie's actually kind of handsome, if I'm being truthful, and almost innocent looking—like Billy Budd.

"I'm trying to find my mom," I say, because it's the truth, and I'm so very tired.

"Get in—I'll help you look," he says. "You're very pretty, you know."

When he calls me pretty, something in my stomach begins to churn, and the man begins to look more like Claggart than Billy Budd. "I think I'll just walk, thanks for the offer, though."

"Bad things happen to girls like you when they stray out of their neighborhoods in the middle of the night," he says. "You should come with me."

"Amber!" a voice yells, and when I look over my shoulder, Father Chee is running toward me in slippers through the cold night and wearing only his black pajamas, making him look sorta like some crazy martial arts ninja or something.

"Who are you supposed to be?" the blond man asks FC when he reaches us. "Jackie Chan?"

"Amber, come," FC says, and then takes my hand.

"Is he your pimp or something?"

"He's my priest," I say.

"Well, maybe another time then," the blond man says, smiling kind of funny, chuckling. He gets into his car and drives away.

"Come," Father Chee says, and then we sorta jog back to The Korean Catholic Church.

"Please tell me what are you doing here in this neighborhood at night?" Father Chee asks when we are inside with the doors locked.

I'm scared for my mom, so I come clean.

As I tell him everything about Mom and our living on Hello Yellow and Mom's not coming home tonight, the adrenaline rush wears off, and I start to get seriously nervous and upset and worried.

My voice becomes all tiny and whiny, which makes me feel like I'll never be as brave and strong as Donna—like I'll never get into Bryn Mawr College.

When I finish, I am crying again, so FC gives me a fatherly hug, patting my back very gently, which is cool of him. He's a good man.

"We should call the police so they will start looking for your mother," Father Chee says.

"Do you think I should consult my attorney first?" I ask.

"You have an attorney?"

So I tell him all about Donna, and then we wake her with

a phone call, using the pay phone in Father's Chee's church, after which FC puts on his penguin suit.

We take a cab to Ricky's house, where I tell Donna the whole story as Father Chee makes coffee.

I can tell that Donna is mad at me for not telling her how bad things were with my mom and my living on Hello Yellow for months, because, very loudly, she says, *"Months?"*

And when I nod, she asks me why I didn't tell her earlier, and I start to cry again because I am so weak and stupid—even though I'm sorta mad at her for not figuring it all out earlier. *Why else would I need to take a shower at her house every morning?*

Father Chee serves us coffee, and then Donna makes a few phone calls.

I hear her talking to the police, and then to some sorta private detective.

At one point I hear her say, "Money is not an issue."

Donna's young assistant shows up without makeup and without her hair done, making her look less intimidating.

"You're getting a raise," Donna says to her assistant.

"Are you okay?" Jessica says to me, and I can tell that she is sincere. I remember thinking how much I hated Jessica in the past, so I start crying even harder now because I'm such a little girl.

"If we're not back, don't tell Ricky anything when he gets up in the morning," Donna says to Jessica. "Tell him I had to go to trial early, let him eat whatever he wants for breakfast, and then take him to school. Oh, yeah. Feed the dog a can, and then let him out. Okay?"

Jessica nods, and then FC, me, and Donna are in her Mercedes driving back to Hello Yellow.

We call Mom's name and search the parking lot with flashlights.

Mom's not in the parking lot.

Mom's not on Hello Yellow.

"Grab your things," Donna tells me, so I get my trash bags from under Hello Yellow and Father Chee takes them to Donna's car. "Where else might she have gone?"

"She might have met a man?" I say hopefully, because it's better than any alternative of which I can think. "She was always trying to find a man with an apartment so we'd have a home."

"Did she ever leave you alone for an entire night before?" Donna asks.

"No," I say, but then feel like I shouldn't be lying now. "Well, not very often. Sometimes. But tonight is different. I feel like something very bad might have happened. I sorta just know it somehow. You have to trust me on this. Seriously, Donna, I'm really scared."

"Okay," Donna says, and I can see in her eyes that she is worried—that this is bad. Very bad. So terribly messed up.

The three of us drive around aimlessly looking for Mom.

We cruise the ghetto, all of the major Childress streets slide past the passenger-side window; we pass all the bars and liquor stores of which we can think and then go back to the bus lot when it is time for the bus drivers to pick up schoolchildren.

Mom's boss confirms that my mother did not show up for

work today, and none of the other bus drivers have seen her. Mom didn't call out sick either.

I start to feel as though I am very alone in the world.

When we get back to Donna's house, Ricky is gone, and BBB has shredded the arm of Donna's leather recliner.

When Jessica comes back from dropping off Ricky, she apologizes for the mess, and Donna says, "My fault. I forgot to tell you to lock up Bobby Big Boy whenever you leave the house."

Even though Donna doesn't say anything about my dog ruining her expensive furniture, seeing the damage makes me cry again for some reason.

I'm so tired.

After a few phone calls, Donna convinces the local police to come interview me. She leaves Father Chee in charge, and then the lawyers shower and dress and get ready to go to Donna's ongoing murder trial.

Father Chee just sits next to me on the leather couch BBB ripped earlier, and we take turns petting B Thrice.

FC doesn't say anything stupid, like most adults would, but just sits with me, which I appreciate.

Right after Donna and Jessica leave, two nice uniformed officers come and ask me a bunch of questions about where Mom and I were living, Mom's drinking problem, and her long list of past boyfriends, all of whom I describe in great detail, while the cops write it all down.

Donna told me to tell the truth, and so I do.

I give all of the same answers to the private detective Donna hired, who shows up seconds after the police leave. He's a twitchy man with a big yellow mustache and acne scars all over his face. He also writes down my answers—all the secrets I have been keeping for months now.

When we finish, it's almost noon, which means that—besides the hour or so of sleep I got on the bus—I have been up for thirty-some hours straight.

"Are you okay?" Father Chee asks me.

"I'm so tired," I say, and then because I really need to, I snuggle up to my Man of God, resting my head on his shoulder, and cry some more.

Somehow I fall asleep.

PART THREE

Puke and Cry

CHAPTER

13

It takes them nine days to find my mother's body, but when they do, the story is the lead on every TV news station and is on the front page of every local paper, especially since my mother's killer is immediately linked to the other rape-murders that had happened in the area, so I'm sure you know all of the gruesome, unreal, sadistic, and childhood-ending details. I'm not going to list these details here, because I don't want to give the facts any more credence than they already have.

I'm pretty numb now.

Maybe even numb enough to be an official nihilist like Joan of Old.

For some things there are no explanations—no reasons, and so, when these things happen, there is nothing to talk about really. And it is best not to dwell on said things for too long, because you will find that life has no real meaning if you do.

Maybe you think I am only saying this because I am in a state of denial or shock, but that's just not the case. I'm being honest, maybe for the first time.

★ ★ ★

With Father Chee and Donna, I go to identify the body, even though Donna says I don't have to.

For some reason, I need to see.

I insist.

I'm a real cat about it.

Maybe I want to know, just so I won't be wondering for the rest of my life—like I do with Dad. And as selfish as it might seem, knowing that my mother is definitely dead is better than thinking she might be out there somewhere having abandoned me in an effort to live an easier life without her stupid daughter to worry about.

I go to the morgue.

I see the facts.

It's worse than anything I could have ever imagined.

My howling stops them from uncovering more than Mom's head and shoulders.

I don't want to see any more.

I crumble.

I melt.

I evaporate.

They cover what's left of my naked mother back up with a sheet and push her into a wall, which is when I realize that she is in some sorta freezer.

I do not talk for three days.

I sit.

I stare.

I see my mother's naked dead body in a dark freezer.

Sometimes I shake.

It seems like I am in a constant nightmare.

Donna brings me soup and crackers and toast—and takes care of BBB's needs.

At my request, Donna pays to have my mother cremated.

Fire. Warmth. It's better this way.

I promise to pay Donna back, and she says it's not necessary.

The very next day, at my request, Father Chee performs a private ceremony at the bench where Mom and I used to feed ducks.

BBB is the only other person invited to the ceremony, because this special childhood place is mine alone—it's what I have left, so I don't want to share it with anyone except FC and BBB. Not even Donna and Ricky are invited.

Father Chee does a very good job eulogizing my mom, especially since he never met her. He says a lot of things about Mom going to heaven and my seeing her again, which is pretty nice, especially since Mom was never baptized or confirmed as a member of the Catholic Church—and I'm pretty sure she never went to confession—so I know FC is supposed to say Mom was going to hell and all.

Maybe the Pope is pissed?

I don't care.

FC says he doesn't care either.

I'm not going to tell you exactly what Father Chee says at

Mom's funeral, but it was very beautiful—as beautiful as Private Jackson's best haiku, which is saying something. True.

We spread Mom's ashes on the water and grass around the bench—and I pray flowers will bloom there in the spring, which is a girly and maybe silly sentiment, but a nice thought too.

CHAPTER
14

Donna takes me in, buys me a bed, gives me my own room, and begins sorting through the legal red tape involved for her to become my legal guardian, which is complicated since no one knows if my father is still alive or where he might be—and I don't know of any living family I may or may not have since my mom left her home out west early on in life, hitchhiked east at the age of thirteen, and never told me anything about her parents whom she hated and refused to even name. I never even knew my own mother's maiden name.

Donna says she knows enough people to keep me out of the foster care system at least until I turn eighteen this summer, provided that I will state before a judge that I want to stay with Donna and Ricky, which I do.

★ ★ ★

The police arrest a man with huge brown glasses and strange hair.

I am sure you read all about him in the papers or see him on television.

His face is everywhere.

He becomes famous.

He admits to doing what he did, but his lawyer stresses that the whole thing was random, an accident even, because my mother's killer went off his medications, but is now back on meds, as if that matters at all to anyone.

Along with the families of the other victims, the prosecution contacts me and says I will be made to testify, which I will hate doing, even though I have Donna to help me out—and I'm not going to tell you about the trial, because it will prove to be too horrible.

My mother's killer uses my name whenever he talks to the press.

Through the media he apologizes to all of his victims' family members, but the only name I really hear him say is Amber Appleton.

He says he is sick.

He says he deserves whatever he gets—and his unfeeling mechanical voice makes me shiver.

He has a long criminal history.

He is a registered sex offender.

Looking into his eyes makes you believe that life can be absolutely meaningless.

He is like every other man who makes people disappear in horrible unimaginable ways.

He reminds me of a Nietzsche quote I found while doing

Joan of Old research: "A casual stroll through the lunatic asylum shows that faith does not prove anything."

Donna tells me this man will go to jail for life, that he will be punished in terrible ways over and over again by the other inmates—and I tell her I don't really care about any of that—in fact, I never want to talk about that man ever again, and I do not really care what happens to him.

CHAPTER 15

I do not go back to school.

I lose fifteen pounds.

I am always cold.

I become very jumpy; any old noise will scare me horribly.

Donna tries to get me to see a therapist, but I refuse.

★ ★ ★

I cannot stand listening to Ricky's autistic nonsense, and I yell at him a lot—until he finally gets the message and just leaves me alone in my room.

★ ★ ★

I decide to quit being Amber Appleton, which isn't to say that I change my name or anything. I just decide that I can't keep living the way I used to live—swinging for the fences, believing that things are going to work out, that everything is worth fighting for, and that I am brave and strong enough to change my reality, because I'm not and I can't.

Joan of Old was right.

I get her now, and what she said about life being a hell that I was only beginning to experience—that makes sense suddenly.

CHAPTER 16

I'm not a kid anymore.

CHAPTER

17

Ty, Jared, and Chad-in-a-backpack come over to Donna's and—in my new bedroom—they say a lot of dumb things.

At first, they say they are sorry, and ask what they can do, and when I don't say anything, they get sorta fidgety, and start talking about the recent Halo 3 games they have played in The Franks Lair, and how they are organizing an all-night video game tournament to help the football team raise money for new safer pads and helmets and other sundry equipment.

This seems important to them.

Back in the day, that news would have pissed me off, because Lex and company are obviously just using my boys—but listening to Ty, Jared, and Chad go on and on, I can't even shrug.

I just stare at my boys with what I suppose is a very blank look on my face until they leave.

That night I tell Donna I don't want to see Ty, Jared, and Chad anymore—but she doesn't respond to my request.

CHAPTER 18

Father Chee jogs to my house every single morning and comes up into my bedroom—even on Sundays, before he presides over Mass.

He never fails to show up.

If I am up, he'll ask if I want to talk.

For weeks, I do not want to talk, so FC just sits next to me for an hour, and we sorta breathe together.

We just sit on the edge of my bed breathing, occupying the same space, which is okay with me, because I really like my Man of God, even if I am mad at God Himself.

If I'm not up, or if I am pretending to sleep, or if I am just lying there like usual, staring at the ceiling, Father Chee will kneel by my bed and bow his head.

If I ask him what he is doing, he'll say he is lifting me up to God, asking God to help me be whoever I need to be at this moment of my life.

He comes every day, and I don't mind his coming.

CHAPTER 19

Franks sends me a card that reads:

> Dear Amber,
> We were very shaken by the news.
> I am always here if you need me.
> We miss you down in The Franks Lair.
> I'm praying for you, and will be
> looking forward to your return.
> Be well,
> Franks

I throw his card away.

I throw away all of the flowers and cards from classmates and community members.

I don't even sniff or open any of those.

I do not want any of these flower arrangements or sympathy cards to exist, so I ask Donna to burn them in the backyard, but I never see any smoke rising past my window, so I don't think she is honoring my request.

CHAPTER 20

This zombie-type mom in need of extra cash starts coming to "tutor" me, since I'm not going to school right now.

She's large.

She smells like mothballs.

She never laughs or smiles or tells a joke.

She reminds me of a robot caked in meat.

Her name is Mrs. Redman.

My real teachers give her assignments that I am supposed to complete. At first, there are little handwritten notes on the assignments—encouraging words from my real teachers—but these notes disappear after a few weeks or so, which is when I realize that my teachers have given up on me. It didn't take them very long.

Because I still want to go to Bryn Mawr, I do all of my assignments and show Mrs. Redman my work three times a week when she comes to visit me.

She gives me all A's, even when I answer incorrectly on purpose.

I think she is afraid of me, or something.

CHAPTER 21

"Father Chee?"

"Yes, Amber?"

"Why does God allow men to go mentally insane?"

"I don't know."

"You'll never lie to me, will you?"

"No."

"Promise me. That you won't tell me lies like everyone else. That you won't BS me."

"I promise—I will never lie to you."

CHAPTER
22

Prince Tony calls me on the phone from time to time, but I don't really listen to what he says to me. It's all crap about the seasons of life and the ebb and flow and other blah-blah stuff adults tell you when they don't know what the hell to say. "Do you understand?" he always asks me at the end of the conversations, and I always say yes.

CHAPTER
23

"Father Chee?"

"Yes, Amber?"

"Why are dogs more humane than humans?"

"I don't know."

CHAPTER
24

Right about the same time my mom's name starts showing up in the news, Private Jackson begins sending me one haiku a day in the mail.

He doesn't write a letter stating that he is sorry for my loss, nor does he ask how I am doing or any of that other crap that doesn't help. He just sends poems. And his haikus are not aimed at inspiring me or making me feel better or helping me deal with the loss. With words, he simply takes snapshots of simple things for me—like a leaf, a bottle cap, a snowflake, a bird in flight, an ant, a single breath—and when I read these haikus I sorta trip out on the image that is never good or bad, happy or sad, exciting or boring.

These images just are.

I begin to really look forward to reading PJ's haikus, and going to check the mail is the only time I leave my new bedroom other than to use the bathroom.

Covering the four walls with Private Jackson's haikus—one page a day—I slowly make my room into a cocoon of poetry.

Here is the first one he sends me:

I WAKE AND SIT UP
SQUIRRELS SCRATCHING FROM INSIDE
MY WALLS ARE ALIVE

At first, I read it—like a million times, wondering if Private Jackson was trying to communicate with me through metaphor.

I puzzled out all sorts of interpretations too.

Maybe it was a metaphor for the madness—or the chaos I was feeling as of late, which is sorta hidden in my chest and mind, but real?

I had been in my new room for days now.

Maybe it was a metaphor for the madness of the man who killed my mother?

Maybe PJ was telling me that I needed to wake up and see that things were still alive and moving around me, even though my mom was gone and I felt so all alone?

Maybe he meant something else, and I was just too dumb to understand?

But then I remembered what Private Jackson stood for, what he was all about—all of the Zen stuff.

I instantly understood that PJ woke up in the middle of the night and heard squirrels in his bedroom walls, so he took a mental snapshot of the moment and wrote me a haiku.

Nothing more.

The moment just was—free of the emotions and judgments or any of the other illusionary things we humans feel the need to attach to everything we encounter.

Reading Private Jackson's haikus after my mother's murder—I totally got why he had been writing haikus all this time, ever since 'Nam, training his mind to allow things to exist without all of the complicated emotional baggage.

Everything simply is—always and forever.

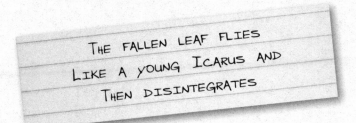

THE FALLEN LEAF FLIES
LIKE A YOUNG ICARUS AND
THEN DISINTEGRATES

I totally get haikus now. True.

And Private Jackson is my favorite writer.

CHAPTER 25

"Father Chee?"

"Yes, Amber?"

"Why does God allow horrible things to happen to good people?"

"I don't know."

CHAPTER 26

One day—on Donna's iPod—I listen to Dinosaur Jr.'s "Puke and Cry" a million times in a row. I just set it to repeat the one song over and over again, and then I listen for several hours—tripping out.

I pretend that the lead singer—J Mascis—is singing me the song over and over again from Donna's living room downstairs. Mascis—who has long silver hair, because he is old now—keeps on singing, "Come on down. Come on down. Come on down," like he really wants me to come down from my little cocoon of haikus and misery.

I don't come down, but I like pretending there is an obscure rock star who wants me to.

The battery finally runs out, and when I take the headphones off, my ears are ringing, J Mascis is gone, and Donna is calling to me, asking me if I want some soup.

CHAPTER
27

"Father Chee?"

  "Yes, Amber?"

  "When will it stop hurting so badly?"

  "I don't know."

CHAPTER 28

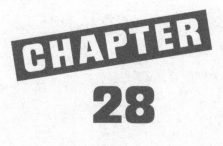

GRASS TEA BOILED AND DRUNK
MY DOG ROLLS THROUGH TOMORROW'S
CUP-THERE'S ENDLESS TEA

CHAPTER
29

After a month or so, Old Man Linder pays me a visit on behalf of the entire Methodist Home.

Donna comes into my room and says that I have to come down to see Old Man Linder because he can't walk up steps. Donna's murder trial ended a week or so ago and she has taken some time off from work to care for me, which I told her not to do. She dotes on me now, even though I hardly talk to her.

"I only go down once a day to check the mail," I tell Donna. "Tell Old Man Linder he'll have to come up here if he wants to talk to me."

"The man has tubes running up his nose and is attached to an oxygen—"

"Yeah, I know him," I say, like a total cat.

"He can't walk stairs. He said it could kill him, but he really wants to talk to you, Amber. I don't think he leaves the home much. Please just come down. He's an old man and I think it might be good for you to—"

"No," I say. "Tell him he can come back tomorrow around one fifteen when I'll be checking the mail. That's when I will next come downstairs."

"Amber, what's happening to you?" Donna says in this really dramatic fashion that pisses me off.

When I don't answer, she leaves.

Ten minutes later, Donna returns and hands me a cup of hot cocoa and a Snickers bar, and then shakes her head at me before exiting my poetry cocoon.

I hear Old Man Linder breathing really hard on the steps.

One footstep, clunk, heavy breathing.

One footstep, clunk, heavy breathing.

One footstep, clunk, heavy breathing.

His oxygen tank makes an awful clunk each time he sets it on a higher step.

"Mr. Linder," Donna says, "perhaps—you really shouldn't—"

"Don't tell me what I can and can't do! I'm old enough to be your grandfather, thank you very much!" Old Man Linder says, and then sucks in an awful breath like he has been underwater for the last two hours or something.

He and Donna fight about whether he should be walking up the steps for another few minutes before I yell, "Donna, your making him yell isn't helping!"

And then I only hear footsteps, clunking, and heavy breathing.

When Old Man Linder reaches the top of the stairs, he looks like he might fall backward and die. His face is completely white, which makes me feel like a total cat, so I walk into the hallway, grab his arm, and escort him into my room.

When he squeezes my shoulder football coach–style, I know that he is going to be okay—that he probably won't die in my room.

He points to the Snickers and cocoa on my dresser. "Compliments of Door Woman Lucy."

I nod.

"How you holdin' up?" he asks me, and then sits down on the wooden chair that goes with the desk Donna bought for me.

I shrug.

I can see that his clear air tubes look sorta fogged up, and I wonder if that is bad.

"What are all those papers on your wall?"

"Haikus."

"Hi-whats?"

"Short Japanese poems."

"You can read Japanese?" he says.

"They're written in English," I say.

"By you?"

"No, by Private Jackson."

"Who's Private Jackson?"

"He was in 'Nam back in the day. Now he writes haikus. He's my favorite poet."

"I'm not going to get into all that, kid," Old Man Linder says, adjusting the nozzle on his oxygen bottle, which produces a hissing sound. "I know you've suffered a horrific, senseless, and cruel loss, and while I won't pretend to know what that must feel like—I will say that I'm old enough to know that life throws you a few nasty blows before she's done with you, but each time you're knocked down, you have to pull yourself up by the bootstraps, and—"

"Please don't," I say to Old Man Linder. "Please."

He looks confused.

He's wringing his hands.

He's so old school.

He's so out of his league.

"I was nineteen years old when I lost my best friend in World War Two. I never did feel the same—"

"Please stop."

He shakes off my request, smiles knowingly, and says, "We miss you down at the home. Joan of Old wants a rematch. She's still contesting your last battle. Stating that the kiss was a violation of the damn rules, not that Old Man Thompson will ever side with her." Old Man Linder forces a laugh. "But some of the older feebleminded broads have taken Old Joan's point of view. If we don't make some sort of public statement quickly, the fans will think—"

"It was just a stupid game. It wasn't real."

"The Wednesday Afternoon Battles are something to look forward to and—"

"I'm retired. Joan of Old can have the title by forfeit."

"Forfeit? Retired? *Are you kidding me?* You haven't even begun to peak and you—"

"I'm done making old people smile. It's over."

He pauses for a second, gathers his thoughts.

So softly, Old Man Linder says, "Amber."

When I look into his eyes they are moist, and I can tell that he loves me like I am his own granddaughter, but I can't play that game anymore for him, so I look away.

"Life goes on," he says. "Whether we choose to enjoy it or not. So you might as well find a way to enjoy the parts you can. You can't just give up on life, Amber."

"Why not? Everyone else does. Everyone. Why don't *you* get up there this Wednesday and tell jokes? Why don't any of you take on Joan of Old yourselves? I'm tired of carrying all you people. I can't do it anymore. I can't be the Princess of Hope for you, because I've got no hope left! Didn't you read the papers? Don't you remember what happened to my mom? How can anyone have hope after something like that? And yet you expect me to snap out of it and carry on for you? Give you a laugh once a week? Get well just so I can play some stupid game with old people every Wednesday afternoon? For what? Why should I?"

And then I break out in tears.

I sob for minutes.

"I shouldn't have come," Old Man Linder says. "I was just trying to—"

"Just leave, okay?" I scream.

It takes Old Man Linder a long time to stand, and from the sounds he is making, I think he is crying now too, which makes me feel even worse, but I don't try to stop him from leaving and I don't say I'm sorry.

I just want him to leave.

I can't be what he needs me to be anymore.

In fact, I was never really who he wanted me to be—I was a fake.

For the next few minutes or so, I listen to him take one step at a time, setting down his oxygen tank with heavy clunks—Old Man Linder sucking air like a madman.

I hear Donna apologizing for me downstairs, and Old Man Linder says he shouldn't have come again, which is when I realize that I crushed him—that I kicked him square in the metaphorical balls and knocked what little hope he had right out of him, the lightweight. It's so easy to crush men like him. I pity Old Man Linder. How did he ever make it to old age?

After I hear the front door open and close, Donna comes up to my room and says, "You should be ashamed of yourself. This isn't you, Amber. You're better than this."

"Fuck you," I say—still sobbing—shocking myself.

Donna looks at me for a second or two—like I had slapped her—and then her bottom lips starts to quiver, which is something I never even thought was possible.

I see a tear slide down her cheek, and then she is gone.

So even the mighty Donna can be crushed, I think.

CHAPTER 30

WRITING HAIKUS ONE
AFTER THE OTHER, KNOWING
ONLY THE MOMENT

CHAPTER
31

"Father Chee?"

"Amber?"

"What is it: is man only a blunder of God, or God only a blunder of man?"

"So you are quoting Nietzsche now?"

"You know his work?"

"Yes."

"Does reading Nietzsche ever make you doubt your faith?"

"Yes."

"But you still believe in God?"

"Yes."

"How do you keep believing?"

"I have faith."

"Why?"

"Because when I asked Him for help, God sent me a young, hopeful girl who was able to convince a group of shy Korean women to sing The Supremes—making ordinary women into divas—doubling my church's membership. This was a great miracle that I saw with my own eyes. It boosted my faith much."

"What if that young, hopeful girl never recovered from the blow God sent her way? What if she never sang with those Korean women ever again, and people stopped coming to your church and the Pope fired you and then you got sick and were about to die all alone feeling like your life meant nothing—and then some mentally insane man appeared and killed you in a strange and bizarre and terrifying manner? Would you still have faith in God then?"

"I don't know."

CHAPTER
32

THE SUN IS NOT A
BALL—IT'S AN ENDLESS WHITE STREAK
TIME'S AN ILLUSION

CHAPTER 33

"Father Chee?"

"Yes, Amber?"

"If I had followed my mom on the night she was killed, do you think I might have been able to stop that man from doing what he did?"

"I don't know."

CHAPTER 34

Four-leaf clover: A
Miracle, mutation, or
Happy accident?

CHAPTER
35

"Father Chee?"

"Yes, Amber?"

"Why do some people go through life never knowing a single major tragedy, and then others have horrible things happen to them over and over again?"

"I don't know."

CHAPTER
36

BITING INTO MY
YELLOW-GREEN APPLE—LIPS AND
FINGERS GET STICKY

CHAPTER
37

"Father Chee?"

"Yes, Amber?"

"Do you believe that I was a pretty good person before my mother died?"

"I know it. You still are a good person."

"So it really doesn't matter if we are good or not—bad things will still happen to us regardless?"

"Yes."

"Why?"

"I don't know."

CHAPTER 38

Outside my window
Sparrow makes a nest out of
What I threw away

CHAPTER 39

"Father Chee?"

"Yes, Amber?"

"Why didn't God turn the other cheek when Adam and Eve ate the apple? Why did He have to punish all of mankind for eating a damn apple?"

"It is a metaphor for wanting to know more than what we can handle. God tried to protect us from the consequences of knowledge, but we failed to listen."

"Do you think I ate some metaphorical apple? Do you think my mother was killed because I pissed God off somehow? Did I fail to listen or something?"

"No. I do not think this. Not at all."

"Then why was my mother killed?"

"I don't know."

CHAPTER
40

How many pieces
of bread separate these words:
Needy, fine, wasteful?

CHAPTER
41

"Father Chee?"

"Yes, Amber."

"Why do you keep coming here every day?"

"Because you are worth visiting."

"Why?"

"Because you will come through this and be stronger on the other side. You will help people again someday."

"Do you really believe that?"

"Yes. It is inevitable."

"So why do you need to come if it's inevitable?"

"No need. I like visiting Amber Appleton. I want to be here when you are reborn—when you finally come through this and are stronger for it."

"Is that why bad things happen—to make us stronger?"

"Maybe, but truthfully—I don't know."

"I miss my mom. She was a terrible mom, but I miss her. I really do."

"I also miss my mother."

"What are your parents like? Are they here in America or in Korea?"

"My parents were very good people. They are both dead now."

"How did they die?"

"They were murdered."

"Seriously?"

"Yes."

"Why didn't you tell me this before?"

"You did not ask."

"How were your parents murdered?"

"Many years ago. In a detention camp."

"What's that?"

"It is a prison where people who criticize the North Korean government are taken."

"What did your parents say about the government?"

"They said that people should be allowed to believe in Jesus and build churches."

"That's a crime?"

"It is in North Korea."

"And they were killed in prison?"

"Yes."

"Why would JC let them be killed after they stuck up for Him?"

"I don't know."

"Is that why you became a priest here in America? Because of your parents?"

"Yes."

"Why?"

"So my parents' death would mean something."

"How does your being a priest make your parents' death mean something?"

"They gave their lives for a good idea. Now I use my life to tell other people the good idea."

"What's the good idea?"

"That no matter how much evidence we have to prove that life is meaningless, we should believe that life makes some sort of sense—and that the story of Jesus is a good story, simply because it teaches us that we should be kind to others. That we should do whatever it takes, that we should sing soul music if it makes the lives of others better. That we should try to be good people, and love everyone."

"Do you love the people who killed your parents?"

"I pray for them, and all like them."

"But do you love them?"

"I don't know."

"You think that I'm going to be like you, don't you? That's why you come here every day?"

"I think you are going to be much better than me."

"Why?"

"Father Chee cannot do the soul clap so well."

For the first time in many weeks, I smile—and Father Chee laughs out a single note—*ha!*

"I'm sorry your parents were killed for believing in JC," I say.

"I am sorry your mother was taken from you for no good reason at all, Amber. I am truly sorry for your loss."

"But there is nothing either of us can do to bring our parents back, right?"

"There is nothing we can do to bring them back, but we can honor their memory by moving forward."

"Why should we do that?"

"Maybe it is better than sitting in a room forever?"

"Why?"

"You know why," FC says.

"It's not fair."

"Life is not fair. You are correct."

"Then why should we be fair?"

"Because we can."

"I don't know, FC. I mean I totally dig your coming here every day. I do. True. But I don't think I can go back to being who I used to be."

"Who were you?"

"Amber Appleton. Aka the Princess of Hope."

"You were, are, and will always be a hopeful person, until you die."

"Why do you say that to me? Even now, when you know I've got nothing left. Why do you put that on me?"

"Because I have faith, and it is riding on the Princess of Hope. I believe in you, Amber Appleton. I've seen your powers."

"Don't do that to me."

"What?"

"Put your faith on me. I can't take that kind of pressure right now, okay? I just can't take it!"

"I did not mean—"

"Just don't," I say, and then go to the bathroom.

I stay in the bathroom for a long time—until I hear FC walk down the steps and leave Donna's house.

CHAPTER 42

The fly that died by
Smashing into my window
Pane, I dispose of

CHAPTER
43

Ty visits my bedroom solo and says, "I brought you this." He places a clear vase with a single rose and some baby's breath on my dresser, and then adds, "How you feeling?"

"Crappy," I say from under my comforter; I don't even sit up.

"I've been thinking about you a lot, Amber."

I haven't thought about Ty even once in the last few weeks, so I don't say anything.

"I don't really know what to say about what happened," Ty continues, "and it seems like you don't want to talk about it, so I'm just going to talk about other stuff, okay?"

With my head still on my pillow, I just look at Ty, who is leaning his butt against my new dresser.

He swallows once and says, "The Marketing Club regionals are next week."

"I know."

"We've been practicing pretty hard. The team and all. Maybe Ricky told you, but Franks has us debating and practicing our pitches in the morning instead of playing Halo 3. We debate at lunch too. We're on a video game hiatus until after regionals. We're all pretty nervous and excited. We think we can place this year, no sweat."

"Good luck."

"You're really not going to compete this year, are you?"

"No."

"You would take first place if you did. We'd all do better, if —"

"Well, I'm not competing, so I'm not taking any place. And The Five will just have to be The Four, because I'm out."

Ty smiles sorta weird and then says, "I'm going to win regionals for you. I'll even give you the red ribbon. I'm going to do it for you. Then we'll take The Five to nationals. Would you come to Vegas with us if I won?"

"No."

"We miss you. All of us. The entire Five."

"I'm sorry my mother's murder has inconvenienced you."

Ty's eyes narrow as if I had sucker-punched him. "Why you being like that?"

"Like what?"

"So mean."

"Because I'm a cat — a real bitch."

"No you're not. You're the coolest girl I ever met. I've always admired you, Amber. And maybe I didn't say it before, but —"

"Just leave."

Ty looks at me for a second, and then says, "I thought maybe sometime The Five could like maybe share a sundae at Friendly's? We could all go to the one in Hampton, so no one would know, if you are afraid of being seen outside the house. You could sneak out one night. I got my license last week. It was my birthday, remember? I sent you an invitation to my party. Did you get it? Ricky came."

I remember throwing it out, but do not say so.

"Maybe Ricky told you my dad bought me an old Volvo station wagon. I've been driving Ricky to school and all. My ride's outside actually. So I was thinking maybe I could take you out sometime?"

"No."

"No?"

"Hell no," I say, and then I walk over to my desk and pretend to do my assignments.

Ty stands there for a few minutes, and then he leaves.

★ ★ ★

A week or so after Ty visits solo, I receive an envelope with a second place Marketing Club ribbon in it. A note reads:

AA,
I tried to win for you. I really did.
Franks said I was robbed by the judges.
My Friendly's offer still stands.
Ty

PS—M.C. regionals weren't as much
fun without you. Everyone else agrees.
Even Franks said it. If Ricky hasn't told
you already, no one made nationals.

CHAPTER
44

"Amber?"

"Yes, Father Chee?"

"I am sorry."

"For what?"

"For putting unneeded pressure on you. For putting a cross on you when you are already suffering. It was wrong of me. Selfish."

I don't say anything.

"Unless you ask me to keep coming, I will no longer come to visit you every day. In fact, I will never come again if you do not ask me to come. I want to help you, yes, but I also have been coming here because I need to believe that you are someone I need you to be, so that my faith will be increased. This is not fair to you. You spoke this truth the last time we talked. So this is the last time I will come to your room uninvited. The Korean Divas for Christ miss you very much and would love to sing with you again, but they will be just fine if you choose never to return to us. It is your life to do with as you wish, and you should make the decisions you think are best. I will be praying that you are who you need to be, always.

And for selfish reasons, I hope that I will see you again soon. But Father Chee will also be okay either way, so do not worry about him. Goodbye."

When Father Chee turns to leave I want to hug him and tell him to stay—that I want him to keep coming every day—but for some reason, I say nothing.

FC does not come the next day, and I am equal parts surprised, angry, and sad.

CHAPTER
45

FLOWERS ARE IN THE
GROUND, WHERE WE CANNOT SEE THE
FUTURE WONDERMENT

CHAPTER 46

Easter comes and goes.
  I do not go to church.
  I do not celebrate the resurrection.

CHAPTER 47

Sun streaming through the window, my carpet is warm enough for bare feet

CHAPTER
48

Jared and Chad-in-a-backpack visit me again for the first time in weeks.

"I know you told us not to come," Jared says.

"But we came anyway," says Chad.

"Did Ty really come here solo?" Jared asks.

"Yeah," I say.

"He's growing a beard," Chad says.

"What?" I ask.

"Ty says he's not going to shave until you come out of your room and agree to go to Friendly's with us," Chad says.

"He's calling it a friendship beard," Jared says. "Says it's an outward sign of his support for the reunification of The Five."

"And he grew a full beard in days!" Chad says. "He's beginning to look like Bin Laden."

"What? Why?" I ask.

"Because his beard is getting all long and pointy at the chin," Chad says. "Not because he actually wants to look like a terrorist or anything like that. Ty's a patriot. Red, white, and blue—tried-and-true."

"No, why is he growing a beard? Seriously."

"As an outward sign of his support for you," Jared says. "Just like I told you. It's a friendship beard."

"But I'm not seeing the beard, because I'm in my room, so why would he grow one?"

"He sorta sent us here today to tell you about it," Chad says. "Show her, brother."

Jared flips open his cell phone, hits a few buttons, and suddenly bearded Ty is smiling through the little square screen. His beard is sort of pointy at the chin, but he looks nothing like Bin Laden.

"We wanted to see you anyway," Jared says, "because we miss you a lot and we feel really badly about your missing Marketing Club regionals and refusing to be a part of The Five. But Ty is really worried about you. He's really upset."

Jared says, "So what should we tell him?"

"Tell him?" I say.

"What's your reply?" Chad asks.

"I don't know," I say.

"Will you—maybe go to Friendly's with us?" Chad asks.

"I'm not going anywhere right now," I say.

"But maybe you *maybe* will—like—go to Friendly's again with us in the future?" Jared asks.

I sigh. This is ridiculous.

"Okay," Chad says. "We'll take that as a maybe and leave before you change your mind."

When they leave, I sigh and shake my head.

I hear Donna ask Chad and Jared how it went, and they say "Pretty good" just before I hear them exit through the front door.

CHAPTER 49

Air goes in and out,
Of my nose, throat, lungs, blood, heart,
Brain—and so I am

CHAPTER 50

"Do you notice anything different?" Donna asks me. She's sitting down on the side of my bed, rubbing my back lightly with her hands. She's been doing this lately. She also has been combing my hair at night. I don't say anything to her about this—because I secretly like it when she rubs my back and combs my hair, as if I were a little girl again and she were my mom.

Donna's not my mom—my mom is dead—but it still feels good.

I don't say anything to Donna, because I'm still being a cat.

"When was the last time you saw Bobby Big Boy?" Donna asks me after rubbing my back for—like—fifteen minutes or so.

I think about it, and suddenly, my heart starts beating really fast.

It's been days—maybe weeks.

No, it can't be.

When *was* the last time I saw BBB?

I haven't thought about BBB even once for so long.

I am a terrible pet owner.

I sit up.

"Bobby Big Boy?" I yell.

"Shhh," Donna says, "he's sleeping downstairs."

"Is something wrong with him?"

"Well. He's been acting a little funny," Donna says. "So—I'm just going to say this, Amber—I called a veterinarian today."

"Why?"

"Bobby Big Boy has had a lot of diarrhea lately. He hasn't been eating regularly. He's been lethargic—looking sort of *unthrifty*. And today when I took him for a walk he—well—he collapsed."

"What?"

"He recovered. He's okay now. But I'm taking him to the vet in a few minutes, and I wanted to know if you wanted to go with me."

I run downstairs and find BBB in his room, lying on his bed.

His eyes are glassy.

He doesn't even pick up his head when I walk into the room.

I pick him up in my arms and kiss him.

"I'm sorry, B3. I'm so so sorry I've neglected you. I'm here now. I'm here."

His eyes look so sad—defeated.

I hate myself for neglecting him, for not noticing that he was suffering—I'm such a cat, such a bad pet owner.

I finally leave the house.

CHAPTER
51

Donna drives B Thrice and me to the veterinarian. Ricky stays home and does math problems.

"Do you think Bobby Big Boy might die?" I ask Donna in her Mercedes, with BBB curled up in my lap.

"Let's not jump to any conclusions," she says.

"So you think this could be serious?"

"He's a relatively young dog, and pet medicine is good these days. We're taking him to the best veterinarian in the tri-state area. Dr. Weissmuller at Weissmuller Pets of Childress."

"We're taking you to the best, Bobby Big Boy. You hear that? The best."

When we get to Weissmuller Pets of Childress, I carry BBB into the waiting room and a woman wearing black scrubs asks us if we have been there before, and when we say we haven't, she asks for BBB's medical records or anything that would prove he's had all of his shots.

"Where did you take him before you started living with us?" Donna asks me.

"Nowhere. He was never sick before," I say.

"So you've never taken your pet to the vet before?" the lady asks me—sending me tons of attitude, cocking her head to one side and resting the end of her pen on her puffy apple-red kiss-shaped lips.

"Listen, I found him in a Nike box when I was living on a frickin' school bus. We were so poor we couldn't even afford to eat—like ever. My mom was killed a few months back by a psychopath, so I don't need any extra crap from you, okay?"

"Oh, *oh, my God*. You're *Amber Appleton*, aren't you?" the woman says, so nicely now. "I'm so sorry. The name on the file says Roberts. I didn't know. Let me get the doctor right away. Just give me ten seconds."

She disappears into another room.

I can see that all of the other pet owners waiting to see the doctor are staring at me now. Regular, work-weary people. A collie is barking at B3, a poodle is hiding under a chair, and this little kid with a runny nose is holding an evil-looking ferret with pink eyes.

"Ms. Appleton?"

When I turn around, a man in peach-colored scrubs is smiling at me.

"Right this way," he says.

In a room with photos of dogs taped up all over the walls, I put BBB down on a silver examination table. He lies on his side and breathes slowly.

"What is wrong with you, my friend?" Dr. Weissmuller says to BBB, shaking his paw like formal men in suits do whenever they meet.

"Bobby Big Boy has been tired lately," Donna says, "he's not eating much, he threw up yesterday, he's had diarrhea—and today he collapsed while we were taking a walk."

Dr. Weissmuller feels BBB's belly.

"What do you feel?" I ask.

"His abdomen is distended."

"Is that bad?" I ask.

"I don't know yet," he says, and then removes a long needle from a drawer. "I am going to stick this into the place where I think there is a tumor, and if blood comes out—then we'll know something."

Dr. Weissmuller inserts the needle into BBB's belly.

Blood comes out, but BBB doesn't move or even whimper.

"You see the blood?" he asks.

Donna and I both nod.

"So we should do an ultrasound to see if the tumor is on the spleen or liver."

"What's the difference?" I ask.

"If the tumor is on the liver—there is nothing I can do for your dog. If it's on the spleen, we can operate."

"How much is the ultrasound?" Donna asks.

"Seventy-five dollars."

Donna nods once and says, "Do it."

Dr. Weissmuller picks BBB up so gently and takes my doggie into another room, leaving Donna and me alone.

"I don't have any money to pay for this," I say. "I blew through my Rita's money back in January."

"Don't worry about that."

"Can I borrow the money from you?"

"I'll pay, don't worry, Amber."

"What about the surgery?"

"If BBB needs surgery, I think I can afford it," Donna says.

I shake my head—and I even cross my arms. I know that I mooch off Donna all the time, but taking responsibility for BBB has sort of become symbolic to me after all that has happened: it's one of the few things that I can control, and so I simply say, "No."

"No?"

"BBB is *my* responsibility. I'm going to pay for the surgery if he needs it," I say.

"How?"

"I'm not sure yet."

"Amber, you just need to worry about getting yourself together now and—"

"Stop," I say, and then we wait in silence.

After a few long minutes, Dr. Weissmuller returns and gently places BBB down on the silver table. "The tumor is on the spleen."

"So what now?" Donna asks.

"The tumor is bleeding into the abdomen. I will remove the spleen and we'll do a biopsy. They send me the results in less than a week. If the tumor is benign—your dog will live."

"I can't take two deaths in one year," I say to Donna, crying.

Dr. Weissmuller says, "I recommend surgery. Again, I will take out his spleen, and if the tumor is benign, your dog will live."

"What if it is benign, and we do nothing?" Donna asks.

"Your dog will eventually bleed to death—internally."

"How much is the surgery?" I ask.

"There can be complications, and maybe your dog will need blood transfusions—all told, the cost should be around two thousand dollars. Should I leave you alone to discuss this matter?"

Donna nods and Dr. Weissmuller leaves the room.

"Can I borrow the money?" I ask Donna.

"I'll pay for all of it, Amber."

"No. I just want a loan. I want to take care of this myself."

I can see that Donna wants to help me. Her eyes are kind and her face is compassionate, but she doesn't understand that charity is for old people and cripples.

I bury my face in BBB's fur.

"Dr. Weissmuller's going to get you feeling better, and then I'm going to get better too. I'm going to take you to see Ms. Jenny just as soon as you are healthy. You stay alive, BBB, and I'm going to be a better pet owner. I promise."

I cry harder like a chick as I hold BBB close to my cheek.

"Dr. Weissmuller?" Donna says.

Even though Donna protests, I sign all of the forms; I agree to pay for the operation in installments over the next few years, Donna co-signs, and then we leave.

As we are driving home, suddenly, I'm saying, "Will you drop me off at Private Jackson's house?"

"Why?" she asks.

"I really need to see him."

"So does this mean you're officially out of your room?" she asks, sorta surprised and maybe even hopefully.

"Something like that," I say.

"Okay," Donna says.

I give her directions and she drives me to PJ's house.

When Donna drops me off on the curb, she asks if I want her to come pick me up, and when I tell her I'll walk home, she says, "Amber, are you sure you're okay?"

"Yeah," I say. "I just need to spend some time with PJ. I'm cool. Really."

"Okay," she says. "But call if you want me to pick you up. Cool?"

I nod once and then walk toward PJ's house.

CHAPTER
52

It's dark, so I know that Ms. Jenny has already gone for her run.

I also know that PJ is home, so I knock on the front door.

When PJ opens the front door, he doesn't say anything about my mom or about me or why the hell I haven't visited him in months—he doesn't even ask if I liked the haikus he has been sending me every day. He only says, "Please come in. I'll put on the tea."

When I enter his house I see the blank spot on the last wall of his living room—the hole that I have not yet covered with doggie haikus—and it makes me feel really depressed.

I sit down on the couch as Private Jackson makes tea.

Ms. Jenny comes looking for BBB, and when she doesn't find him, she jumps up on the couch and ducks her head under my hand, so that I will pet her.

I pet her with all I got.

When PJ brings me the tea, it is green—like always.

I sip it.

He sits and sips his cup.

I sip mine again—and then I start sobbing.

I sob so hard I drop my teacup and Ms. Jenny jumps off the couch and hides under the coffee table.

I can't stop crying.

I can't stop shaking.

Snot is running down my nose—spit down my chin.

It all comes out.

Everything.

My dad leaving us.

Being homeless.

My mom's murder.

BBB's having a tumor.

I'm not even an adult yet.

It's not fair.

It's really not fair.

I close my eyes so hard—trying to stop the tears.

I start to cough wildly.

I feel like I might die.

And then Private Jackson is next to me on the couch.

He's moved toward me for the first time.

I throw myself at him.

He hesitates for a second or two, but then he puts his arms around me.

I bury my head in his yellow button-down shirt, and he holds me.

After a few minutes, I stop coughing, but I can't stop crying.

I soak his yellow button-down shirt with hot tears.

We stay entwined like this on his couch—father-daughter style—for a long time.

When I finally let go, Private Jackson turns his face from me quickly and says, "I will get you more tea."

Before he leaves the room, I see that his face is also streaked with tears.

He stays in the kitchen for a long time—longer than it takes to make green tea.

When he returns, he hands me a new steaming-hot cup.

When I sip, he says, "I just wrote a haiku in the kitchen."

He has a piece of paper in his hand, so I ask, "Can I read it?"

He hands it to me.

It reads:

THE SUN SETTING THROUGH
PINE TREES AT THE EDGE OF TOWN
MAKES ME SQUINT AND SMILE

"It's good," I say. "But it doesn't capture the present moment."

"Maybe sometimes—on special occasions—every so often, it is best to capture a different moment, maybe, when the present moment is not the right moment for you. It is sometimes nice to think that more moments are always coming. Always. Like the moments when you come to visit me."

"True," I say, and then sip my tea, realizing that what PJ just said is like—revolutionary for him, so I don't push it. I simply enjoy the present moment—having released so much emotional baggage—as this moment bleeds into the next one.

Silence.

We sip our cups for an hour, not saying a single word, just occupying the same space.

When I finish, I stand and say, "You're a good man, Private Jackson."

"I will wash the teacups now," he says.

"I'm going to bring BBB here in a week or so to visit Ms. Jenny, cool?"

"Ms. Jenny will be looking forward to the visit very much," he says, and then takes our teacups into the kitchen.

I let myself out of PJ's house and then walk through the darkness, navigating the Childress streets back to Donna's house—thinking about Dr. Weissmuller cutting open Bobby Big Boy and removing his spleen—and before I know it, I'm praying again, asking JC to be with Dr. Weissmuller, to help him to be exactly who he needs to be, so that BBB will be okay. And then I sorta promise JC that I will try to return to my hopeful self if He spares BBB's life—even after what happened to my mom—which is a pretty good bargain for JC, as far as I'm concerned.

I'm still sorta mad at JC, but I've missed Him too. True.

I sorta need to pray, and all.

Praying keeps me sane.

Maybe it's my true favorite?

★ ★ ★

When I get to Donna's house, I find Ricky in the kitchen eating Ritz crackers and peanut butter.

"I'm sorry, Ricky," I say.

"Ricky Roberts is supposed to leave Amber Appleton alone because her mother was killed and it wasn't fair, so she is mad at everyone for now, but she will snap out of it in the future. Yes. In the future."

I snap both of my fingers and then give Ricky a kiss on the cheek.

"Amber Appleton kissed Ricky Roberts! Yes!"

"I'm sorry I was mean to you, Ricky," I say, and then I notice that Donna is in the doorway watching the apology.

So I walk over to Donna, say, "I'm going to school tomorrow," and then I give her a big old hug before I go up to my room and stare at the ceiling all night — wondering how in the hell I will pay for B Thrice's surgery.

PART FOUR

We're Not Alone

CHAPTER
53

I don't sleep a wink.

Around five thirty, I get up and make omelets.

Eggs, milk, peppers, mushrooms, tequila—all whisked up in a big old silver bowl.

Omelet jizz in the pan.

Sizzle.

Sizzle.

Sizzle.

Fold over: O to D.

Flip, flip, flip.

Plates in the oven.

Oranges halved.

Donna's juicer used.

Coffee put on.

The paper I get ready for Donna.

The table I set.

"Good morning, Amber," Donna says, big old smile on her face.

"Hope it is," I say, and then serve the omelet.

"Amber Appleton is making omelets for Ricky Roberts, yes-ssssss! Tuesday is omelet day. Yes."

"Is it Tuesday?" I ask as I serve Ricky, noticing the Tuesday Chase Utley jersey. "I haven't really been keeping track of the days."

"Tuesday — all day," Donna says from behind the business section.

We eat omelets.

"How do you think BBB is doing?" I ask.

"I'm sure he's fine. We'll pick him up just as soon as I get home from work," Donna says. "Okay?"

"Okay," I say.

I clean the table when everyone is done eating as Ricky does math problems.

After I have everything in the dishwasher, I go shower, put on makeup, and pick out a killer outfit from the new clothes Donna has been buying me for the past two months. I go with these designer jeans that make my butt look pretty good, and this crazy preppy purple v-neck sweater that makes me look like I might be going to play tennis.

When I come downstairs, Donna says, "You look great. But are you sure you're ready to go back to school? I don't want you to feel rushed."

"Yeah," I say, "I have to execute my plan."

"What plan?" Donna asks.

"The Save Bobby Big Boy Variety Show," I say.

"What's that all about?" Donna asks.

But then — suddenly — Ty is beeping his car horn out front.

"Have to drive to school with Ty Hendrix!" Ricky says, and is out the door, backpack in hand.

"Take this," Donna says, and then hands me a twenty.

"I don't need your money," I say as I put on my backpack.

"You have to eat lunch, Amber. Please."

I take the bill, shove it in my front pocket, and then give Donna a kiss on the cheek. "You're a good woman," I say, and then I'm out the door.

Ty is just about to pull away when I yell, "Wait!"

He smiles all surprised when he sees me running toward his Volvo station wagon.

I'm shocked to see his beard.

It's already three inches long.

He looks like frickin' Rip Van Winkle.

"You comin' to school today?" Ty asks as I climb into the backseat.

"Yep," I say.

"Cool," he says, and then turns up the radio before pulling away.

P!nk's "God Is a DJ" is playing.

I sorta dig that song, which Ty knows, so I sing along—yelling out the curse words that the radio station bleeps out.

Ricky counts to himself—*who knows what he is counting?*

Bearded Ty keeps on looking in the rearview mirror, watching me sing—so much that I worry we might crash, but I only smile at him and sing louder.

P!nk kicks butt. Period. She's another one of my women heroes. She doesn't need a man to take care of her—no way.

We park two blocks from the school.

"Going to play Halo 3 with Mr. Jonathan Franks!" Ricky says, and then we follow him toward the The Franks Lair.

"It's good to have you back in school," Ty says.

"Are you going to shave now?" I ask.

"Not until you agree to go to Friendly's with us."

"Why?"

"Because I made a vow," Ty says. "Respect the sanctity of the friendship beard."

When we knock on Franks' outside door, Jared kicks it open and I see ten or so boys playing Halo 3. Chad, Jared, Lex Pinkston, some other meathead football players, a few guys whose names I don't know, and Franks.

"Amber?" Franks says, and then everyone turns and looks at me.

The Halo 3 game stops.

"I'm back," I say.

"Welcome," Franks says, and then walks over to shake my hand like I'm the president or something.

Everyone looks really nervous—I can feel the tension in the room.

No one knows what to say, because my mom was murdered.

Everyone is looking at me.

"Listen," I say, "I know you are all probably freaked out by what happened to my mom, but it's not contagious. *Right?*"

No one laughs at that one.

Blank faces all over the room.

"Listen. I don't want to talk about my mom. Cool?"

"Cool," Chad says from Das Boot.

Everyone else looks like they think I have the plague or something.

"Listen, to top it all off—and this is no bullcrap story—my dog might have cancer. He had to have an operation last night, which I can't afford. Now I know a dog is not a person or anything, but I went ahead and said I'd pay for it all, and I'm broke. So I need to raise—like—two or three grand. I don't even know if BBB made it or not—I find out later today—but I have to pay regardless, and I'm assuming he did, because he's a fighter."

"BBB has cancer?" Jared says, and sounds truly concerned.

"Damn," Chad says.

"I'm so sorry," Ty says.

"So I'm thinking of setting up a variety show and selling tickets to raise money to pay for my dog's operation. I can get Prince Tony to give us the auditorium, no sweat," I say. "I just need to find some acts. Who's with me?"

"You want us to perform?" Jared asks.

"Yeah, or find performers," I say.

"I'll give you money," Lex Pinkston says. "I have some in the bank. It's yours."

"No. I don't want anyone to give me money. I want to *raise* it for myself. I'm not a charity case."

"What's a variety show?" one of the football players asks.

"How will we find acts?"

And then everyone is talking all at once—sounding very confused.

Until Franks loudly says, "I'm in!"

Everyone gets quiet.

All of the boys look at Franks and he nods confidently.

"Cool," I say.

"I'm in," Ty says.

"Hell yeah," Chad says.

"Why not?" Jared says.

"Ricky Roberts is in—yeah-shhhh!"

And then all of the boys present agree to help.

"First thing to do is shut off those Xboxes, because this is going to take some planning," I say.

Lex shuts off all of them.

"Franks, you're the sales and marketing teacher, so how do we make this kind of money?" I ask.

"Well, we need to advertise all over town and include as many people as we can in the show. It's all about inclusion. People will give because of the situation. People like dogs. Yours is a sympathetic story. But the more people we include in the show, the more parents and community members will buy tickets and make donations. I have a special folder in my car, it's red and it has a lot of ideas for advertising in it. It says 'Advertising Ideas' on the front. Would you mind going and getting it for me, Amber?" Franks says, and then holds out his keys toward me.

"Sure," I say, and then take his keys.

I leave the room and go to Franks' car—an old rusty Jeep with a hardtop—in the faculty parking lot, but when I key in, there is no red folder on the front seat. There is no folder of any color in the car at all—not on or under any seat. I check the glove compartment and the trunk, just to make sure, but there is no folder, period, so I walk back toward Franks' room feeling sorta annoyed, because I want to get this plan rolling.

When I return, Franks has the boys all fired up.

Lex tells me that the football team is going to do a secret performance.

"What are you going to do?" I ask him.

"You'll see."

"I've got a little something planned for you," Chad says from Das Boot.

"I'm going to do math problems on stage!" Ricky says.

"I can do the lighting and stage stuff," Ty says, because he is the head of the theater's stage crew.

"Jared's performing with me," Chad says.

"What?" Jared says.

"Don't be a wuss," Chad tells his brother. "Maybe we'll get prom dates, eh? Girls dig what we're going to do onstage."

"Umm," Jared says. "I don't—I'll handle finances and incoming money."

"And do that thing we are going to do onstage, because you are a Fox brother and not a wimp," Chad says pretty aggressively from Das Boot.

But then the homeroom warning bell sounds and everyone scatters.

"There was no red folder in your car," I tell Franks, and then give him back his keys.

"That's weird," he says, and then eats a few peanut M&M's from his desk drawer.

"What did you tell the boys when I was out of the room?"

"Just brainstormed ideas for acts. That's all."

"So will you be the faculty advisor for The Save Bobby Big Boy Variety Show?"

"Sure," he says.

"Can we make an announcement over the loudspeaker this morning?"

"Sure," Franks says.

"All right. Let's go tell Prince Tony."

Franks and I go up to the main office, and Mrs. Baxter goes nuts when she sees me.

"Amber, come here!" she screams, and then runs around her desk to plant some lipstick on my cheek and give me a big old hug. "I'm so sorry for your loss. I've been so worried about you. Did you get the flowers I sent you?"

"Yeah, thanks," I say, even though I chucked all the flowers without even reading one damn card. "Do you like variety shows?"

"What?" she says.

"Amber Appleton," Prince Tony says from his office doorway. "How the heck are you?"

"Cool," I say, "but I need to book the auditorium for a variety show. It's got to be a Friday night, because that's when the most people will come out. I need to raise money to pay for my dog's operation."

"What are you talking about, Amber?"

"Can I talk to you in your office?" Franks says.

"I'm not sure I —" Prince Tony says, but Franks forces him into the office and then closes the door before I can sneak in.

I'm sorta mad at Franks for excluding me while making the Prince Tony pitch, so I decide to make my own announcement before homeroom even starts.

I walk over to the microphone Franks uses to make the

morning announcements and ask Mrs. Baxter how to make myself heard all over the school.

"You just push the red button, but I don't think you should be—"

I push the red button and say, "Attention fellow Childress High School classmates. This is Amber Appleton. The girl whose mother was murdered. I don't want to talk to you about that, so please do not bring it up, okay? I would like to invite you to participate in The Save Bobby Big Boy Variety Show, which will raise money for my dog's operation, which he had last night. He might have cancer. I have to pay two or three grand for that, and I'm broke. So please help me do this by signing up to be in the variety show, or by buying a ticket—those will go on sale soon after I iron the details out with Prince Tony. Cool? Thanks. Peace out. Amber Appleton."

When I finish my announcement, Prince Tony and Franks are smiling at me from Prince Tony's office.

"Are you cool with my making an announcement?" I ask.

"I think this variety show is a great idea. I'm one hundred percent behind it," PT says, and then takes me into his office so we can discuss dates, while Franks does the morning announcements. PT shows me all of the available dates for the auditorium, I pick a Friday night three and a half weeks from today, and he tells me that Mrs. Baxter will handle all ticket sales, but that we should feel free to collect donations and sell program advertisements around town; PT says that all of the advertisement checks should be made out to the high school. "You can get Mr. Valerie to do the programs. He does all of the theater programs. I'll talk to him about it today.

It's good to have you back in the building, Amber. It's so good to see you."

"Cool to all of that," I say, and then go to my first period class.

No one—not even teachers—asks me about my mom all day, but craploads of people—many of whom I've never even met—want to be in BBB's variety show. At first I write down the names and ideas in a notebook, but after I fill seven pages, I realize that we will need to have an elimination audition, or something, and I'm sorta amazed at how well my plan is working.

During lunch Ricky and I blow off socialization time in the lunchroom and go to The Franks Lair, where kids aren't playing video games but are actually brainstorming marketing techniques for The Save Bobby Big Boy Variety Show.

When Franks sees me, he says, "Amber, will you take a walk with me?"

"Sure. Why?" I ask.

The Five are looking at me really funny.

"Come on," Franks says, and then leads me outside of the building, where it is pretty springlike and sunny.

"The guys want to surprise you with the acts," Franks says. "They want to put together the variety show for you, and then let you emcee the event."

"What? Why?" I ask.

"They think it would be fun."

"So they don't want me to be involved at all?"

"We want you to drum up support and enthusiasm. We want you to emcee and to be the star, but we want the acts to be a surprise."

"I don't understand why they would want that," I say.

"Because they want you to be surprised."

"How will I emcee if I don't know what acts are involved?"

"We'll make you note cards."

"So I have to trust you?" I ask.

"Yeah," Franks says. "Trust your friends too."

"Do you think we can raise enough money to pay for BBB's operation?"

"I do," he says, and then smiles confidently. "We will. I promise."

Franks is a man of his word, so I start to feel better—relieved, excited. "Okay," I say. "Just leave one slot open, because I got an act lined up already. As soon as I confirm the act, I'll put you in contact with the right people."

"Cool," Franks says.

I go back into the lunchroom and buy some food with Donna's twenty.

A billion people ask me to sit with them, which is weird, so I go outside, eat alone, and start to worry about how BBB is doing.

After I finish my turkey hoagie, I go to the pay phone by the gym, drop in some change, and dial Weissmuller Pets of Childress.

"Hello, Weissmuller Pets. How may I help you?"

"May I speak with Dr. Weissmuller please?" I ask.

"He's with a patient, can I take a message?"

"It's Amber Appleton, I just want to—"

"Hold on, Amber, I'll put him on the line. Just hold for a second, okay?"

"Okay."

I hear easy listening music for a few long moments—before Dr. Weissmuller says, "Hello?"

"This is Amber Appelton. Bobby Big Boy. My dog. Is he okay?"

"The surgery went well. Your dog's tumor was sent out for a biopsy. BBB is recovering, but he is fine."

"Thank you so much, Dr. Weissmuller. I'll be in later today."

"Bobby Big Boy should be ready to go home by seven tonight."

"Thank you," I say, and hang up, trying hard not to cry like a chick, but of course, I do leak a few tears.

I say a little thank-you prayer to JC, and then I finish my school day—working on my prom dress a little in Life Skills and daydreaming through my real classes.

★ ★ ★

By the end of the day there are posters and signs hung up all over the hallways.

The Save Bobby Big Boy Variety Show
Presented by Amber Appleton
April 24—Friday Night
Save the Date

Some have pictures of Bobby Big Boy on them and I wonder how that came to be.

Weird.

Bearded Ty drives Ricky and me home in his Volvo station wagon, and as we drive, I ask him why The Five want to keep the acts a surprise.

"Don't you like surprises?" he asks me.

"Sure," I say.

"So?"

"Ricky Roberts is going to do Stump the Mathematician."

"Well, I know one act, eh?" I say.

Ty looks at me in the rearview and smiles through his beard.

CHAPTER 54

After I get Ricky doing math problems at the kitchen table, I ride Donna's bike through the ghetto to the Korean Catholic Church for the first time without BBB, doing the "I hope you are having a great day!" trick the whole way there, which always makes me feel good, because I dig lighting up people's faces.

When I get there, Father Chee is not out front because he is not expecting me. I haven't talked to him since I told him I couldn't be what he needed me to be anymore.

The church door is locked, so I knock, and after a few minutes, Father Chee appears.

I ride my bike inside, and Father Chee locks the door behind me.

"You left your room," FC says to me.

"I'm out," I say as I hop off Donna's bike. "And I'm sorry."

"For what?" FC says with a smile.

I give him a big old hug.

"Welcome back," FC says as he pats my back all fatherly.

When we let go, FC asks, "Where is BBB?"

So I tell him all about B Thrice's tumor, The Save Bobby Big

Boy Variety Show, and also about how we will know whether BBB is going to live within a week.

"I will pray for BBB," Father Chee says. "The KDFCs have missed you. Want to say hello?"

"Hell yeah," I say, and then we walk into the sanctuary.

The KDFCs are sitting around with English-Korean dictionaries. They are all writing Korean into what looks like new songbooks.

"Jesus sent us Aretha Franklin's Greatest Hits," Father Chee explains, and then yells something in Korean.

The Korean Divas for Christ look up and then attack me, giving me so many long drawn-out hugs that I think I might pop!

In English, they all tell me that they are sorry about my mom, and then they say a lot of things to me in Korean, which Father Chee translates into English.

These things they say in their native language are so heartfelt, so beautiful, The KDFCs make me cry, which makes them cry and hug me even more.

Finally, I tell them about Bobby Big Boy's tumor, and The KDFCs start hugging me again and shaking their heads and talking very quickly in Korean.

So I tell them about The Bobby Big Boy Variety Show and ask them if they will perform — if they will do a few Supremes songs to help me raise money to pay for BBB's operations.

The KDFCs look down at their feet.

"What?" I say.

Father Chee says something in Korean.

Yung Mi says something back.

Sun says something to Yung Mi.

Na Yung shakes her head, and offers her opinion.

Hye Min yells at Na Yung.

And then all of The KDFCs are bickering in Korean.

Father Chee tells me, "Some of the women want to perform, but others think that their English is not good enough yet, and that they will embarrass you and themselves."

"Are you kidding me?" I ask them very loudly. "You guys are frickin' pros."

"We good backup singers," Sun says, "but we need good English-speaking front woman. True diva."

"Amber is the true diva," Na Yung says.

"No, no. I'm emceeing," I tell them.

"Why not sing with them?" Father Chee says.

But I don't want to sing with them. I know I should sing because I am one of The Korean Divas for Christ—even if I am not actually Korean by birth, only by association—and also I shouldn't ask people to do something that I am not willing to do, which I fully realize, but the truth is I'm not really feeling up to the task of rock-starring in front of all my classmates, especially after my mother's death, and so the bickering continues amongst The Korean Divas for Christ, until I change the subject and simply help them translate "(You Make Me Feel Like) A Natural Woman."

While Father Chee jogs me home, he says, "You have to realize that you are the only white person many of our church members have had any meaningful contact with. Walking into an English-speaking high school like yours terrifies them."

"I can understand that," I say. "Believe me."

"But if you would sing *with them*—behind you, a true diva—I think they would sing at the variety show."

"I'm not a true diva," I tell him. "I'm just a crappy English teacher who uses R & B as a teaching tool."

"Well then, I will pray that Jesus sends us a true diva to lead The KDFCs, so that they will feel confident enough to participate in your variety show," Father Chee says, and then he suddenly stops running, so I stop pedaling.

I'm straddling Donna's bike.

We look at each other.

"Are you okay?" FC asks me.

"Yeah," I say.

"Are you sure?"

"No. But I'm moving forward."

"You are out of your room. This is good."

"Because Bobby Big Boy needs me."

"Many people need you, Amber."

"One thing at a time, FC."

"You are stronger than you think."

"Hug?" I ask, because I can't take too many compliments right now.

"Of course," he says, and then hugs me all fatherly.

"Will you pray for me?" I ask.

"Every day," FC says, smiling at me. "Almost every hour."

And then I ride my bike back to Donna's house and cook chicken in a pan, slice that hooey up, and make a chicken salad with honey-mustard sauce and kick-ass croutons.

When Donna gets home, we eat.

"How was your first day back?" Donna asks me.

"Ricky Roberts is going to Stump the Mathematician onstage April twenty-fourth, Friday night, in the Childress High School Auditorium so that we can raise money for Amber Appleton."

"For Bobby Big Boy," I say. "We're doing a variety show to pay for BBB's operation."

"You are, eh? Prince Tony went for that?"

"Franks backed it big-time. Do you know any real-live divas?"

"Divas?"

"To be The KDFCs' front woman. They won't perform without an English-speaking front woman because they are too embarrassed of their English, even though I taught them pretty well."

"Why don't *you* be their front woman?" Donna asks me.

"Hello? Have you ever heard me sing?"

"Something will turn up," Donna says. "I talked to Dr. Weissmuller."

"So did I," I said.

"So you know that BBB is fine."

"Yeah," I say. "Until we get the biopsy anyway."

"One thing at a time," Donna says with some honey mustard sauce dribbling down her chin.

★ ★ ★

When we pick up BBB, his belly is shaved and stitched up, and he is wearing a little lamp shade on his head.

I carry BBB to Donna's car, and we take B3 home.

Bobby Big Boy is a little sluggish at first, and doesn't dig wearing the lampshade one bit—I know because he claws the hell out of it within the first forty-eight hours—so we eventually take it off, and BBB is eating and crapping merrily in no time at all.

CHAPTER 55

A week later, I call Dr. Weissmuller after school and he tells me that my dog is cancer free.

BBB and I celebrate by taking a bike ride over to the Methodist Retirement Home.

We hit Alan's Newsstand, and Alan says, "I'm sorry about what happened to your mother, and I bought two tickets to The Save Bobby Big Boy Variety Show."

"From whom?" I ask.

"Kids have been asking me for a week to buy tickets. Must have been three hundred kids asked me already. Better be a good show."

"It's going to be the bomb," I tell him as I pay for the Snickers and the hot chocolate with some of the lunch money Donna has been giving me.

"The what?" Alan says.

"You won't be disappointed," I say, even though I don't even know what the hell The Five are cooking up.

And then BBB and I are stashing Donna's bike behind a bush and offering Door Woman Lucy the regular bribe to get B Thrice into the building.

"You get the Snickers and hot chocolate I sent you?" DWL says to me.

"Yeah, thanks," I say.

"Ain't right, what's been happening to you. Ain't right at all."

"Tell me about it."

"Your little boyfriends been 'round here selling tickets to some show they say you puttin' on."

"Boyfriends?" I ask.

"Tiny kid in a wheelchair. Tall funky-lookin' white kid. Cute black kid with a beard."

"They're not my boyfriends."

DWL sips her hot chocolate and then smiles at me sorta weird.

"Strange times, DWL. Strange times."

"What's this show you putting on all about, anyway?"

"It's a variety show."

"To honor your mother's passing?"

"No, it's for Bobby Big Boy here. He just had surgery. See his scar?" I hold up BBB's belly. "It cost me almost three grand, so I have to raise money."

"Well, you let me know if you need any help, Sister Amber."

I nod once, smile at DWL's calling me Sister Amber for the first time, which makes me feel pretty cool, and then BBB and I walk into the old people's home—through the depressing hallways with the dusty fake plants.

When we get to the common room, I can't believe what I see.

All of the old people are seated in two long rows.

Old Man Linder is singing a song with Old Man Thompson. Both are wearing red sports coats.

They're singing some ancient song about makin' whoopee, and as I listen to the lyrics, I think they are actually singing about sex!

The old people are smiling and laughing and singing along so happily as Old Man Thompson sings his heart out and Old Man Linder echoes the verses in spoken word—and suddenly I realize that Old Man Linder has taken me up on my challenge.

He's gotten up in front of his peers.

He's entertaining the people.

He's giving them something to look forward to—something to break up the boring days and weeks.

He's keeping hope alive!

BBB and I watch the performance from the back of the room and laugh every time one of the old men punch the air in front of them, or try to move their ancient hips to the beat.

The performance is not all that lively.

My boys don't sing that well.

But as I look at how much fun the old people are having—many of them singing along with the two old men in front of them—I realize that this is enough, that these old people are getting a little fuel from my manager, and I feel something warm heat up my chest.

When they finish the old-time sex song about makin' whoopee, Old Man Linder sees me standing at the back of the common room. "Amber?" he says.

Fifty blue-haired heads turn around slowly, and then everyone is staring at me and BBB.

I walk toward my elders and say, "Hey."

When no one says anything, I give Old Man Linder a hug, whisper, "I'm sorry," into his big hairy ear, and then—to the crowd—I say, "Who knew these old guys could sing so well?"

No one says anything, and Old Man Linder looks a little nervous.

"Listen," I say. "I'm okay."

"We were really worried about you," Old Man Thompson says.

"We didn't think you'd ever visit us again," Big Booty Bernice says.

"I hope they fry that horrible man who killed your poor mother," Agnes the Plant Talker says.

"Are you really okay?" Old Man Linder says.

"Where's Joan of Old?" I ask.

"She had a heart attack," Old Man Thompson says.

"What?" I say.

"It wasn't fatal," Old Man Linder says. "She's in the hospital wing. I hear she goes in and out of consciousness—but when she's awake, they say she's still with it."

"Well, I'll have to visit her after the show," I say, and then sit down, allowing B Thrice to curl up on my lap. "I want to see what else you two got up there."

Old Man Linder smiles proudly, snaps back into character, and—in an old-time radio voice—says, "How many of you remember this gem from 1927?"

Old Man Thompson and Old Man Linder start snapping their fingers and tapping their toes, and when they sing the next song all of the old people get really excited and start to sing along in rousing unison—everyone is waving index fingers in the air, nodding out the beat, and singing their dusty old lungs out.

Because they repeat the chorus so many times I sorta figure out the song's called "Side By Side," and it's about two people with no money who don't know what's going to happen, but at least they have each other to travel through life together. The old people love this corny old song, and I have to say—seeing them sing it so passionately makes me feel something good. True.

My old men are moving people this afternoon.

When the song is finished, Old Man Linder says, "Thanks for coming to the Wednesday Afternoon Old-Time Sing-Along with The Red Coats—Albert Linder and Eddie Thompson. Until next week, when we will be singing more of the songs you remember and love—make sure you stay alive at least seven more days! Because you won't want to miss what we have in store for you! Reminisce, people. Reminisce!"

All of the old people clap for a few minutes while The Red Coats bow, and then resuming once again is the endless talk of grandchildren, jigsaw puzzles, who died last week, the weather over the past eight decades, and—of course—the many family members who never visit.

I leave BBB curled up in a pile of Knitting Carol's yarn and step out into the hallway with Old Man Linder.

"You were really good up there," I tell him. "You had everyone into it. True."

"Listen, I was mad at you for a week or so, kid. I could have died climbing those damn steps, and then the way you treated me," Old Man Linder says—oxygen tubes running out of his nostrils. "But then, I thought, you know what—the girl's got a point. I'm not dead yet, and I have to do something to keep myself alive. I can't always depend on others. So I thought up the sing-along with Eddie, who carries me up there with his golden voice—if you didn't notice. I'm the ham. He's the voice. But I always loved to sing. And the old chippies favor men who sing in public. Can't keep them off me lately."

The old man winks at me.

I smile at Old Man Linder.

"Are you okay, Amber?"

"Truthfully, no. But I enjoyed your singing very much—and I'm out of my room, at least."

"That's a start."

"It's something."

"So?"

"I would like to visit Joan of Old," I say.

"You sure? I haven't been to see her yet, but I hear she's in bad shape."

"Yeah, I'm sure," I say.

I follow Old Man Linder through a bunch of depressing hallways full of mauve wallpaper and mauve carpets—finally, we arrive at the hospital wing, which is just another mauve hallway with special hospital-looking rooms.

When a nurse pops out of one of the rooms, Old Man Linder says, "Excuse me, but do you know which room is Joan Osmond's?"

The nurse doesn't answer, but points to a door down the hall, so we walk toward it.

Joan of Old is a tiny mountain range under a sky-blue blanket—her sunken pink wrinkled face sticking out, her small head resting on a pillow.

"Can I get a few minutes alone with Joan?" I ask Old Man Linder.

My manager says, "Sure. I'll wait out here for you."

I walk into the room and close the door behind me.

I pull up a chair next to the bed.

"Joan?" I say.

Joan of Old doesn't move.

I can hear her struggling to breathe.

Her mouth is open slightly.

I reach under the blanket and hold her hand.

It's freezing cold.

"Squeeze if you can hear me," I say.

Nothing.

"I guess you heard all about my mom and my depression. I've been in a room for months, pretty much being a bitch to everyone. I've been crying a lot too. True. But what you probably don't realize is that I cried a whole bunch before my mother was killed too. The Amber you saw during our battles—that was all an act. I'm not very strong. I'm not very hopeful. I'm not very much of anything. I'm just a stupid girl who can tell a few good jokes at pivotal moments and knows how to work a crowd. If you only knew how much I internalized all of your insults. Word. You really have me thinking I have a dinosaur face, which freaks me out a lot. True."

Joan of Old doesn't squeeze my hand at all.

I can still hear her breathing.

"I'm starting to think that you are right about life, Joan. Maybe it's all meaningless? I mean—I still dig JC and all. I still pray, and I still believe in certain people. But that guy who killed my mom—he's not human, and he scares me, because he *is* human, and yet he did what he did, which will never make sense, no matter how long I think about it. It's so random. So vile. It makes me get why you are so mean and cranky. I bet you weren't like that before your husband died, right?"

Suddenly, Joan of Old squeezes my hand and scares the hell out of me.

"Why are you telling me these things?" Joan asks.

"Were you awake that whole time?"

"Yes."

"You rotten old lady! Why didn't you say so?"

"Because I'm gathering information for our last battle—when I will finally make you cry."

"You can't be that evil," I say.

Joan of Old smiles up at me from her pillow, and her wrinkly pink eyelids bore through my forehead.

I shiver.

"Why'd you really come in here, Amber?"

"I don't know. I really don't. Are you going to die?"

"We all die eventually," Joan of Old says. "That's just about the only thing God got right."

"Okay," I say, "I think I'm going to leave now."

"When do we battle next? My doctors say I could die any day now."

"Sorry, I'm retired," I say.

"You have to give me one last shot at the title."

Suddenly, Joan of Old just seems too absurd for me to handle, so I walk out of the room.

"Amber? Amber? *Amber?*" Joan of Old says as I walk down the hall with Old Man Linder.

"What did the old broad say to you?" he asks me, dragging his oxygen bottle behind him.

"She faked like she was sleeping so I would tell her personal things that she could use against me the next time we battle."

"I wouldn't worry too much about that."

"Because I'm retired?"

"Because she's going to die any day now. And ding dong the wicked witch will be dead."

"You know what's the weirdest thing about that?"

"What?" Old Man Linder asks.

"I'll miss her."

"I miss everyone from my past, Amber. I really do. It's the curse of old age."

We walk the rest of the way in silence, and just before we reenter the common room, I say, "Will you and Old Man Thompson sing one of your songs at The Bobby Big Boy Variety Show?"

"No one wants to hear two old men sing forgotten songs, Amber. Especially one who needs bottled oxygen to breathe. Singing's a young person's game. Who would want to hear me sing?"

"I would."

Old Man Linder smiles at me all grandfatherly, but his eyes get misty and sad.

When he doesn't say anything, I give Old Man Linder a kiss on the cheek, and then—in the common room—I make the rounds with BBB, allowing everyone to check out his scar while they give him a pet on the head.

And then B Thrice and I are walking through the depressing hallways with the dusty plants.

"How'd it go in there today?" DWL says.

"Okay. Even though he said he didn't want to do it, I'm hoping Old Man Linder will change his mind and he'll sing at The Save Bobby Big Boy Variety Show. That would be pretty cool."

"Who asked him to sing?"

"I did."

"Why didn't you ask *me* to sing?"

"Do you sing?"

"You kiddin' me? I'm a pro. I got me a band and everything. They're called The Hard-Working Brothers. We do weddings mostly, but we play clubs too."

"What type of music?"

"Mostly R & B. I'm known for my Aretha Franklin impersonation—but I do The Supremes, Ella Fitzgerald, Nina Simone, all the big names."

I cross myself, and then say, "DWL. You're a diva?"

"Girl—I bring the roof down whenever I sing. I just work this job for the health insurance."

Suddenly, I understand that Father Chee's prayers are being answered—that JC has sent me and the KDFCs a diva. Word.

"Are you for real?" I ask.

DWL laughs and hands me her card. It reads:

Sister Lucy and The Hard-Working Brothers

There is a phone number underneath.

I explain my relationship with The Korean Divas for Christ, our asking JC to send us a true diva front woman, and then, like a frickin' maniac, I pedal Donna's bike all the way to Father Chee's church, telling everyone I pass that I hope they're having a great day, and when I get there, I bang on the door until FC opens.

"Amber, what brings you here today on a—"

"I found us a true diva!" I say, and then hand him DWL's card.

Father Chee reads the card and then smiles knowingly. "So Jesus has sent us a diva."

"Hell yeah," I say.

"I will take care of everything," Father Chee says, and then jogs me and BBB in-a-basket back to my neighborhood, only I don't go home after FC turns around—BBB and I go to Private Jackson's house.

After so much time with people—I'm tired.

I'm not used to people.

I've been alone in a room for two months.

This is all baptism by fire.

I want to go somewhere I can just be—where I can chill and process the miracle of finding a true diva for The KDFCs.

I stash Donna's bike around the back of PJ's house and knock on PJ's door with BBB in my arms.

"Come in, please," PJ says while scratching Bobby Big Boy's head. "I'll put on tea."

I put B Thrice on the floor inside of the door, and even though he had surgery not so long ago, he tears ass toward the bedroom. I'm a little worried about those stitches, but then I just sit down on the couch figuring Bobby Big Boy knows his own limitations.

A few minutes later, Private Jackson hands me a steaming cup of tea.

We sip in silence for a time.

I put my cup down on the coffee table, stand, pull an origami swan from my pocket, and hand it to PJ.

"It's beautiful," PJ says. "It's perfect."

"Open it up," I say.

"No, I want to let it be—just as it—"

"I'll fold you up another one. There's a haiku inside."

PJ nods and then unfolds my origami swan.

He reads my latest haiku for like—an hour, nodding and rubbing his chin.

"Do you like it?" I finally ask.

He looks up at me and says, "It is perfect. Will you do a reading for me?"

"You serious?" I ask.

"I would very much like to hear you read this haiku."

I take the piece of paper from him, and read.

"We cry together—on the couch for different—reasons, but it helps."

"I will hang it on the wall now," PJ says, taking the paper from me.

"But it's not about a dog."

PJ smiles, tapes my haiku to the blank spot on the final living room wall, and then says, "I like you, Amber Appleton, just as much as I like dogs. And I like dogs better than people."

"And I like you, Private Jackson, just as much as I like dogs."

"We are very lucky then," he says, and we both sit there smiling and sipping green tea for a half hour.

BBB and Ms. Jenny come out of the bedroom all glassy-eyed and wobbly, but BBB seems to be smiling, so I laugh and say, "You can't keep a good dog down, eh, BBB?"

I pick B3 up in my arms, kiss the furry spot between his ears, and then tell PJ I gotta go.

"I will wash the teacups," he says.

Outside, I put BBB in Donna's bike basket, and he's asleep before I pedal one block.

CHAPTER 56

For the next two weeks I work on my prom dress, which I am going to wear when I emcee The Save Bobby Big Boy Variety Show, so—in an effort to finish in time—I start going to the Life Skills room before and after school.

Franks and The Five hold auditions for the variety show.

Door Woman Lucy and the Hard-Working Brothers meet with Father Chee and The KDFCs.

Kids I don't even know sell tickets door-to-door.

Mrs. Baxter collects money.

Mr. Valerie sells advertisements and puts together the program.

And I take BBB to see Ms. Jenny every single day.

I drink tea with Private Jackson—and I fill that blank spot on the last wall of his living room.

Everything is moving toward something—but I'm sorta in a daze.

Sometimes I think I see my mother.

Whenever I see a school bus—my heart leaps.

When I see a bleach-blonde in a crowd.

When I close my eyes at night.

When Donna kisses me, sometimes I pretend, and I get to feeling really badly about my wishing Donna was my mom—back when Mom was actually alive.

I wonder if Mom's death was God answering that wish.

I wonder.

I feel guilty a lot.

I sweat through the nights.

I shiver through the days.

The only thing I really like doing—believe it or not—is drinking green tea with Private Jackson. Sipping in complete silence, surrounded by my haikus.

CHAPTER
57

On the day of The Save Bobby Big Boy Variety Show—before school—I finish my prom dress. It is a silver sleeveless with an empire waist and a scoop neck that shows off what little cleavage I got. When I try it on, my Life Skills teacher, Mrs. Tyler, says, "It's the best prom dress ever made in this classroom. A-plus."

I smile at her and begin to look forward to wearing it later.

All day, students smile at me dramatically and say, "See you tonight, Amber," way too much.

I mean, I'm all about a good variety show, but it seems like people are really going nuts for The Save Bobby Big Boy Variety Show.

Too nuts.

I skip lunch, and go right to The Franks Lair.

When I enter, thirty students stop speaking and turn to face me.

Total frickin' silence.

"What's going on?" I say.

"We're finalizing tonight's plan," Franks says.

"Cool," I say.

From Das Boot, Chad says, "If you come in right now, it's going to ruin the surprises."

"Surprises—plural?" I ask.

"Come on, Amber," Jared says. "Just trust us."

"Am I still emceeing?" I ask.

"All's you have to do is show up at the auditorium at six forty-five," Ty says.

"What time does the show start?"

"Eight," Franks says. "See you then."

"Okay," I say, feeling quite weird and a little embarrassed by how little I have had to do with the preparation.

I chill outside for a bit, and then finish up my school day.

Ty drives Ricky and me to Donna's, and after I take BBB out—I actually take a nap. I'm always tired lately. Naps are becoming my favorite. Word.

★ ★ ★

I wake up to Donna yelling, "We have to get you to the auditorium in less than an hour!"

So I get up and shower.

Makeup is applied.

Hair is blown dry.

Silver prom dress is put on my pre-woman body.

Red pumps are put on my nasty feet.

Prayer is said to JC—with much conviction and hope. "Please help everyone to be who they need to be tonight! Amen!"

Ricky is wearing a tuxedo.

"You look dapper, Ricky!"

"Amber Appleton is wearing a silver dress!"

"Are you ready for this?" Donna asks, and I nod once.

Amber Appleton, Bobby Big Boy, and Ricky Roberts are driven to the CPHS auditorium in Donna's Mercedes with the heated seats on.

When we arrive, there is this huge line to get into the auditorium. There are no seat numbers, so if you want a good seat, you have to line up early.

We have to walk past this line to get to the stage.

When the crowd sees me, they actually start cheering—as if I were a rock star.

No bull.

There are hundreds of people lined up—all looking at me with these really sympathetic eyes.

We pass a section of Korean people—maybe forty of them.

We pass a group of women who look a lot like Door Woman Lucy.

And we pass a lot of Childress citizens.

Halfway up the line, some reject starts chanting, "Amber! Amber! Amber!"

All of the morons in line start doing the chant, and I start to blush.

When I notice that Donna is also chanting, I elbow her and say, "Stop."

She laughs at me and keeps on chanting—like a complete dork.

When we get to the front of the line, Ricky heads into the auditorium, and I start to cry.

The first person in line is Private Jackson.

He's in a yellow button-down shirt, like always.

He has his ticket in his hand—as if he's some excited kid waiting to get into a ball game.

He's smiling at me all proud of himself.

I know this is the first time he's been out in public—besides walking Ms. Jenny and getting groceries—probably since he came home from 'Nam.

"What are you doing here?" I ask.

BBB licks PJ's hand.

PJ pets BBB's head, and says, "I wanted a front row seat, so I came early."

"How did you even know about this?" I ask, because I never told him about The Save Bobby Big Boy Variety Show.

"A boy with a beard, he came to my house and told me that you would appreciate it if I came tonight. So I came. Why didn't you tell me about this?"

Ty. I could kiss him.

"Must have been enjoying the tea-drinking moments too much," I say, and then I get PJ through door security, which is pretty much the bearded history teacher who asked if Ricky was okay when I was tickling him in the hallway three months back and a gym teacher I don't know who lifts a lot of weights.

Inside the auditorium, Donna and Private Jackson take center front row seats—the best seats in the house. And I can tell Donna thinks Private Jackson is handsome, because she sits sideways in her chair and leans forward a little toward him, so that PJ will get a good view of her boob crack.

I smile, and then carry BBB backstage.

There are a crapload of people backstage:

Chad in Das Boot, Jared, Ricky, and Franks are in tuxedos.

Lex Pinkston and the entire football team have greased their hair and half are wearing leather jackets and jeans and white T-shirts—so that they look like they have just stepped out of the '50s—and the other half are wearing black pants, purple button-down shirts, and pointy dress shoes.

The KDFCs are all wearing identical beautiful gold dresses.

Father Chee is in his penguin suit.

Door Woman Lucy is in a tight red dress and killer heels—she is also wearing hair extensions and much glitzy makeup, all of which makes her look like Queen Latifah, who is entirely awesome and another woman I admire.

The black men with instruments—whom I assume are The Hard-Working Brothers, since they are the only brothers backstage besides Ty—those guys are dressed in black suits and wearing white shirts, black skinny ties, and old-school sunglasses with green lenses. Whenever I look at one of The Hard-Working Brothers, they all nod at me as if they are a unit—connected or something.

Ty is at a table just offstage, punching away at a laptop that controls the mics and lights and curtain and sound system. He's dressed like every other day in jeans and a red hoodie sweatshirt. I smile at him because he got Private Jackson out tonight, but Ty's too busy with the laptop and doesn't notice me.

There are cheerleaders dressed in their uniforms.

Two hippie-looking kids with acoustic guitars.

A pimply kid in a medieval jester costume with a hat that looks like a red and yellow palm tree.

And then I see two old men in red sports jackets standing off to the side all alone, one with an oxygen bottle, so I run up to Old Man Linder and Thompson and say, "You guys are singing tonight?"

"We're opening up the show!" Old Man Thompson says.

"You know it," Old Man Linder says, and then pinches my cheek.

"I thought no one wanted to hear old men sing?"

"You said that?" Old Man Thompson says.

"That bearded classmate of yours over there convinced me otherwise," Old Man Linder says, and when I look back at Ty, I smile. He looks so serious at his laptop—so loyal, so dedicated, so like a good friend should.

"You have to make power circle!" Sueng Hee of The KDFCs says to me, and then pulls me and BBB toward the middle of everyone.

"You got something to say before we take the stage?" Door Woman Lucy says.

I look around at all of the faces, some of which I love, some of which I do not even know—all of which I can plainly see need me to say something hopeful so that they will be able to rock Childress High School.

"I want to thank everyone for coming out tonight," I say. "It means a lot to me and Bobby Big Boy, who is cancer free, thank God."

I pause, because I know that the night requires more of me.

I have to be more than a teenage girl.

I have to move people—get them pumped up.

I have to be a rock star.

So I say, "Everyone form a big old circle. Arms around your neighbors' shoulders. Feel the love, people! Feel the love! Ty, you too. Get your butt over here!"

Ty looks up from the computer and then takes his place in the power circle.

Maybe more than fifty people are surrounding BBB and me—all with arms around each other, all watching me.

"Bow those heads," I say. "If you don't believe in JC, well then feel free to sub in whatever deity you dig! If you are an atheist like Ricky, then just humor me, okay?"

Everybody except Ricky bows his or her head.

I close my eyes and say, "JC, you got some good people gathered together down here for a good cause. Please be with all of these good people tonight. Help them be whoever they need to be. Please let us rock. Please let us move some people—so they don't ask for their money back. Be with us tonight, JC. Amen."

"Amen!" most of my people say, and then start to unlink their arms from their neighbors' shoulders.

"Get those arms back around those shoulders!" I yell.

Everyone does what I say.

I start stomping my left foot.

Stomp! Stomp! Stomp!

Everyone catches on.

Fifty-some feet are stomping now.

The floor below us seems to be moving.

"If the people in the house are feeling all right tonight, say 'Yeah!'"

"Yeah!"

"If the people in the house are feeling all right tonight, say 'Hell yeah!' "

"Hell yeah!"

"I can't hear you!"

"HELL YEAH!"

Stomp, stomp, stomp, stomp!

"If you're ready to rock Childress Public High School tonight say, 'Woo! Woo!' "

"Woo! Woo!"

Stomp, stomp, stomp.

I can't think of any other cool empowering jazz to say, so I end with, "Bring it in for some love! Everyone put a hand in the middle of the circle."

I quickly see that Das Boot is going to mess up the unity, so I say, "Scratch that. Everyone put a hand on Chad's head!"

We all circle Das Boot.

We all put a hand on Chad's head—well, most of us do, and the rest put hands on the shoulders of people who have their hands on Chad's head.

"Watch the hair, people," Chad says.

"Thank you for helping me pay my vet bill," I say. "I love you people. All of you. On three, we say, 'Go time.' One, two, three!"

"Go time!" everyone yells.

And when they back away from Das Boot, they look pretty pumped up.

Suddenly, on the other side of the front curtain, the crowd is chanting, "Amber! Amber! Amber!"

And I think, *Damn, I really am a rock star*.

"You look good in that dress," Ty says.

"Thanks, I made it myself," I say, and then he returns to his laptop.

"How was the prayer?" I ask Father Chee.

"God was very pleased," FC says.

"How do you know?" I ask.

"He told me!" FC says.

"Did He tell you if tonight was going to work out?"

"Yes, He told me that too."

"What did He say?" I ask.

"He says it's time for you to take the stage," FC says, and then points to Franks, who is standing by the edge of the curtain waving me over. "Better hurry."

I carry BBB over to Franks, who says, "Okay, Amber. Before each act, I give you a note card. You read the info on the card, and then you announce the act any way you see fit. Cool?"

"Cool," I say.

Franks hands me a card, and then I walk out onto the stage with BBB in my arms.

A spotlight hits me.

The house lights dim.

I step up to the microphone stand.

The crowd hushes.

I see PJ and Donna smiling up at me.

I hold BBB up over my head.

"Cancer-free!"

People cheer.

"Now we have to pay the vet bill."

The crowd laughs, but I'm not sure why.

"Thanks for coming out tonight."

I scan the crowd. Packed house.

"Ladies and gentlemen, I have a special treat for you this evening. Backed by tonight's house band—The Hard-Working Brothers—singing the old-time classic 'Makin' Whoopee,' the best two men the Methodist Home has to offer—let's give it up for Albert Linder and Eddie Thompson, better known as The Red Coats!"

The curtain rises, and The Red Coats start snapping their old fingers.

The Hard-Working Brothers start playing the old-time song, and Old Man Thompson starts to sing "Makin' Whoopee" in this good but corny old-time singing voice.

With his oxygen bottle and all, Old Man Linder doesn't really sing, but in a speaking voice sorta echoes Old Man Thompson—and it works.

The Hard-Working Brothers are a pretty good band too.

From offstage, I look out into the audience and I see some old people singing along.

Cool, I think.

After The Red Coats finish their number, the crowd claps, and I announce various other acts—some fellow classmates sing and play instruments, some do dance routines, the kid in the medieval jester costume actually juggles knives and flaming tennis balls, which gets Prince Tony out of his seat. PT tries to stop the juggling act, but gets booed so badly that he eventually allows the kid to finish.

When I announce the Mackin' Mathematician, Ricky takes the stage and Franks throws a couple dozen or so cheap calculators into the audience. "Ladies and gentlemen, I have a genius here with me tonight," Franks says.

"Yes," Ricky says into his microphone.

"Anyone who caught a calculator can ask Ricky to multiply any number and he will do it in his head in less than five seconds—providing you with the correct answer. You are welcome to check his math using the calculators, although I assure you this will not be necessary."

"Yes," Ricky says, standing center stage in his tuxedo.

Franks hops off the stage and walks the cordless microphone into the audience. "Who's first?"

Some regular-looking dude raises his hand and says something to Franks.

"Ricky, this gentleman wants to know what is one-hundred fifty-seven times five-hundred twenty-one."

"Eighty-one thousand, seven hundred and ninety-seven. Yes."

"Is he right, sir?" Franks asks.

The man punches the numbers into his calculator, and then nods, looking amazed.

Fifty hands go up in the air.

"One thousand, two hundred sixty-eight times one-two-nine-six-oh, Ricky."

"Sixteen million, four hundred and thirty-three thousand, two hundred and eighty."

"Five times nine," some little kid wants to know.

"Forty-five," Ricky says. "Forty-five."

"Sixty-five times three-hundred thirteen thousand, one-hundred thirty-one."

"Twenty million, three-hundred and fifty-three thousand, five-hundred and fifteen."

"Five hundred and sixty-eight point thirteen times five-hundred sixty-seven point seventy-seven," some wise guy wants to know, throwing decimals at Ricky.

"Three hundred and twenty-two thousand, five hundred and sixty-seven point seventeen."

Ricky does several more math problems in his head—each time the difficulty is raised—and he answers all of the questions correctly, before he says, "Ricky Roberts is hungry," and then walks offstage.

The crowd claps for Ricky, and Donna looks so proud in the first row.

There are a few more singing and dancing acts before I make this announcement: "People, it is my pleasure to introduce my good friends Chad and Jared Fox, performing The Spinners classic 'Working My Way Back to You' accompanied by The Hard-Working Brothers and the Childress High School cheerleaders!"

Chad, Das Boot, Jared, and The Hard-Working Brothers take the stage.

My boys look good in their tuxedos, although Jared looks like he is about to crap his pants.

The Hard-Working Brothers' drummer starts the song and the bassist plays some funky notes.

In this really affected put-on voice, from Das Boot, Chad starts singing about how hard he's working to get back his woman.

When his brother begins to sing, Jared starts clapping and sorta moves his weight from one foot to another.

Suddenly, the cheerleading team comes flying across the stage doing cartwheels—their skirts flying up and down.

It is the strangest thing I have ever seen.

As Jared and Chad sing, the cheerleaders do all sorts of acrobatics—throwing girls up into the air, building human pyramids, and doing spirited jumping jacks with pompoms.

People in the audience actually start to get up and dance.

My boys are a hit!

Chad is doing circles around the cheerleaders with Das Boot, singing to them.

Jared is still moving his weight from one foot to the other, backing up his more confident brother—looking sorta like he is about to have a heart attack.

And I can't help but laugh.

When the song ends, the crowd goes wild, and Franks hands me the next note card.

I take the stage and say, "And now performing selected scenes from *West Side Story*, ladies and gentlemen, I give you *the Childress High School football team?*"

Lex and a bunch of his teammates walk onto the stage wearing purple shirts and pointy dress shoes—snapping their fingers in a crouched sneaky position.

The rest of the team enters from the other side of the stage wearing the leather jackets and jeans—also snapping their fingers while in a sneaky crouched position.

What ensues is a street war orchestrated through fabulous dance moves, and set to heart-racing jazzy recorded music.

And as I watch the football team perform selected scenes from *West Side Story*, I am amazed by how good they are. They are frickin' pros.

As the quicksilver of fake knives flashes, people in the audience are on the edges of their seats!

These boys were born to do musical theater!

Suddenly I understand why our football team never wins any games.

The Jets and the Sharks get a thunderous round of applause as they link arms and take a bow center stage, and I have to say, I'm impressed.

"Ladies and gentlemen," I say, "we've come to the headliner, which combines two very talented groups of people—people I know well and love very much. I give you The Korean Divas for Christ, Sister Lucy, and The Hard-Working Brothers!"

People clap as the curtain rises.

The strings and brass are set up stage right, the drums are deep center, The KDFCs are lined up on risers, tiered in all their golden glory stage left, and Sister Lucy is front and center holding a microphone.

"Come on out here, Sister Amber," Sister Lucy says.

I carry BBB out to center stage, and Sister Lucy puts her arm around me.

"You know, they say the way to a woman's heart is to give her enough chocolate," DWL says, and the audience laughs at that one. "Before she knew I was a diva, when she thought I was just a door woman at the old people's home, when she was homeless herself, every week Amber brought me a hot chocolate and a Snickers bar. Might not sound like much to some, but I liked it well enough. It was something to look forward to on Wednesdays. I'm sorry about what happened to your mom, Sister Amber. It ain't right. So this one is for you."

When Lucy lets go of me, I walk to the side of the stage, and an electric organ starts playing.

I look over by the horn section at the keyboard synthesizer and I suddenly realize that Father Chee is playing it—he's playing with the band!

Sister Lucy starts singing and her voice is deep and rich and divine.

She's singing about Mother Mary.

The KDFCs are doing these slow hand motions I didn't teach them—and then they are echoing Sister Lucy beautifully, like pros.

They're doing an R & B version of The Beatles' "Let It Be."

The Hard-Working Brothers kick in with the drums and the bass and guitar and then the horns too.

The people in the audience are standing now.

Their hands are swaying back and forth over their heads.

I listen to the lyrics and understand what Sister Lucy is telling me—and then I'm crying like a baby.

Jared puts his arm around me during the saxophone solo.

From Das Boot, Chad reaches up and holds my hand.

BBB licks my under-chin.

Toward the end of the song, Sister Lucy really starts to push it—showing off her vocals—and this is when I know that she is indeed a true bona fide diva.

I'm so proud of The KDFCs, who sound and look great.

There is still a light that shines on me, I think as Sister Lucy sings the line.

Listening to Sister Lucy sing — backed up by The KDFCs — I feel like JC is there with me, and that everything is going to be okay somehow.

It's a pretty powerful moment.

Maybe even holy.

And then the song is over.

"Let it be, Sister Amber, let it be," Sister Lucy says to me. And then, to the crowd, she says, "Childress Public High School — you people ready to dance your butts off?"

The crowd cheers, and then Father Chee hits some funky old-time piano chords on the synthesizer, The Hard-Working Brothers start playing, and Sister Lucy is rocking "Think" by Aretha Franklin.

The KDFCs are shoulder dipping, booty shaking, making circles with their open hands, and whenever Sister Lucy points at them, they all shout, "Think!" or "Freedom!" They are rocking so hard — I'm amazed.

The crowd is going frickin' nuts.

There are people dancing in the aisles.

Everyone is on his or her feet.

And when I look down at the first row, Donna is dancing with Private Jackson. PJ sucks at dancing — but he is dancing! That's a miracle!

So I start dancing with Jared and Chad and BBB — and then I even try to get Ricky dancing, but that doesn't fly so well.

Sister Lucy runs through "Come See About Me," "Baby

Love," "O-o-h Child," "I Want You Back," "(Sweet Sweet Baby) Since You Been Gone," "Freeway of Love," and when she gets to "Respect," everyone on stage is soaked with sweat — and everyone in the audience is drenched with sweat too.

The roof is officially off the Childress High School Auditorium.

Sister Lucy rocks the Aretha Franklin signature song, and The KDFCs get to shine on this one too, as they do all kinds of hand movements, shoulder dip with tons of attitude, and sing, "Sock-it-to-me, sock-it-to-me, sock-it-to-me. Just a little bit. Just a little bit."

When they finish the set, the crowd claps and whistles for ten minutes, and The KDFCs are beaming with pride.

JC is definitely in the house tonight.

Sister Lucy announces the names of the band members and The KDFCs, making all the Koreans in the house cheer like mad, which is when I realize that The KDFCs' families have come to support them, thanks — no doubt — to Father Chee. And I think, *Cool, we're bringing people together tonight.*

I can't believe how well The Save Bobby Big Boy Variety Show has gone.

I'm so amazed.

I'm so thankful.

But then Franks is telling me that Ty is going to post the total amount of money we raised on the big movie screen at the back of the stage, and that I'm supposed to thank the crowd for coming, so I do, with BBB in my arms.

When I turn around and point to the movie screen at the

back of the stage, behind The Hard-Working Brothers' drum set, Ty does his computer thing, the $0000.00 numbers on the huge screen start to spin and "We're Not Alone" by Dinosaur Jr. starts playing very loudly, probably because Ty knows it's one of my very most favorite songs.

$375.15 flashes on the screen.

People cheer.

I nod and think, not bad.

But then the numbers start to spin again.

$657.15

Nice!

People cheer even louder.

$2,019.89

People start to cheer like mad.

$3,998.23

I've accomplished my goal!

I'm so happy.

$5,002.11

Could we have possibly raised that much?

What will we do with the extra money?

I look back behind the stage curtain and Franks and The Five are smiling at me. People are clapping like mad now. Everyone is smiling, and I notice that there are people crying in the audience, which makes me feel very strange.

$7,628.54

This can't be right.

$23,425.76

I almost crap myself.

$62,981.72

"What is going on?" I yell to Franks, sorta laughing now, because there is no way we raised that much money.

He winks at me from offstage.

$121,521.09

Suddenly I notice news cameras in the aisles, camera crews and news reporters.

$215,671.87

The last number flashes on the screen several times and then the words Grand Total appear for a few seconds.

Suddenly—Bobby Big Boy and I are standing on the stage alone now, and the auditorium is completely silent.

The screen goes blank.

What the hell is going on?

These words flash up on the screen:

A Message From Amber's Nemesis

Suddenly, Joan of Old's head is on the screen, which completely shocks me for obvious reasons. The shot is a close-up, so her wrinkly face is gigantic. I can see the pillow behind her head, and it looks like she is having trouble breathing. Her wrinkly eyelids look really pink and her skin looks like wax, or maybe ancient cheese.

"I'm probably already dead by now," Joan of Old's pink wrinkly enormous eyeless head says. "For those of you who don't know, Amber and I used to battle every Wednesday afternoon. Her strange little boyfriends recorded this several days ago, which was fortuitous, because I am probably gone and buried by now, yes—but especially because I vowed to make Amber cry before I died, and I always keep my word, Ms. Appleton, Princess of Hope. Today is the day I defeat you, once and for all. The doctors say this is the end of the road for me. It's about time. My body is going to return to dust. Good riddance! Now I understand the town is having some sort of pep rally for you because of what happened to your mother and because you were so constantly on your guard that you are no longer able to defend yourself, like Nietzsche said. I hear you've lost hope, and—regardless of my philosophical views—you're far too young for that. What will you have to look forward to in old age, if you become a nihilist before you hit eighteen?"

Joan of Old starts coughing very badly here, but then recovers.

"I want to say two things to you before I die. One. My Lawrence was a German philosophy professor, hence my obsession with Nietzsche. Here is a quote I never got around to sharing with you: 'We should consider every day lost on which we have not danced at least once. And we should call every truth false which was not accompanied by at least one laugh.' That was my Lawrence's favorite quote. He used to dance me around the house every night. Every. Single. Night. And how we would laugh. He was a beautiful man, who died far too young, but he would have absolutely loved you. Keep making people laugh, Amber. At least until you are old and gray. Laugh at yourself and others will always laugh with you. Even mean old defeated women like me."

Joan of Old coughs again.

"Two. I've got some bucks left over—and I'm leaving my entire estate to The Amber Appleton Community Service College Fund, which is what your friends have established without your knowing it. My son Teddy hasn't come to visit me in eleven years, so screw him! Bye-bye, Amber. See you in hell."

Joan of Old smiles the last grin of a dying woman—which is huge and beautiful—and then she says, "I finally got you, didn't I?"

I'm crying now onstage even though I'm not exactly sure what is happening.

The film cuts to the old folk's common room at the home. My old able-legged silver-haired friends are gathered around my wheelchair-bound silver-headed friends. With his oxygen bottle by his side, Old Man Linder steps forward and says, "Kid, you were the only one who came to visit us when we needed a good laugh. Life is a long, long race, and the finish is often lonely. Even our own flesh and blood—many of our sons and daughters—abandoned us at some point, so when we heard about what happened to your mother, we all wrote you into our wills. Some of us are giving more than others, but you should be all set covering your Bryn Mawr tuition over the next five years or so. Maybe there'll be some left over for law school too."

The audience is clapping now, camera crews are rolling film, women are crying, and I'm still not sure what the hell is going on.

But then Franks and The Five walk out onto the stage.

Franks has a live microphone. He says, "I've never met a person with more spirit, I've never met a person with more hope and love in her heart, I've never met a more deserving person than Amber Appleton. She never thinks of herself first. She's always thinking up some crazy scheme to help others, whether they want help or not. Well, Amber, this time it was The Five who thought up a plan to help you in your time of need."

Ricky, Chad on Das Boot, Jared, Ty, and Lex Pinkston dressed as a Puerto Rican gang member—they are all smiling at me.

"You are loved, Amber Appleton," Franks says.

"So this money is for me?" I ask.

"It's your college fund."

"What about Bobby Big Boy's operation? How will I pay for that?"

"She wants to know how she's going to pay for her dog's operation," Franks says into his microphone, and the audience starts laughing—as if everyone is in on the joke except me.

Dr. Weissmuller stands up in the third row, smiles, and yells, "On the house!"

The audience cheers again, and then some bright loser starts yelling, "Speech! Speech! Speech!"

The chant catches on, and then Franks is handing me the live microphone.

I'm still crying a little.

"Thank you, everyone. I'm not really sure this is real, or what it means exactly. I hope my mom is looking down on us tonight," I say and then pause, because I start to cry a little harder.

I swallow and think about my mom.

She'd have liked to see this.

She would have crapped her pants when that last number flashed up on the screen.

"I don't know what else to say. I'm speechless. Thanks."

I hand the live microphone back to Franks, and he says, "Thanks for coming, everyone. You make me proud to live in Childress—the town that takes care of its own. Drive home safely!"

And before he sees me coming, I give Franks a big old teddy-bear hug right onstage—getting my arms halfway around his big belly and sinking my tear-streaked face into his chest.

Surprisingly, he hugs me back, and I smile and close my eyes—savoring the moment.

"You're a good man, Franks," I say. "You really are. True."

"How about you give the rest of us some love, sweetheart?" Chad says.

But before I can answer, I'm rushed by a bunch of reporters who stick cameras in my face and ask me all sorts of personal questions about my mom.

Before I can even think, Donna is onstage, yelling, "My client has no comment at the present moment! Boys, let's get her out of here!"

So I say a quick goodbye to PJ, FC, The KDFCs, DWL, The Hard-Working Brothers, Old Man Thompson, and—

"Get the hell out of here already before those reporters lynch you," Old Man Linder yells at me, and then squeezes my shoulder like he always does.

The Five gets me the hell out of there, leaving Das Boot behind, because it doesn't fit into Donna's Mercedes. No worries. Mr. Fox will take Das Boot home in the Fox family van.

In the car I pet BBB, hug my boys and thank them for getting everyone to participate in the show, filming Joan of Old, and raising money for my college fund, which is pretty amazing. I even thank Lex, who is still dressed as a Puerto Rican gang member and is somehow smushed in the car with us—making us The Six and no longer The Five.

Donna says, "Sundaes at my place!"

After a quick stop at the food store, I wash my hands, make proper sundaes in Donna's kitchen for my boys, and then we celebrate the night by sharing ice cream and sword fighting with spoons. True.

After everyone is finished eating, the boys go to Ricky's room to play Halo 3, and Donna and I wash dishes in the kitchen.

"What the hell happened tonight?" I ask.

"The town of Childress came together and tried the best they could to make a wrong right. And I'm not talking about the money. They came together in the auditorium, gave their time to say that they care."

"Why?"

"Because most people are good," Donna says, and then passes me a rinsed bowl.

I stick it into the dishwasher and say, "Did they make a wrong right?"

"What do you think?"

"It doesn't bring my mom back. It doesn't erase what happened—which is still messed up beyond imagination. Whack."

"No, it doesn't. And yes, it still is."

"So I really have access to all that money?" I ask, shoving a handful of spoons into the dishwasher utensil bin.

"No," Donna says while rinsing the last ice cream bowl. "You have a college fund that you can use to pay college and graduate school tuition. I drew up all of the papers."

"What happens if I don't use the money?"

"Why wouldn't you use the money? You're still planning on going to Bryn Mawr and then Harvard, right?"

"Yeah, but maybe I'll get scholarships—like you did."

"I thought of that."

"You did?"

"If you get to go to school for free, you can donate the money to the charity of your choice."

"Really?"

"Really."

"So I could like—donate all of the money to the Childress Public High School Business Department so that Franks could maybe build a killer classroom and get out of the basement? Or maybe, at least, he could get some windows put in and he wouldn't have to buy all of his own supplies using his own personal money?"

"You could do something like that. Absolutely."

I smile, thinking of all the good hooey I can do for others with the money.

CHAPTER 58

When the junior prom rolls around, Donna rents Ricky and me a stretch limo. I wear my silver dress. Ricky wears his tuxedo. Donna has flowers for both of us. We take a crapload of pictures in the backyard, and then we go to Ty's house and pick him up. He's still got the beard, but he looks dashing in a navy blue tuxedo. Mr. and Mrs. Hendrix take pictures of Ricky, Ty, and me for — like — an hour, and then we jump into the limo and tell the driver to take us to Jared's and Chad's house, where they are waiting with their dates — Carla Winslow and Sally Craig — from the cheerleading squad. These girls are bimbo airheads, but for my boys, I'm super nice to both of them. Mr. and Mrs. Fox take pictures of all of us in various poses for another hour, and then we are in the limo again — off to the local Hilton reception room where our junior prom is held, with Mr. Fox following us in the Fox van, which transports Das Boot for Chad.

When we arrive, we get Chad into Das Boot, and then we make our entrance.

Franks is a greeter, which means he has to check our breath for alcohol.

So we walk in all staggering, pretending to be hammered.

"Want some vodka?" I ask Franks.

"I'll probably need some by the end of the night," Franks says to me, and we all laugh.

"How do I look, Franks?"

"All of you look great," Franks says, and Carla and Sally giggle at that one.

At the prom we eat good food, we dance to the music the DJ plays, we mix in with Lex Pinkston and all of the football players and their cheerleader dates. I split the slow dances equally between Ricky and Ty. And when they play "Always And Forever" at the end, all members of The Five and Sally and Carla dance in a big circle with our arms linked—and our teachers watching and waiting to go home. It's all pretty silly, really.

When the prom is over, we put Das Boot into the Fox van, hop into our limo, and drive to Ty's parents' beach house in Long Beach Island, or LBI. Mr. Fox follows us down with Das Boot, because he is a good dad.

Ty's parents' house is actually right on the beach, so after we get Das Boot into the house and Mr. Fox leaves, we put Chad in a backpack and hit the sand to do some stargazing.

Barefoot, but still in our tuxedos and dresses, we run along the edge of the ocean, the water licking our ankles—laughing and singing like the kids we are.

Somehow we decide to spend the entire night on the beach so we can see the sunrise.

We pick out a spot in front of Ty's parents' house.

We lie down on the sand making this big pile of teenagers.

We look up into the universe, and we get pretty quiet as we marvel.

Everyone falls asleep except me.

I think about my mom.

I get up and cry a little down by the ocean, so that the others won't hear.

After a few minutes, Ty appears and puts his arm around me—in a brotherly sorta way.

When I turn around surprised, he holds me, I sob into his overly starched tuxedo shirt, and his friendship beard scratches my forehead.

Hours later, the sun comes up.

Ty and I are simply sitting together on a sand dune.

When The Five finds us, I snap out of my sadness and yell, "I'm making breakfast!"

And then in Ty's parents' beach house, I make killer omelets for everyone.

CHAPTER 59

By doing some Internet research, I learn that you have to fill out a visitor's application and get it approved before you will be allowed to visit any prisoner in a maximum-security facility. There are these rules you have to read and agree to follow with a signature. If you are not eighteen you need to have a guardian sign the forms as well, and since I don't want Donna or anyone else to know that I am going to visit my mother's killer, I wait until my eighteenth birthday to fill out the form and send it in — which I do after the barbeque party Donna throws for me in the backyard.

My eighteenth b-day party is sorta a big thing, as Old Man Linder, Old Man Thompson, and some old people from the home come, The KDFCs bring their families along with FC, the Franks family shows, The Five are, of course, there along with many of my fellow CPHS classmates, Prince Tony, and Mrs. Baxter — and even PJ and Ms. Jenny show up, which is sorta cool, because in a sexy summer dress, Donna flirts with PJ and he doesn't leave early. Sister Lucy and The Hard-Working Brothers do an encore outdoor performance with The Korean Divas for Christ, which rocks hard-core, and brings the neighbors out of their houses and into our back-yard. I am embarrassed by the many super-cool presents. And later that night, after everyone has left, I fill out the visiting-prison form and drop it in the mail—which is my birthday present to myself.

My mother's killer has to agree to see me as well, and I worry that he'll refuse.

I also worry about Donna getting the reply letter, so every day I sneak away from my summer job at Rita's water ice when the mail is delivered at two, just so Donna won't inter-cept the letter from the prison.

After a few weeks of waiting, I get a very official response.

The letter states a date and time.

I am granted a fifteen-minute non-contact visit—meaning we will be separated by Plexiglas, which is just fine with me.

I'll only need five minutes with my mother's killer, so I'm cool.

The day before the non-contact visit, I call Ty and ask him if he will ditch work at one of his dad's bank branches—where he does his summer nine-to-five as a drive-thru bank teller. I ask if he'll take me somewhere secret, and promise never to tell anyone about it for as long as he lives, and in exchange, I'll finally go to Friendly's with him just like old times, so he can finally shave off his friendship beard. We still haven't been to Friendly's since my mom died.

"What time do I pick you up?"

"Eight AM. And make sure you have a full tank of gas."

"Cool."

The next morning I call my boss at Rita's and tell him I am having woman problems so he won't ask any questions, and he doesn't.

Bearded Ty shows up right on time, I jump into his Volvo station wagon, and he says, "Where we headed?"

"Get on the turnpike and go north."

"Cool," Ty says, and then we are off.

I give him directions for almost two hours, and when we pull into the parking lot of the maximum-security prison, he says, "Um, Amber. What the hell are we doing here?"

"I have a non-contact visit scheduled with my mom's killer."

"What? Why?"

"Because I need to face him and then move on."

"I'm not sure that's a good idea."

"Trust me."

"Amber, um—"

"Just wait here, okay? I'll be back in less than an hour."

"I don't like this," Ty says, and I notice that his friendship beard is almost six inches long now. It has to go—and soon.

"Get ready to lose that beard," I say, and then walk across the parking lot.

Ty yells my name from his car a few times, but he doesn't follow me into the prison.

Inside I have to walk through a metal detector, show my driver's license, my CPHS school ID, and my visitation permission letter—and then I am frisked and searched by a large woman in a guard uniform. She's packing heat too.

When she concludes that I have no weapons on me—that

I am only a harmless girl—she leads me down a hallway and through two sets of guarded and locked doors, where she has to yell, "Visitor coming through—searched and clean!"

At the end of the fourth hallway, she opens a door and says, "This is it. I'll wait for you here."

Right before I step into the room, I get really nervous, and for some reason I just can't make my legs carry me into the visitation room, so—in my mind—I conjure up my all-time Amber-and-her-mom number-one moment to give me courage.

I wasn't going to tell you this, but my mom's last boyfriend—A-hole Oliver—well, he didn't exactly throw us out of his apartment.

The whole deal went down something like this:

Mom, BBB, and I were watching the debut episode of *Buffy the Vampire Slayer* from the season one DVDs, which I had borrowed from Jared and Chad. Buffy was just about to save her new friend Willow from the vamps when A-hole Oliver came home and told us that he wanted to watch the Sixers game, so I immediately turned off *Buffy*—right at the good part—and handed AO the remote, because it was his apartment and his DVD player and I really didn't feel like arguing with A-hole Oliver, because he was pretty stubborn and would cut you down in a heartbeat with one of his mean, straight-for-the-jugular insults.

He put on the Sixers, which didn't really bother me all that much because AO pretty much controlled the TV whenever he was home, so I wouldn't have expected anything different. But Mom, she was sorta into *Buffy* after watching season six—which Chad and Jared gave me for my birthday the year before, saying that season six was the best because that one has the musical episode, *Once More, With Feeling*—and it was actually Mom's idea to borrow season one from my boys so we could watch the whole series in order, together, mother-and-daughter style.

I think that maybe Mom dug the show because Buffy kicks so much apple bottom for a regular chick, even if she is a slayer. She's really like a role model for women. But Buffy keeps it real too. She may be a superchick, but she still hangs out with her dorky friends Xander and Willow, who are totally like real people even if one falls in love with a demon and the other becomes a powerful witch, so you sorta believe in Buffy—like she's real—even though she kills vampires and monsters and lives on a hellmouth. The show gives regular chicks like Mom and me hope. True? True.

We watched the Sixers for a while, nobody saying anything, and then A-hole Oliver went into the kitchen and didn't come back for a few minutes.

"Why did you make us turn off *Buffy* if you aren't even going to watch basketball?" Mom yelled to her man.

"I'm listening to it," AO said from the kitchen, making himself a sandwich.

I was shocked when Mom got up from the couch, took back the remote, and put the *Buffy* DVD back on.

AO returned to the living room, sandwich in hand, and said, "I'm watching the Sixers!"

"We were watching *Buffy*," Mom said, which surprised me because my mom never stuck up for herself at all.

"When you start kicking in some more bucks for rent, you

can control the TV," AO said. "You're responsible for two of the three people living here and you don't even cover your half of the bills. So as long as I'm picking up the *entire* cable bill, we watch the Sixers whenever they're on."

Oliver sorta pushed Mom aside, ejected the *Buffy* DVD, and threw it at me like a Frisbee, but too hard. The disk rose up, hit the wall over my head, and then fell behind the couch. BBB began to bark.

"Hey, what the hell?" I said. "That's not mine. You're paying for it if it's scratched."

AO pointed to the DVD player and said, "That machine's not yours either. Nothing in this apartment is yours. You don't own anything besides that found mutt. And if it weren't for me, you'd be out on the streets—and don't you forget it."

"I work," I say.

"And do I take any of your water ice money?" AO asked me as if he was a hero or something.

"No."

"Well then," AO said, and then sat back down.

I looked at Mom and could tell that she'd had enough of Oliver, but I wasn't ready for what she said next.

"Amber, go into your room and put all of your clothes into trash bags. Pack up all your belongings. Don't forget your comforter."

"Why?" I said.

"Because we're moving out," Mom said with this real determined look on her face.

"Where are you going to live?" AO said with a laugh, flashing a mouthful of half-chewed lunch meat—laughing at us. *"On your school bus?"*

Mom went into the kitchen; I followed her. When she grabbed the trash bags from under the sink, went to her room, and started stuffing all of her clothes into the bags, BBB and I went to my room and did the same thing. We didn't have that much stuff, so we only filled six bags.

With coats on, bags in hands, we walked past A-hole Oliver, and he said, "You'll be back. See you in a few hours."

We walked out of AO's apartment complex, and then my mother kissed me on both cheeks, held my head in her hands, and said, "Oliver was an asshole. I'm sorry I made you live with him for so long. We're never going back to his apartment. I promise."

I smiled at her, and for some reason we both began to cry right there on the sidewalk, hugging each other, as BBB watched.

"It might take me some time, Amber," my mother whispered into my ear, "but I'll get us into our very own apartment. We can make it without Oliver. I'll get a better job or maybe find a better man. Something will come along for us."

"I know," I told my mom, but the truth is that I was very scared, because Mom had a lot of alcohol on her breath and I sorta understood without Mom saying it that right then and there, we were officially homeless. But we were also free, and Mom's standing up to Oliver and taking a chance, well that was something I could respect. It kicked a little apple bottom—Buffy-style. Or at least that's what I thought at the time, three weeks before Mom asked A-hole Oliver to let us back into his apartment and he refused, even after Mom brought me to him and begged him to let us back in if only for her daughter's sake.

"Promise me something right now," Mom said while looking me in the eyes, still holding my cheeks with her hands, five minutes after we had first left AO's apartment. "You'll never ever let a man treat you the way Oliver treated me."

"I won't."

"Tell me that you won't live your life afraid, but will grow up and live a better life than your mother could ever imagine."

"I will," I said.

We were both crying in public, with our six trash bags of belongings circling our feet, and for some reason, right then and there, I felt like I was saying goodbye to my mother, that she was going to descend into a place that doesn't allow you to return — that this was the beginning of the end or something for her. It was like she had snapped — as if her mind had begun to turn on her and she knew it. It was like she was on her deathbed in some stupid movie and I was vowing to fulfill her last wishes. But it was also sorta like a beginning for me, because what I promised my mother — I didn't take that vow lightly then, and I sure as hell don't take it lightly now.

So standing there in the doorway of the prison visitation room, just before I face my mother's killer, I take a deep breath — remembering all that has happened, all that I have survived, how strong I've become — and once more I say, "I won't. I will."

When I walk into the room, another security guard — a

young skinny man—shows me to a little booth that is sorta like a desk with dividing walls to separate me from the other visitors, even though there are no other visitors in the room right now.

My mother's killer—he's seated on the other side of thick Plexiglas and is staring at me.

On the desk are headphones I am supposed to put on that have a little microphone stick that hangs out over your mouth—sorta like what a helicopter pilot might wear.

My mother's killer already has his headset on.

He's staring at me—blankly.

Huge brown glasses.

Crazy hair.

Orange jumpsuit.

His wrists are handcuffed to the belt that circles his belly.

I try not to think about what he did to my mother, but I can't help it—a wave of anger rushes through my limbs.

I take a few deep breaths.

He nods toward the headset and mouths the words: PUT IT ON.

I look into his eyes and shiver.

There is nothing there.

He is not human.

He is a thing.

There is nothing left in his eyes.

Nothing.

He is a monster.

Seeing the daughter of his last victim—no emotion registers on his face.

Nothing.

So I do not put on the headset.

Instead, I pull out an origami swan from my pocket and show it to him.

No emotion registers on his face.

I unfold the swan with trembling hands.

My poem is written in huge letters.

With an open hand, I hold my words up to the glass and watch my mother's killer read what I have written to him—how I am responding to his murdering my mother.

> You may exist in
> This world—but I exist too
> And I will not yield

The face of my mother's killer does not change.

He nods toward the headset again and yells, PUT IT ON!

He's trying to yell through the glass, he obviously wants to say something to me, but he doesn't get to call the shots today.

I see the guards behind him stiffen.

I keep my haiku up against the glass and shake my head no.

Suddenly, the man lunges toward the glass.

Attacks my haiku with his head—banging it against the glass several times before the guards come and drag him out of the visitor's room.

I don't even flinch.

Only when they have him completely out of the room do I lower my haiku from the glass.

I leave my poem there on the desk; I want it to stay in the prison.

"What the hell did you write on that piece of paper?" the young skinny guard asks me.

When I don't answer, he walks past me and picks up my haiku.

I walk out of the visitor's room, and the woman guard escorts me past security, through the metal detector, and out of the prison.

Surprisingly, I'm feeling a little better having faced my mother's killer.

He has not defeated me—and if a man like him can't beat me, I know nothing will.

There is life all around me.

Sky.

Clouds.

Trees.

Endless air.

Birds flying overhead.

There is a good bearded boy in a Volvo waiting for me.

All this, right now, is mine to experience.

I need to drink it up for Mom, for all of those who cannot—and for me too.

I'm only eighteen.

These are the days.

I'm still a kid if I want to be.

And I do.

Bearded Ty gets out of the car when he sees me walking across the parking lot, but he doesn't say anything. His face expresses concern. I can tell he cares about me—deeply. And I can tell he is still a kid too—in spite of the hideous friendship beard.

"I did what I had to do," I tell him.

"Do you want to talk about it?"

"No."

"Okay."

"Do you want to open your presents?" I ask.

"Presents?"

"For driving me today."

"I'm not sure this is the appropriate—"

"We're opening your presents. Get in the car."

We get into his Volvo station wagon.

"Here's present number one," I say and then hand him a small but heavy wrap job.

"This is sort of weird," Ty says.

"What?"

"Opening presents in the parking lot of a maximum security prison."

"We're celebrating our freedom. We're celebrating our ability to be kids when everything is trying to take that away from us. It's a choice, Ty. We can do whatever we want."

"What are you talking about?"

"Come on, just open it already. You're going to like this present. I promise."

Ty rips off the wrapping paper. "Batteries?"

"Open 'em up. You'll only need two."

"For what?"

"For present number two."

"What?"

"Just do it."

Ty gets two batteries ready and then opens his second present.

"An electric razor," he says.

I grab the box, open it up, and put the batteries into the electric razor.

I flick it on and it makes a buzzing noise.

BZZZZZZZ.

I look Ty in the eyes and I say, "I think it's time to shave off that awful beard."

"I'm not shaving until you agree to go to Friendly's with The Five," he says, and then laughs sorta strangely, as if he's no longer sure about his plan. "Remember?"

But then suddenly, I want to look into his eyes—I want to know that there is something inside of Ty. Something human. The opposite of what I saw while looking through the Plexiglas—gazing into the eyes of a monster.

I search those brown orbs.

They are innocent.

They are the color of bark.

They are alive.

They are boyish.

They are full of possibility.

They are full of hope.

They are gorgeous.

They are beautiful.

They give me fuel—they make my chest feel so warm.

"Well, then, we'll go to Friendly's," I say. "Just as soon as we pick up The Five. You have my word. So this is the part where I get to shave off your beard."

BZZZZZZZZ! says the electric razor

"You have to trim it with scissors first," Ty says.

So I show him the scissors that came with the electric razor.

"You're gonna do it in my car? Right here?"

"Yep," I say.

He swallows once, and then says, "Please, Amber. Not in my sweet ride."

So we step out of the car and I carefully snip Ty's beard down to the skin with scissors—so much hair falls to the asphalt of the maximum-security prison parking lot.

Carefully—I shave Ty's face with the battery-operated electric razor.

A boy emerges from underneath all that facial hair.

"How's it feel to be clean-shaven?" I ask when we are back in the Volvo.

"The people at the bank are going to be pleased," Ty says. "My parents will probably write you a thank-you note."

★ ★ ★

Ty and I eat a late lunch at McDonald's—cheeseburgers, salty fries, milk shakes—and then we ride the rest of the way home from the maximum-security prison listening to pop music on the radio, and when a good song comes on that we both know, we sing it loudly.

When we get back to Childress, we stop by Chad's and Jared's house.

"You shaved the beard!" Jared says. "Does that mean we're going to Friendly's?"

When I nod, the Brothers Fox smile and Jared carries Chad into the backseat.

We pick up Ricky just as Donna is getting home from work.

In the kitchen, Ricky says, "Ty Hendrix does not have a beard. Yes. Where did his beard go?"

"You're going back to Friendly's, eh?" Donna asks as BBB runs around our legs and licks my boys' hands when they bend down to pet B Thrice.

"You wanna come with, Donna?" I ask.

"You kids go and have your fun," she says.

"You haven't ridden in my Volvo yet, Donna," Ty says. "It's a sweet ride."

"You really want me to come?" Donna asks.

"Come on, sugar," Chad-in-a-backpack says. "You know you want to sit next to me in the backseat. I'll keep my hands to myself. Promise."

We all laugh, and Donna says, "I'm paying then."

I put BBB in his room, put on the classical music station, and it's playing Chopin's "Minute Waltz," which makes BBB start jumping and dancing, so I watch him for a while—my best buddy, BBB—and then I lock B Thrice's bedroom door and we all pile into Ty's Volvo station wagon, and someone suggests that we ring and run Franks' house, so we drive there, and Jared runs up to the door, rings the doorbell, and then runs back into the car. When Franks' redheaded wife steps outside and looks around clueless, we all laugh, and Ty hits the gas.

At Friendly's Donna orders one of every sundae and some fries too. We all sword fight with the long dessert spoons, getting whipped cream and cherries and caramel and chocolate sauce and nuts all over the place. We laugh our heads off. Donna takes it all in with a wise smile. And in my head I say a little prayer to JC.

I don't get it, JC. I don't understand the plan. I miss my mom. To take her like that when I'm not yet even a woman—it's not really fair, is it? But I'm glad there are times like this. I'm glad there are friends like this. I am glad there are Friendly's sundaes. That's all for right now.

Donna is smiling. All my boys are eating ice cream. I have a whole booth full of good friends. And I think to myself, you cannot give up, Amber. No matter what happens.

I won't. I will.

Suddenly, as I think about my mom, I feel like I might start crying.

Before I burst into tears, in my mind, I start pumping myself up with accolades to stop the waterworks, and I'm using a super-mega sports announcer voice:

The indomitably hopeful one!

The girl of unyielding optimism!

The teen of merriment!

The fan favorite!

Your undisputed champion!

"Amber—Rock Star of Hope—Apple-TOOOOOOOOOON!"

I yell across the Friendly's, and everyone in the joint turns and looks at me like my head is on fire.

"You are *such* a freak," Jared whispers to me, and all of my boys smile and laugh.

I smile right back at them and fill my mouth with a spoonful of delicious coffee ice cream.

Maybe I am a freak—but I'm one hopeful misfit, and you could be worse things in this world. True? True.

I spread hope.

I'm a hope spreader.

I guess that's what I do—licentiously—that's why I'm still circling the big flaming ball in the sky. (That's the sun—sucka!)

Acknowledgments

I would like to thank my wonderful and tenacious agent, Doug Stewart—D, you are simply amazing—and my brilliant editor, Alvina Ling, for believing in both Amber and me and for pushing me to tell the best story I possibly could. I am wildly blessed to be working with such smart and hip and kind professionals. Props to their assistants, Seth Fishman and Connie Hsu. Thanks to all at Sterling Lord Literistic and Little, Brown and Company who worked on this manuscript and/or helped to get my words out into the world. Much love to all of the friends and family members who continue to support me and my career—but an extra nod to the people who played a special role in the creation of this book (whether they know it or not) and the people who keep me feeling hopeful: my wife, Alicia Bessette; Sister Megan; Brother Micah; K-Hen; Mom; Dad; Barb & Peague; Bill, Mo, and Owen Rhoda; Flem; fellow Bardbarian, Scott Humfeld; Scott Caldwell (Mr. Canada); Myfanwy Collins; Justin Dunn; K-Rob; BD; veterinarian extraordinaire, Dr. Corey Shagensky; Roland Merullo; Old Man Harry and Grandmom Dink; Uncle Pete; my webmaster, Tim Rayworth; my photographer, Dave Tavani; LL; The WMs; Chris Barrett; everyone who attended the TSLP launch party; and many many more....

Reading Group Guide

1. So many times, Amber claims to be "sorta like a rock star." What exactly does she mean?

2. At the beginning of the novel, Amber is homeless and living on a school bus with her alcoholic mother. She has every reason to give up hope. What keeps Amber moving forward?

3. Is Amber a mature or immature seventeen-year-old?

4. When Amber's mother falters, several adults emerge as parental figures. Which of these characters plays the most important role in Amber's life?

5. How is Amber able to keep her homelessness a secret? What does the secret say about Amber? About her community?

6. Why does Amber feel such an intense need to take care of others?

7. Amber creates her own unique language by mixing and matching popular catchphrases with her own quirky expressions. Why does Amber speak the way she does?

8. Why does Amber seek out relationships with men like Father Chee, Mr. Franks, Private Jackson, and Old Man Linder? What do they all have in common? What makes each man uniquely important to Amber?

9. All of Amber's friends are boys, and Donna seems to be the only woman on whom Amber relies. Why?

10. What role does humor play in Amber's life? Joan of Old tells Amber, "Laugh at yourself and others will always laugh with you." What does she mean by this? Do you think Joan's statement is true?

11. Why do so many people end up caring about Amber?

12. Amber claims to be a "hope spreader." Have you ever known a real-life hope spreader?

Check out *Boy21*,
by Matthew Quick.

Turn the page for a sneak peek!

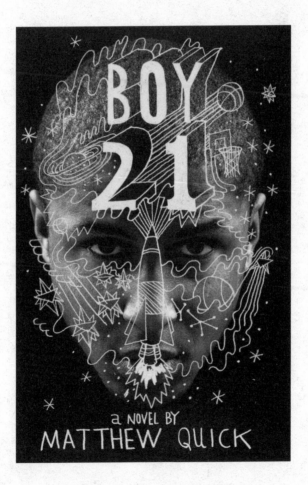

PREFACE

Sometimes I pretend that shooting hoops in my backyard is my earliest memory.

I'm just a kid, so Dad gives me one of those smaller basketballs and lowers the adjustable rim. He tells me to shoot until I can make one hundred baskets in a row, which seems impossible. Then he goes back inside the house to deal with my pop, who has recently returned legless from the hospital, clutching my dead grandmother's rosary beads. Our house has been silent for a long time and I understand that my mother is not coming back, but I don't want to think about what happened, so I do as my father instructed.

At first, I can't even reach the rim when I shoot, even though the hoop has been lowered. I keep shooting for hours and hours, until my neck is stiff from looking up and I'm sweaty. When the sun goes down, Dad puts on the floodlight and I continue to take shots, because it's better than being inside listening to my pop cry and moan — and, also, it's what Dad told me to do.

In my memory, I shoot through the night and don't stop for days and weeks and months. I don't even break to eat or sleep or use the bathroom. I just keep shooting hoops, zoning out, pretending that I will never have to go into my house again — that I will never have to remember what happened before I began shooting hoops.

You can lose yourself in repetition — quiet your thoughts; I learned the value of this at a very young age.

I remember the leaves falling and crunching under my feet, the snowflakes burning my skin, the yellow long-stem flowers blooming by the fence, and then being scorched by the powerful July sun — through it all I kept shooting.

I must have done other things — like go to school, obviously — but shooting hoops in my backyard is the only thing I remember from childhood.

After a few years, Dad began speaking more and shooting with me, which was nice.

Sometimes, Pop would park his wheelchair at the end of the driveway and sip a beer as he watched me perfect my jump shot.

The rim was raised every so often, as I grew.

And then one day a girl appeared in my backyard. She had blond hair and a smile that seemed to last forever.

"I live down the street," she said. "I'm in your class."

I kept shooting and hoped that she'd go away. Her name was Erin and she seemed really nice, but I didn't want to make friends with anyone. I only wanted to shoot hoops alone for the rest of my life.

"Are you ignoring me?" she asked.

I tried to pretend she wasn't there, because back then I was pretending the whole world wasn't there.

"You're really weird," she said. "But I don't mind."

My shot clanked off the rim and headed straight for her face, but the girl's reflexes were good and she caught the ball just before it smashed into her nose.

"Do you mind if I take a shot?" she asked.

When I didn't answer, she fired and the ball went in.

"I play a little with my older brother," she explained.

Whenever I shot around with my dad, the shooter got the ball back after a made basket, so I passed the ball to her and she shot again, and then again, and again.

In my memory, she hits dozens of shots before I get the ball back, but she doesn't ever leave my backyard—the two of us keep shooting for years and years.

1

One week before our senior year of high school begins, Erin's wearing her basketball practice jersey and I can see her black sports bra through the armhole, which is sort of sexy, at least to me.

I try not to look—especially since we're eating breakfast with my family—but whenever Erin leans forward and raises her fork to her mouth, her right armhole opens up, and I can see the shape of her small breast perfectly.

Stop looking! I tell myself, but it's impossible.

I don't hear one word that's said over our eggs and sausage.

No one notices my staring.

Erin's so charismatic and beautiful that my dad and pop never pay any attention to me when my girlfriend's around.

Like mine, their eyes are always on Erin.

When we get up to leave, my legless pop yells from his wheelchair, "Make the few remaining Irish people in this town proud!"

My father says, "Just do your best. Remember—it's a long race and you can always outwork talent in the end."

That's Dad's personal life motto, even though he ended up alone and working the night shift, collecting tolls at the bridge, where he needs neither talent nor a good work ethic.

Mostly because of Pop, my father's life has been pretty dreary. But his eyes always seem hopeful when he says that I can outwork talent over the long haul, and so for him—and for me too—I try my best to do just that.

The nights Dad watches me play basketball, I truly believe that those are the best in his entire life. That's one reason I love b-ball so much: for the opportunity to make Dad happy.

If I've had a good game, Dad's eyes water when he says he's proud of me, which makes my eyes water too.

When Pop sees us like that he calls us pansies.

"You ready?" Erin says to me.

Even though I don't want to, when I look at her face and into her beautiful shamrock-green eyes, I think about kissing her later tonight, and I begin to stiffen, so I quickly wipe the thought out of my mind.

It's not time for romance—it's time to get strong, and basketball season's only two months away.

2

Something you maybe need to know: People call me White Rabbit.

Whenever they serve cooked carrots in the lunchroom, Terrell Patterson sneaks up behind me and yells "Feed White Rabbit!" as he dumps his carrots on my plate as a joke, and then everyone follows his example, until there's a huge mound of orange.

This started last spring.

The first time it happened, I got really mad because people kept walking by and scraping what they didn't want onto my tray, which wasn't very sanitary, especially since I hadn't finished eating my lunch.

Erin—who sits next to me in the cafeteria when it's not basketball season—just started eating the carrots off my plate enthusiastically and thanking people until they got confused.

She kept saying, "Delicious! May I please have some more!" all crazily, until people were laughing at *her* instead of at what everyone was doing to me.

I actually like carrots, so I ate some too, because I saw that Erin's plan was working and I don't really care that people laugh when I eat those orange vegetables. *I'll have better eyesight than everyone,* I thought, and then just left it at that.

The only problem is that the carrot dumping became a weekly event, and it's really not funny anymore. I hope people forgot about it over the summer, but I doubt it.

I'm one of the few dozen white kids at my high school. I'm quiet like a rabbit. Eminem's character in the movie *8 Mile* is nicknamed B-Rabbit; Eminem is the most famous white rapper in the world; and I actually sort of look like him.

But the main reason people call me White Rabbit is because we had to read this very sad book by John Updike. It was about a long-ago white basketball star named Rabbit who grows up and lives a miserable life. I'm not a star, but I *am* the only white kid on our varsity basketball team.

Wes, who plays center and is the only other basketball player in the Accelerated English track, told all my teammates about the Updike book—well, just the part about there being a white basketball player with an embarrassing name. My teammates all started calling me White Rabbit.

The nickname stuck and now everyone in the neighborhood calls me that too.

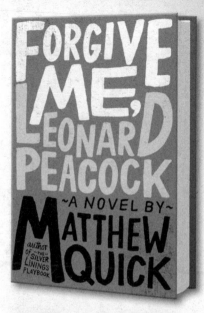

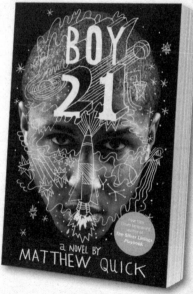

WHICH 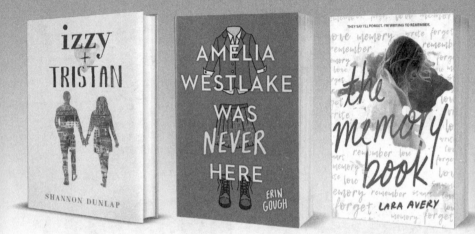POPPY WILL YOU PICK?

Find more Poppy at TheNOVL.com!